Pride and Patience:
A Pride and Prejudice Variation

Lorraine Hetschel

DEDICATION

To my husband and family for their love and support.

I would like to thank Simon Richardson at simonrichardsonenglish.com for his meticulous help with editing and thank Betty Campbell Madden for her many hours of editing, making this book a pleasure to read. I also thank the readers at fanfiction.net for encouraging me on this journey.

I would not have been able to accomplish this without your help.

CONTENTS

INTRODUCTION

Mr. Darcy finds out what life will be like with Elizabeth married to Mr. Collins. How will he react? Can he let her continue with such a small-minded man? Once assumptions are corrected, can Mr. Darcy be anything other than a friend to Elizabeth.

1: HUNSFORD PARSONAGE

The carriage stopped in front of Rosings. Mr. Darcy descended first, allowing his cousin out after himself. He hated this annual trip to visit his overbearing aunt. He looked out so as to observe his surroundings. The formal gardens surrounding them had barely recovered from the cold winter. The distant woods were more inviting.

"Another boring Easter lies ahead of us," Colonel Fitzwilliam managed.

"It might not be so bad. Eventually she will stop trying to convince me to marry Anne." Mr. Darcy's attempt at sarcasm was weak, drawing a grunt from his cousin. "The footmen are already opening the door. It is time to get this over with."

Within minutes, the two gentlemen were standing in front of Lady Catherine de Bourgh. She sat in her regal manner and asked outright if Mr. Darcy had set a date for his wedding.

"I am not engaged to anyone," was his simple response. He had been saying the same thing for too long. He was tired of refusing to marry Anne at each visit. And when he left, she would pretend the engagement was official. She would tell everyone the news. He would then have to spend too many hours refuting her claims during the season. Matchmaking mammas thought that the comparison of their daughters to

Anne would help their cases. It never did. Then, in a year, the same would happen again. If only he could find the bride he sought so that she would no longer encourage this false engagement.

"Of course, you are engaged to Anne. You must set a date soon. Her health will not last forever."

Mr. Darcy barely restrained the roll of his eyes. "I am not engaged to Anne, nor do I have any intentions of becoming so. Neither does Anne, if you ever bothered to ask her."

Lady Catherine was about to respond, when the door opened, and Mr. Collins entered moments after being announced, out of breath but eager to show his respect. He spoke with little eloquence, and it was another fifteen minutes before anyone else could interject.

Lady Catherine finally cut him off. "Mr. Collins, I am having an important discussion with my nephews. Will you kindly leave us?"

Mr. Collins turned to depart immediately and was apologizing most profusely when Mr. Darcy stopped him. "That is not necessary. We have nothing further to say. Mr. Collins, my aunt informed me that you are recently married." He decided that meeting the parson's ridiculous wife was preferable to his aunt's company. She must be ridiculous if she had married this parson.

Mr. Collins bowed as deeply as he could. "Yes, I married quickly after my proposal was accepted following the ball at Netherfield. Your esteemed aunt insisted I marry speedily, so that I would not delay my return to my parish. We married at the beginning of the year after a short courtship. We are very happy together."

Mr. Darcy blanched as he remembered whom Mr. Collins had paid his attentions to the previous autumn. Surely it could not be her. "I wish to pay my respects to her. Will you escort me to your house?"

"You are most gracious!" Mr. Collins continued praising him as he skipped out of the house, but Mr. Darcy did not listen.

Colonel Fitzwilliam followed behind Mr. Darcy, cautiously wondering what could have taken his cousin. The wife of the small-minded parson would be no one in particular to require this condescension. He whispered his thoughts to Mr. Darcy, but he only shrugged in response. Mr. Collins continued quickly ahead of Mr. Darcy and Colonel Fitzwilliam. So quickly, in fact, that he had reached the parsonage ten minutes ahead of them.

Mr. Darcy and the colonel entered the house with mixed emotions. The colonel was more curious than he had ever been before, while Mr. Darcy was white as a sheet. His complexion worsened when he entered the parlor where Mr. and Mrs. Collins were waiting for them.

Mr. Collins spoke very grandiosely in his glee. "Mr. Darcy of Pemberley, Derbyshire, and Colonel Fitzwilliam of His Majesty's Army, may I present to you Mrs. Elizabeth Collins, my wife of just over three months."

Colonel Fitzwilliam moved forward when he saw that his cousin was in no mood to either move or speak. His polite congratulations were enough for the two of them. He watched with concern as Mrs. Collins lifted her head high after her polite curtsey. She attempted to move away from her husband, but he moved closer and wrapped an arm around her waist. She was effectively trapped. The colonel observed that she seemed squeamish at such closeness. He entered into conversation easily with her and asked many questions about her family and how she liked Kent. He had hoped the parson would release his wife, but it was not to be.

Mr. Darcy stood in silent mortification. Elizabeth, who had spent so many nights in his dreams making passionate love to him, and whom he had seen many times in the halls and rooms around him as he had daydreamed of a future with her, was married to the odious parson. Mr. Collins put his arm around her waist with such a familiarity that he had only dreamed of for himself. Elizabeth looked lovely, despite a cap covering her hair. He looked at the cap, which covered all of her curls. Her hair was as dark as he remembered, but he could barely see it as it was so tightly bound. Not even one curl escaped the cap.

She looked at her husband in disgust, but he did not register her emotions and moved closer. When the colonel asked how Mrs. Collins was enjoying Kent, Mr. Collins stepped forward, disliking his lack of opportunity to speak before this moment. "My Elizabeth is very happy here. We are of one mind, and she is an excellent mistress. Why, just today she told me that this is the second month she has missed her courses. It is very likely we will have a child before next winter. I am thrilled that I chose my wife so well."

Mr. Darcy abruptly recovered his faculties and left the room without a bow. The images he had dreamed of were now replaced in his mind with images of Elizabeth submitting to her husband. The front door slammed shut behind him, and he walked away.

2: REJECTION

In his anger, the gardens spun around him and he soon realized he was lying in his bed at Netherfield, drenched with sweat. It had been a dream. The sun shone in through the window, bathing him in light. He stepped out of bed and donned a robe, before hastily going to the window. It was still fairly early in the day. The memory of the ball returned to him. The night before, he had danced with Elizabeth downstairs. He then witnessed Mr. Collins' attentions towards her for the rest of the evening. Indeed, he had been so attentive that she could not dance again.

The dream had startled him. He had dreamt of Elizabeth before, but he had believed it to be a simple distraction or, at worst, an infatuation. He had assumed it would disappear when he traveled to London and was no longer in her presence. But now, he could only think of Elizabeth's future. He knew his dream was no prophecy. Elizabeth would never marry Mr. Collins. In his reasoning, she was far too independent and intelligent to consent to such a scheme. But she would marry someday to someone worthy of her. It chilled his blood that he could not be that man. He had to put her out of his mind or this torture would never end. He had no intentions towards Miss Elizabeth, and he had to remember that.

His valet entered, having heard his master moving about. "Good morning, sir. Do you wish to ride this morning?"

Mr. Darcy sighed. "Yes, a ride would suit me perfectly, Davies." He scolded himself for allowing his thoughts to wander as far as they had. His valet worked his magic quickly and quietly, realizing his master was in a terrible mood. Half an hour later, Mr. Darcy was outside, walking toward the stables.

The ride helped dispel the image of Elizabeth in Mr. Collins' arms, but nothing could help him determine why he was unable to stop thinking of her. He had to forget her. He jumped over a fence and found himself in a field of lavender. The scent was intoxicating, especially since it was her scent. He looked around, almost believing that he could see her at the other end of the field. His mind would oft play such tricks on him.

However, this was no trick. Elizabeth Bennet was indeed standing on the other side of the field. Caught up in her own thoughts, she had walked on without noticing the horse and rider watching her. At the sound of the horse's neigh, she looked up. She sighed as she recognized Mr. Darcy. After being accosted by Mr. Collins, the last man she would wish to encounter was now before her. She turned away, but it was no use. He had come to greet her.

She was feeling irresolute enough without his presence. Her mother's absurd notion that she would marry Mr. Collins to save her family was enough to put anyone into distemper. If not for her father's love, she might have been forced to accept his proposal. He usually did give in to his wife in order to keep peace in the house. But she could not think of that now; she needed to keep calm in Mr. Darcy's presence.

He rode forward and dismounted in front of her, bowing as he righted himself. The greetings were out of the way within moments. Mr. Darcy noted that she was in low spirits when she barely responded to him.

"Has something happened to upset you?"

"Nothing that concerns you, sir," Elizabeth quipped.

"I understand. I noticed that Mr. Collins spent an unusual amount of time at your side during the ball. Has he done something to upset you?"

Elizabeth prevented the smile which threatened to erupt. Of course, he had been watching her most of the evening, although she could not understand why. A woman with so many faults could not easily entertain such a man. She thought of how to reply. "Perhaps he has."

Mr. Darcy shuddered. The man had proposed, then. "You refused him."

"That is not of your concern, sir."

"I wish to offer you comfort if I can, Miss Elizabeth. He is unworthy of your notice."

Elizabeth stiffened at his compliment. "On the contrary, he is very eligible."

"How so?" He could not disguise the incredulity he felt.

"He has a very fine living in Kent, and he will inherit Longbourn when my father dies." Elizabeth felt no need to give him the satisfaction of being right, despite her determination not to marry Mr. Collins.

All at once, the color drained from his face. Such would indeed be enough inducement for her mother and father. Perhaps they had forced her to accept. Perhaps she had felt obliged to accept. "You could not be happy with him," was the only reply he trusted himself to make.

"I would thank you to stay out of my personal affairs. I believe I am the best person to determine who will and who will not make me happy."

"That might be true, but in a moment of weakness, you could be blinded by the needs of others. I only wish for your happiness."

"Would you prefer me to become an old maid? Mr. Collins said that he is the best offer I am likely to ever receive." Elizabeth stood transfixed. Why should he care if she were happy?

Mr. Darcy stood silent, warring within himself as to whether he should speak his heart or not. Seeing her again, especially with her refusing to give him the satisfaction he needed, told him that he would be happy with no one but her. No one else had her vivacity or wit. He stepped toward her and said, "He is wrong."

"How can you be so sure?"

"Because I have every intention of proposing to you. Despite the mortification of your low connection and the degradation that your family, in particular your mother and youngest sisters, will bring, I am in love with you. Please, will you consent to being my wife?"

As he waited for her response, he closed his eyes, thinking his torment to be finally over. He was, therefore, completely unprepared when her hand made contact with his cheek in a terrible slap. Off guard, he stumbled backwards. Upon opening his eyes and righting his posture, he could not help but notice that she was utterly livid. So transfixed was he by her beauty, he barely registered her words.

"Only the deepest love will convince me into matrimony, and you, sir, are the most arrogant, selfish being I have ever met. I have no intention of ever seeing you again, let alone considering marrying you. You have insulted me, and I will have no further words with you." She turned and ran away.

It was another quarter of an hour before Mr. Darcy realized the full weight of her words. Mortified, he mounted his horse and rode away, but in his haste, he did so in the wrong direction. His stomach rumbled terribly when he finally stopped and realized his predicament. Looking around, he found a row of tenant houses in the distance. He moved toward them to get directions to Netherfield.

Upon his return, he found that Mr. Bingley had already left for London, and his sisters were eagerly awaiting him for a conference. He did not feel up to the task, so he pleaded the need to change his attire after galloping over the muddy roads. The delay gave him the strength he needed to appear passive and aloof, which he needed now more than ever.

Pacing in the drawing room, Mr. Darcy listened to Miss Bingley and Mrs. Hurst explaining how unsuitable the Bennets were for their social standing. "My brother is infatuated with her pretty face. She has encouraged him unduly. It would be well if she felt affection for him, but I am sure I saw nothing of it."

Mr. Darcy turned to Miss Bingley. "I thought so too last night, but upon reflection, I cannot see Miss Bennet being so mercenary."

"How can you say that? Her mother will stop at nothing to see her daughters married."

"Mrs. Bennet is a matchmaker for her daughters, and you are right that she is dangerous. However, I have seen no evidence that Miss Bennet or Miss Elizabeth would willingly attract the attention of a gentleman without some affection." He shook his head as her words swirled around in his mind. "I must speak plainly. Your brother is besotted with a woman who returns his affections. We should be happy for him."

Miss Bingley stared open-mouthed at him. The previous evening, Mr. Darcy had offered a different opinion. Obviously, something had changed his mind. Had he seen Miss Elizabeth during his ride? Had he offered for her? She took a deep breath. "I see where your allegiance lies. You are attached to Miss Elizabeth. I suppose with your marriage, Charles could do worse than to align with you."

Mr. Darcy closed his eyes. Would the pain ever diminish? "I am not and have never been attached to any lady." He wondered how often he would need to say those words. First to Lady Catherine and now to Miss Bingley. Suddenly, he realized that he could not remain in Hertfordshire. He must go where he could forget her. "I simply wish for my friend to be happy. I will join him in London. I am eager to see my sister, and there are plenty of business matters that need my attention. I will depart as soon as my bags are packed." He turned toward the sisters. "Thank you for your hospitality. You will make a splendid mistress someday."

3: RECOVERY

The roads were muddy and filled with ruts. His horse could not reach any kind of speed or he would injure himself. Darcy felt stuck in the slow monotony as he slowly became drenched. Thoughts welled up inside him as one hour became three. Would the blasted rain ever end? His precipitance was not beneficial if it kept him in such terrible weather with such gloomy thoughts. Elizabeth hated him. He could see that now. Where had it come from? Would his dream become a reality? He had no power to change her mind. Would he see her in Kent as his dream predicted?

Finally, London appeared. The cobblestones were easy to maneuver over, and he was at the Hurst's home very quickly. He was shown into the study, where a footman helped him to remove his boots and take some rest. Mr. Bingley joined him shortly. "You could have asked for a room to change. There are always rooms ready to use. Not that your boot prints will pose a challenge for the staff to clean. Why have you followed me with such haste? Has some calamity befallen someone?" His normally joyful voice quickly turned apprehensive.

"I know of no calamity. I simply could not stand to entertain your sisters for one more day. I shall enjoy London's society for the winter."

"You will not return with me to Hertfordshire?"

"I see no purpose in returning. You are fit to become an estate owner. There is little guidance I can give you at this time of year."

"I thought you would help me with the neighbors. You are better at speaking with the landed gentry."

Mr. Darcy laughed. "That is a gross falsehood. You are better at speaking in any situation that does not involve settling matters of estate business. Everyone admires you, and my presence seems only to irritate those you wished to please. I shall not return at this time; perhaps I will visit to congratulate you on your nuptials in the spring."

Mr. Bingley beamed. "You approve of Miss Bennet! I must say that I love her dearly."

"I believe she will be well suited for you, and she will help you settle in with the landed gentry more than I could do. Mrs. Bennet keeps an excellent table. Her daughter will be the same. I will hear all about it in your letters. Just promise me one thing…" He trailed off.

"Anything. You are an excellent friend." Bingley had completely missed that Darcy was struggling with his request.

"Do not write of Miss Elizabeth Bennet. I find I would not appreciate hearing her name. I must go." He slid on his boots and stood without tying them. He walked quickly out of the door before turning to his friend. "I hope you have better luck than myself, although I have no doubts about your success. I wish you very happy. Good day." He did not wait for Mr. Bingley to respond because he felt he was very near tears.

A month later, a letter arrived from Netherfield Hall for Mr. Darcy. Miss Darcy had seen it and brought it to him. She hoped a letter from a friend would improve his spirits, which had been low ever since his return. Unfortunately, it did not appear effective as he stared at is as though a serpent might jump out at him. "I doubt it can give me any information that I wish to hear."

"Open it anyway, dear Brother. I am worried about you."

Mr. Darcy looked up at his sister. She did appear very worried. He had been selfish, wallowing in self-pity for so long. He needed to make an effort for her. "Hand me the letter. I promise I will be myself again shortly, Georgiana."

He read the letter as quickly as the blots would allow.

Fitzwilliam,

I will not trouble you with the trivial dai-- accounts as ----- letters will do. Jane has accep--- my hand, and I am the ------- man alive. My sister -------- her regard, but now that we are ------ in our feelings, Jane has been ----- vocal about her adoration of --. Even you could not doubt her -----. She is such an angel.

Despite the c---, our engagement is not the only festivity we are celeb-----g. Last week, Mr. Collins ---- married and took his bride to K--t. I am certain I am not the only one glad to be rid of him. Mar-------------s excited to be able to come out sooner as she is the next eldest in line.

I beli--- the carriage is bringing my angel to -----. I cannot stay here, writing to you. Come if you will in a month to ----------- me in person.

Your serva--,
CB

Mr. Darcy put the letter down. He attempted to make sense out of the blotted letters. Mr. Collins was set to marry Elizabeth in November. It was impossible to hope he could have been rejected and found another prospective bride in such a short time. Her parents had forced her to accept, or she had willingly accepted to save her family. He knew she could not love him. It was over. He turned to his sister but had to look away quickly as he felt a tear slipping down his cheek. He must show her a brave face. "He is to marry Miss Bennet. You will enjoy meeting her when she comes to London. She is perfect for him: kind, gentle, and intelligent."

"Shall we travel to Hertfordshire, so I may meet her this winter?"

"No," Darcy replied, a little too quickly. How could he return to Hertfordshire now and witness Elizabeth's chosen path? Even her absence would be too much to bear in his current state. He needed to learn to be indifferent to her first, although he could not tell his sister that. "My business will not allow me to travel immediately. I have been away too long as it is. I am feeling very tired. I think I shall retire early." He kissed her forehead before leaving as quickly as he could for his chambers, despite its still being early in the morning.

4: TRAVEL

The sunlight crept into Mr. Darcy's room the next morning as the city awakened. While he was not drunk, too many nights of too little sleep had left him with a severe headache. He put that aside as best he could, knowing he must stabilize his thoughts and move on. The woman he wished to marry was already married. Georgiana needed him to be a brother upon whom she could rely. He might as well marry someone from his society. A wife who could be the sister Georgiana needs would suit him. He could never love her. No, his heart lay elsewhere, but he could and would be a kind husband to whomever he chose.

While he was being dressed by his valet, he could not help but feel that his legs moved like bricks. His body did not like his resolution, but he was determined. He walked to the study like a man heading to the gallows. Once inside, he found the daily post, among which he was certain to find invitations for a great many balls and dinner parties. Normally he avoided the majority of these functions, but he could not do so now. He needed to find a wife worthy of Pemberley.

An hour after scrutinizing each invitation, he had selected five dinners and one ball that would take place in the following fortnight, along with a few others that would occur later in the month. The London season was in full swing, and once he began attending functions, he knew he would be overwhelmed. The writing of the acceptance notes was accomplished quickly, and he put the notes on the salver to go out with the next post before he could change his mind.

With his *business* accomplished, he found his way to the music room where Georgiana was practicing with her music master. He did not mind that the playing was frequently interrupted either by words of encouragement or instruction. He liked spending time with Georgiana and seeing her at her favorite occupation. He briefly wished she would come out this season, so that she could attend with him, but he ought to have a wife first. It would make everything easier. Georgiana had said she was not ready, and he would respect that for now. He doubted she would ever declare herself so. Mr. Wickham had destroyed her confidence too thoroughly.

His mind raced back to the last time he had spoken that man's name. He had been talking to Elizabeth – Mrs. Collins, he ought to remember – about what, he could no longer remember. In a fury, she had blamed him for refusing the man friendship *when he had been most desperate*. What lies had Wickham told her? At least she was not in danger from him, for she was no longer in Hertfordshire. The only danger for her now was from her husband. She deserved so much better. He did not think he would ever be reconciled to her marriage.

He was so out of sorts that he jumped when Georgiana grasped his hand. "I am sorry Georgiana. I have been wool gathering." He looked around. The music master had departed already. How had he not noticed that the music had stopped? How long had he been lost in his thoughts?

"I worry about you, Brother. I know something has upset you. What can I do to please you?" He could tell she spoke in earnest, and she deserved an honest answer. However, he could never deliver this.

"You please me greatly, Poppet. I believe being cramped inside for so long is the reason for my sour mood. I have accepted an invitation to the Crawleys' home for tomorrow night, and I will resume my fencing practice this afternoon. Shall we spend the rest of the morning shopping? I have not seen enough of you, despite our being in the same house for some time. I intend to mend my behavior."

Georgiana squealed at the idea of shopping and spending more time with him. They walked through the streets of London as they went from shop to shop, purchasing gloves, hats, and ribbons to Georgiana's contentment. He put every thought into her happiness, and they had a most enjoyable morning and afternoon tea as a result.

Once the tea was finished, they parted ways. Mr. Darcy walked to the nearby gentlemen's club while his carriage took Georgiana and their purchases home. That evening, he was the outgoing brother he had once been. It cost him a great deal of energy to maintain such a façade, but he was determined not to hurt Georgiana any further.

The following evening, he went out for his first foray into the London season for the year. It was a disaster. All manner of ladies flocked to him throughout the entire dinner, making obscene innuendoes or smiling so hard that they could scarcely respond to his inquiries. Everyone seemed so focused on earning his regard that they forgot to even pay attention to what he was saying. At the end of the evening, only one thing had been accomplished: the London world knew he was earnestly looking for a wife.

The following morning's newspapers held two columns about his return from his determined bachelor state. He felt sick and used, but there was nothing else for it. He was determined to have a wife before he traveled to Kent for his Easter visit to Lady Catherine.

A month into his plan, he realized his big mistake: he kept thinking that the right woman would present herself to him. But every woman he met paled in comparison to the Elizabeth Bennet he remembered. No other woman had the power to move him as she had done so effortlessly. He could not envision any of the ladies of the Ton by his side, and not one of them seemed as if she would be a good influence for his gentle sister. The Easter visit loomed closer day by day, week by week.

Mr. Darcy stopped reading letters from Netherfield. While they did not ever contain information about Elizabeth Bennet, they were still far too romantic and happy for his mood. He knew he would never have what Mr. Bingley felt, and it tore at him to know he deserved his own pain for having insulted Elizabeth when he had proposed to her. If only he could have had another chance to get it right.

February and March came and went with no resolution. He claimed business was still too hectic to travel to Hertfordshire for the wedding. He did not yet feel ready to face her or her family. He had found no one worth marrying, so much so that he had begun to consider marrying his cousin, Anne. While she would not be an ideal wife, she was of good family and wealth. It would please many in his family for him to make that choice. No other in London was any better choice.

The week before Easter arrived. His valet packed with the usual care for the visit. He tried to picture what his aunt would say to his decision, albeit not quite entirely made. She would certainly lord it over everyone that she had foreseen the engagement years ago. She would not forsake appearances by becoming undone, like Mrs. Bennet was wont to do, he added in his mind. He briefly wondered if the cost of occasionally having to listen to her would be worth being the husband of Elizabeth Bennet. Yes, it definitely would be worth that occasional sacrifice. But this would never be; she already had a husband. A husband who did not deserve her. A husband she had chosen with her eyes open.

Colonel Richard Fitzwilliam was in a fine mood during the carriage ride. He was quite talkative, and nothing Darcy could say made any difference.

"I am tired of my men complaining like children about their rations. They eat better than most peasants. Nothing but a king's feast would appease them."

"Undoubtedly."

"Mother is in a fine mood, scurrying around all the parties.

She is as eager as the other matchmaking mamas to marry you to someone. She has almost forgotten that I am still single, and I have no intention of regaining her notice."

"Hmmm." He did not even look across the carriage at his cousin.

"Lady Catherine is undoubtedly prepared to entertain us."

"Of course."

"I wonder how many minutes we will be in the drawing room before she will remind you of your duty to marry Anne. Care to make a wager?"

"No."

Colonel Fitzwilliam searched his cousin's face. It was distraught. "Has my mother offended you with her ways?"

"No."

"Are you worried about Lady Catherine? I have always thought it must be difficult for you to keep her cries of duty at bay."

"No."

The carriage ride continued at its normal pace, but Darcy thought it moved too quickly toward a future for which he was not yet ready. While Darcy continued to respond evasively to all the colonel's inquiries, his mind quarreled with itself. Could he really agree to marry Anne? His hopes had already been dashed. If Elizabeth could not be his bride, would Anne be such a poor choice? While she could not be the partner he envisioned in Elizabeth, she would keep to her rooms and allow him to make all the decisions. Life would be simple. Society would calm. It would not help Georgiana other than to give her a female companion, but perhaps that would be enough. Anne would at least never be cruel to his sister. Could he really ask her to marry him? Once said, he would never be able to take the words of proposal back. Lady Catherine would not allow it.

This was the reason he kept evading his cousin. He could not say the words until he was absolutely certain of his choice. Perhaps he would wait until he had seen Elizabeth. Would he see her before the church service? Did he want to? Surely it could serve no purpose.

"Have you heard much about Mr. Collins?"

"Hmm." He could not respond. His words caught in his throat. Yes, he knew much of Mr. Collins. He was an oaf who did not deserve his bride.

"If he is anything like Lady Catherine's other parsons, then he is a blithering sycophant. It should be mildly entertaining, which is more than Lady Catherine's entertainment usually is."

"I suppose."

"And he is married. Although, who would marry such a person is baffling. Can she be sensible?"

"No." Could she be considered sensible? He had said the word in hopes of his cousin changing the subject.

"Oh well. Two new people should liven the environment. How soon should we call on them? We have no invitation, but that hardly matters. Mr. Collins will undoubtedly be at Rosings to welcome us. Do you suppose we could call on them immediately? Then we would know what to expect."

"No."

Colonel Fitzwilliam attempted a few new topics, but they were all shut down. Darcy could not even be persuaded to talk of Georgiana. His mind was too full. He had to steel himself for his final heartbreak. How would she respond to him? Would she be embarrassed to see him again? Would she be angry that she had not accepted his proposal, now that she knew how wrong she had been to accept Mr. Collins?

5: ROSINGS

"Fitzwilliam Darcy! Richard Fitzwilliam! I have been waiting too long! I was certain you must have met some calamity on your drive!" Lady Catherine was always ready to scold someone into listening to her advice. "You should have had your carriage checked for necessary repairs before beginning the journey."

Colonel Fitzwilliam stepped forward. "No calamity befell us. I was simply delayed leaving my barracks. You know there is always more to accomplish than I ever imagine. Do not blame Darcy's fine carriage. Undoubtedly, he had it checked before we set off. He always sees to such things."

"I knew you were the cause of the delay!" Lady Catherine bellowed, as though her previous remark had not been uttered. "You should find a wife, so you can retire. No nephew of mine should have to work for a living. It is far too long since you became eligible. Your mother is neglecting her duties."

"That is impossible." Darcy cut in. "And this is hardly relevant. We are here. Will a servant show us to our rooms? If not, I am certain we will be able to find them ourselves."

"You most certainly will not! We have servants specifically for this task. I am no pauper." She turned around. "Stevens, show them to their rooms immediately. Then, send Mrs. Hall for some refreshments. We will eat in one hour."

Darcy and Richard walked away behind Stevens. An hour later, Darcy was standing in the drawing room by the window, staring over at the parsonage. Was Elizabeth there now? Was she happy? He noticed Mr. Collins coming down the lane. Would Richard really want to return to the parsonage today? Was he ready to see her? The time had come. Within minutes, Mr. Collins entered the drawing room. With scarcely so much as a bow to him, Darcy returned to staring out the window. He tried to block out the effusive praise Mr. Collins heaped on his patroness and her family.

Richard could barely contain his merriment. He had expected to find Mr. Collins ridiculous, and he was not disappointed. He would bait him to continue speaking whenever there was a lull in the conversation. Lady Catherine seemed to enjoy the attention. After the tea had been consumed, Richard requested an introduction to Mrs. Collins.

"That is an excellent idea, Fitzwilliam. When you return, Anne will be well rested and will be ready to see you. Darcy, she is very eager to see you again. In fact, if you had been on time, she would have been here to greet you." Lady Catherine enjoyed the luxury of one more barb. Her plans had been foiled by their tardiness. With that out of the way, she added, "Go to the parsonage with Collins. Darcy, you know his wife, if I understand correctly. She also has guests, one of which, I will warn you, has a somewhat lively disposition. Miss Bennet and Miss Lucas have made a welcome addition to my evening parties."

The cousins left the drawing room in the wake of Mr. Collins' profuse joy. This attention from the nephews of his esteemed patroness was more than he could fathom. He skipped ahead with barely the patience to wait for the butler to open the door. His patroness hated it when someone of any rank opened a door themselves. Proper order had to be maintained, especially with her nephews on his trail. Realizing he should warn his wife and cousin, he skipped faster until he was practically running home.

The colonel laughed at the scene once they were outside, lifting Darcy from his stupor. While they had been cooped up inside the house, Darcy's desire to see Elizabeth again, even if he would only see her as another's wife, had consumed him. Now that he was walking towards her, he was reluctant to make his nightmare come true. He remembered how heartbroken he had felt over the winter. His legs shook, and he paused. He truly felt as if he could not go through this.

"Darcy, you are pale. Are you not enjoying such simpering? This is likely our only entertainment, unless Mrs. Collins and her guests are truly good company." Richard stopped, noticing his cousin's increased distress.

"I met her guests while I was staying in Hertfordshire. They are too silly to offer true entertainment." He could not stop thinking of Elizabeth, but neither could he forget about her sisters. From his aunt's words, she must have been referring to either Lydia or Kitty. Mary could not enliven any evening, he was certain of that. How could he withstand her sister's silliness while watching her in the arms of her husband? No, it was too soon to see her again. "I should warn you, Richard. Mrs. Collins' younger sister will flirt with you so long as you wear your red coat. I am... not inclined to meet them again. I shall go for a ride instead."

Darcy walked away before Richard could stop him. Richard watched his cousin flee, wondering what the meaning of his actions could be. What had Mrs. Collins' sister done to him? This ought to be interesting. He turned and hastened his steps to the parsonage.

Two hours later, Darcy returned to Rosings, tired from both the ride and his emotional state. He had no answers to his mind's constant line of questioning. The idea of marrying his cousin had lost all of its fervor. How could he marry such a frail creature? His life would be barren of conversation. Slipping into the library undisturbed, he found the port and gulped down two full glasses, relishing in the burning feeling and hoping it would rid him of his thoughts for at least one night. After replacing the bottle, he snuck upstairs. Ordering his valet to deliver an excuse for not being able to attend dinner, he slipped into his bed fully clothed.

The liquor did its trick. He did not wake until morning. Opening his eyes, he immediately regretted the action. His head felt ready to split in two. Realizing the futility of staying in bed, he rose to find a glass of water beside the bed. Silently thanking his valet, he drank it down and returned to bed to wait for it to work its wonders. Half an hour later, he was able to rise. His valet appeared promptly to shave and dress him for the day, having waited for four hours past his normal rising time.

Downstairs, Darcy had more than enough to deal with. Lady Catherine was ready with her diatribe against alcohol, so certain was she that it was the only plausible reason that he had not attended dinner. He weathered the storm well, countering each one of her attacks without promising or refusing to marry Anne. He would not be coerced into a decision either way. This discussion was preferable to thinking about Elizabeth with Mr. Collins.

Richard enjoyed the battle from a distance. He rarely intervened, as his assistance was not necessary. The alcohol and sleep had revived his cousin. Lady Catherine was no match for the Master of Pemberley when he had nothing better to do for an afternoon. While there was no shouting, the verbal onslaught was amusing to Richard.

When Lady Catherine left, she felt like she had gained some ground. Darcy, on the other hand, knew he had not relented in the slightest, as did Richard.

"You have recovered from yesterday admirably. This seems to be the best trip to Rosings yet. What with the liveliness at the parsonage, and you and Aunt Catherine bickering about false hopes, I have ample entertainment."

"I am glad you are taking pleasure at my expense." Darcy took a deep breath before asking what he wanted most to hear. "How is Mrs. Collins?" He had a foul taste in his mouth from calling her thus.

Richard smiled at his cousin's discontent. "She is everything

I thought her to be. She is a proper wife for Mr. Collins. Her sister is shy and quiet. Her friend, on the other hand, is engaging and fun. I am certain you would enjoy her charms. Her conversation is perfectly enchanting."

Darcy tried to fathom who Elizabeth's friend might be. The only woman he could remember her talking to was Miss Lucas. She had never seemed enchanting. And the sister could only be Miss Mary Bennet. Lydia and Kitty could never be shy or quiet. He would have to wait for their next encounter to understand this turn of events.

"I believe I am in need of another ride. Will you join me?"

"I have seen enough time on a horse. After tea, you may ride over the valley as much as you choose."

Darcy sighed. He had to face Lady Catherine again in an hour. He silently wished for another port, but he could not drown his troubles any further. He rarely drank to excess. It was not a good example to set for Georgiana even if she were not there. It was also not his way. He never lost his temper, and he always acted as a perfect gentleman should. This being the case, why then was he so out of sorts over Elizabeth?

"You are not apprehensive of having tea with Aunt Catherine?"

"No. Her tricks are old. I am simply bored."

"You were not bored this morning."

"I had been contemplating... some matters."

"You are not considering marriage, are you?"

Darcy's silence was very telling.

"Are you going to marry Anne?"

"I have not yet decided. I could certainly do worse than marry her. It would please most of our family. She has an excellent background, and her wealth would help me keep Pemberley prosperous."

Richard thought for a moment, puzzled. "Is Pemberley in danger of failing?"

"No."

"Have you need of any wealth from a marriage?"

"No."

"Then why consider Anne? She gives nothing other than her name and fortune. She does not even try to hold a reasonable conversation."

"I am tired of searching for a wife. She will allow me to continue my life without needing to be harassed by all of the fortune hunters."

Richard paused his questioning to analyze the situation. "You have never let the fortune hunters bother you before. I think it more likely that you are scared of a woman you have found. Does this have to do with your reluctance to visit the parsonage?"

Once again, Darcy's silence gave his answer.

"What happened?"

"She refused me."

"She must be more extraordinary than I had imagined."

"I have tried for months to forget her. There are none like her."

Richard watched as the anguish played out over his cousin's face. He tried to decide upon which of the ladies at the cottage had bewitched the great Fitzwilliam Darcy of Pemberley. Only one possibility came to mind. If only he could get them together.

"Do you fancy a game of billiards? The strategy involved might take your mind off your troubles."

Darcy nodded, glad the conversation was over. He had not intended to express his heart, although he knew Richard would be a good confidant. They had always been close over the years. This would be no different.

After two games of billiards, they were summoned to tea. They ate quietly while Lady Catherine went over the changes she had made to Rosings and the tenant homes. She liked that Darcy felt obligated to care for Rosings, and she wanted to ensure that when he married and took Anne to Pemberley, he could trust her to keep Rosings well cared for. With Collins, she always knew the happenings in the village. As such, the village rarely wanted for anything. A prosperous village showed off her talents as an estate owner; she never neglected her tenants.

Darcy did not need to hear his aunt praise her own abilities. He knew her ways. They never changed. Her talking allowed him to think, which was dangerous. He thought about the conversation he had had with his cousin. One thing stood out: Richard had not said there was hope for him. He had been hoping to be wrong; that Elizabeth had not in fact married Collins. Richard knew there was no hope. He had all but said so.

The room closed in around him. If he stayed for the rest of this visit, he would eventually see Elizabeth with Mr. Collins. He could avoid her during the week, but he would definitely see her at church. If only he could leave early. He began to contemplate reasons to leave. Certainly, he could claim business. Something could urgently call him back. Could he leave Richard here? If Richard returned early, he would have to return to the barracks. It would not do to force Richard back to work early, but he would not wish to remain alone either. That settled the matter. He could not leave Rosings early. He had to face his demons. He had to live through another heartbreak. As though he had not already been through enough.

The rest of the week passed slowly. During his morning rides, he would occasionally catch a glimpse Elizabeth walking through the park. He always kept his distance. He could not think of a way to approach her. There was nothing he could say. She was trapped, although he had noticed she was happier than he expected her to be. It would seem that she had not a care in the world.

Richard occasionally visited the parsonage, but he never discussed his conversations with his cousin or aunt. Whether he was gone half an hour or half the day, he would not reveal how his time had been spent. Darcy knew better than to ask, but Lady Catherine had no scruples. She did not like the idea of her esteemed nephews spending time with a simple parson and parson's family. Richard, such was his skill in the art of war, knew how to evade each attack.

When Sunday came, Darcy dressed with care. He wanted to be impeccable, such that when he first saw Elizabeth, he could hide his emotions behind his attire, if such a thing were possible. He walked to the foyer with lead in his shoes. Lady Catherine had the carriage ready to go. With her daughter so ill, they needed it, even if it was not normally permissible by the church. Therefore, Mr. Darcy could no longer delay their trip.

6: FIRST REUNION

The carriage stopped in front of the church. A footman opened the door seconds later. Colonel Fitzwilliam, noticing his cousin's distraction, leapt out to offer his assistance to Lady Catherine and her daughter. He did not flinch when Anne smiled at him in thanks. It was an odd circumstance, because she usually only smiled when Darcy complimented her, and only then if she was well-rested. On this occasion though, she was obviously tired from the journey, and he was not Darcy.

Mr. Darcy climbed out of the carriage after a few deep breaths. Mr. Collins was standing at the door to welcome them. Darcy bowed slightly as he walked by. He was not up to conversation with Elizabeth's husband. The mere idea of them being together sickened him, and he needed to concentrate on something else to prevent further discomposure. He sat beside Anne in the back pew. While it was not the best pew, it allowed Lady Catherine full view of the parish. She used this time to observe her tenants and note anyone in apparent distress or discomposure. She also looked for absent tenants. She would spend the next week either visiting those who were in need or sending Collins to see to them in her stead.

Darcy looked straight ahead, hoping not to see Elizabeth. He knew better than to shut his eyes, so he focused on the windows. He could not avert his ears, however. A few moments after taking his seat, her laughter rang out. She was behind him, laughing at something Richard had said. He wanted to turn around but was afraid. Instead, he listened as she recounted something funny about a rabbit she had seen on her morning walk. What he would give to hear that laughter every day! He heard them part as she began to walk to her seat.

Despite his determination to not watch her, he could not prevent his eyes from wandering to her graceful curls as they bounced up and down. It amazed him that something so simple as her walking down an aisle for church could affect him so much. He stared at her, hardly breathing as she took her seat beside two other women. One was Miss Lucas. He expected to see one of Elizabeth's younger sisters, but he did not recognize the other girl.

In his trance, he was startled when Richard sat down beside him. "She is lovely, is she not? And the best part is that Miss Bennet is as beautiful as she is intelligent and witty. She is the most interesting person I have met in some time." He paused to look at his cousin. "Darcy, breathe! Or you will cause Aunt Catherine to worry. You would not want her to discover your affection for Miss Bennet."

Darcy looked at his cousin in shock. Realizing that there was indeed truth to his words, he took a few breaths to calm his nerves. However, it did not take long for the revelation to sink in. She was Miss Bennet still! He looked back to her. Elizabeth was sitting beside Charlotte Lucas, who was wearing a cap over her hair. The sign of a married woman. She was the new Mrs. Collins! The strange girl must be Mrs. Collins' younger sister, now Miss Lucas. All of the conversations he had had before replayed through his mind. They all made sense with this new information. How had he not seen it earlier?

He thought back to the first letter from Bingley. He had said "Mar-" was eager to come out. Miss Lucas must be named Mary or Maria. Part of her coming out must have included coming to visit her sister. He realized he was veering off track. All that mattered was that Elizabeth was not married.

He shook his head as his heart repaired itself. Attempting to push his thoughts aside, he tried to focus on Mr. Collins' sermon. He was speaking of forgiveness and second chances. Darcy smiled. This was his second chance; his second chance at love. His heart swelled with hope at the thought. He continued listening with a quite unbecoming grin spread across his face. Richard attempted to check his humor many times, having deduced what had been happening to his normally stoic cousin. Lady Catherine had to frequently shush him.

After the service, Darcy remained in his seat as the rest of the congregation filed out and milled about outside of the church. Elizabeth waited with Miss Lucas while Mrs. Collins joined her husband to greet the villagers. Darcy watched her, wondering what she was whispering to Miss Lucas. Her curls shook daintily as she spoke. Miss Lucas laughed at something that she said. She no longer looked shy as she responded to Elizabeth. She would be good at drawing people out of their shell, he thought. She would be perfect for Georgiana.

While he was thinking such pleasant thoughts, he was surprised to notice that she was staring back at him with a curious expression. He had been caught. He bowed in greeting as he schooled his features into a neutral expression. She bowed her head, now looking slightly confused. Quickly, she shrugged off her thoughts and whispered again to Miss Lucas, who nodded in response. Almost before Darcy could indiscreetly look at her again, they fled out of the door and into the cemetery. He longed to follow them, but Lady Catherine should not be alerted to his purpose. It would make things unpleasant for them both.

With a heavy sigh but a light heart, he rose from his seat and found the rest of his party. They were talking to Mr. Collins at the door. The rest of the parishioners had already returned home. He caught up to Richard in time to hear Lady Catherine inviting Mr. Collins and his party to dinner. Once again, he smiled. He would see her that evening. It was nothing to remain pleasant with Anne and Lady Catherine on the carriage ride home.

31

"Darcy, are you even listening?" Lady Catherine boomed through his thoughts.

He looked around to see everyone staring at him. What had they been talking about? "Forgive me. My thoughts were on the sermon. What were we discussing?"

"I was asking when we should announce your engagement. We cannot waste any time."

Darcy turned to Richard. What engagement was she talking about? "I am not engaged to anyone at present." Hopefully, soon he could change that statement.

"Of course, you are engaged to Anne. She has been waiting here for you. If you had not been intending to honor your mother's wish, you should have said so. I would have a mind to sue you for breach of promise should you back out now."

"I was never engaged to Anne, nor have I ever wished to be. A mother's wish is not a promise, and you were the only one who knew of this, which is why you waited until my father's death to speak of it. I will not be coerced by you or anyone else."

Lady Catherine sat in her corner and stewed while she watched her nephews glare at her. "If I had known that, she would have been presented at court ages ago. She cannot be presented now. If Darcy will not have her, then Richard will have to do. You would be able to retire."

Richard eyed her carefully before responding. He considered his aunt for a moment. "Why is it so important that Anne marry immediately? Is her illness getting worse?" He looked over and saw that Anne was asleep.

"No, but she will not be able to recover enough to have a season. Who will be fit to marry her?"

All four looked towards Anne. Darcy looked away in time to see a glance of affection from Lady Catherine for her daughter before it was hidden once more behind her own haughty mask. How much she must be weighed down by these circumstances. Her daughter's situation was of her own making. He had never pretended any interest in marrying Anne. His conscience was clear. But that did not make Anne's fate any worse.

The rest of the ride was completed in silence. They descended without speaking, and the gentlemen watched as Lady Catherine and Miss Jenkinson escorted a barely conscious Anne inside. Darcy and Richard looked at each other, silently agreeing that they should find somewhere private to discuss this revelation. They ordered the carriage to be removed and then entered the house. Finding sanctuary in the library, Darcy poured each of them a small brandy.

"This is quite the turn of events. Do you suppose Lady Catherine has actually given up on you as a son-in-law?"

"I doubt it. I did notice that you never answered her question though. Would you marry Anne to allow you to retire from the army?"

"No. I have no desire to have a wife or to be a landed gentleman. I am better suited to the army. Balancing books and visiting tenants holds no interest for me, and being any more a part of society would bore me to death. Besides, I would need to reside at Rosings year-round, which holds no benefit for me while Lady Catherine is mistress."

Darcy nodded.

"What about you? Only a few days ago, you said you had been considering Anne for a wife. Have you changed your mind?"

"Yes. I want a wife who will liven Pemberley, and myself with it." Immediately, his thoughts returned to Elizabeth. She was even more beautiful than he had remembered.

Richard noted the changes that played over his cousin's face. "Tell me about Miss Bennet."

"You have met her."

"And the simple act of seeing her has filled you with hope and relieved your heart. Why did you dread seeing her so?"

A long pause followed this question. Just when Richard thought to repeat the question, Darcy replied, "I had thought her married."

"Married to Mr. Collins! How ghastly a thought! Why did you think she was married?"

"Because she had received an offer from him the same morning I had proposed to her."

"A woman cannot control who offers for her hand."

"That is true, but as he is the heir to their small estate, it seemed likely her parents would force her to accept. It certainly was a good offer for her, from a mercenary point of view. Her mother, in particular, clearly favored the match."

"Her will is too strong to be mercenary. Anyone can see that. What did she say when she rejected you?"

"That only the deepest love would persuade her into matrimony. In my haste, I said some disparaging things about her family." Without thought, he touched the cheek she had slapped. It served him right for what he had said.

"You should never act in haste. It is not your way. Until you have had more practice, continue with your well-rehearsed speeches. I would also refrain from disparaging her family. You must accept them for who they are. Otherwise, she would hold Lady Catherine against you as well."

Darcy nodded, unable to think of a reply.

"What is your plan to woo the young lady?"

"I have not had practice in wooing of late."

"When did you have such practice?"

Darcy thought back to his teenage years when he had been enamored of the pastor's daughter. The affection had been trifling at best. Other than a few well thought-out words, nothing had come of it. He knew he could not offer for her, and he knew better than to trifle with her and risk breaking her heart.

He chose not to answer the question. "I suppose I should ask for her permission to court her."

"Does she have any reason to accept?"

Darcy hung his head. No, she probably still hated him, though he knew not why. Suddenly, he remembered her vitriol at the Netherfield Ball. She had defended Wickham to him. What had he told her? Was he still in her presence and thoughts? Perhaps he was already too late. Bingley would know. Suddenly, he desired Bingley's letters. Though he had not read the last few, he had kept them. They were upstairs now. "I must go." He swallowed the last of the brandy and set the glass on the counter to be washed.

Richard watched him go with mixed emotions. He hoped his cousin would find happiness, but he worried at the same time that he would ruin things once and for all; it had already happened once. He spent the rest of the afternoon thinking over how he might be able to help.

When dinnertime arrived, Darcy headed downstairs, dreading the evening which was to come. In the company of Lady Catherine and Mr. Collins, he was certain he would not be able to have the conversation he wished for with Elizabeth. He wanted her alone, because he knew he would not be able to say anything private in such company. Indeed, Lady Catherine was waiting for his arrival while watching Richard speak with Anne quietly. She bore a shrewd smile as though she knew something or had concocted a plan. Feeling fortified by the conversation in the carriage, Darcy moved to observe the walkway through the window. The view almost completely showed the walk from the parsonage, and he hoped to watch Elizabeth come.

He was so entranced by the walk that he did not hear Richard move beside him. "Did you get the information you sought from Bingley?"

"How did you know that I read Bingley's letters?"

"I spoke with Georgiana. Your sadness seemed to stem from information in Bingley's letters. She said she could tell you were not even reading them anymore. As he is in Hertfordshire and married to Miss Bennet's elder sister, I can only assume that we already discussed your interest in his information. Did you find the information you sought?"

"No. I had asked him to avoid news of Miss Bennet, and he obeyed me to the letter. I cannot find a single thing that I wish to know." Like how much she enjoyed the company of Mr. Wickham, who was apparently still in Hertfordshire. He did not wish to tell Richard of the blackguard. Richard was more vindictive than himself, and it would not do to renew old wounds, no matter how much they had festered.

"Then you must ask Miss Bennet for the information you seek. Be kind and listen to her. Guide her to the answers. On second thought, you might wish to keep your conversation to the weather. You do not appear to be in control enough to have a rational discussion. Are you even listening to me?"

Richard looked over to see Darcy lean towards the window, completely oblivious to the rest of the room, including his conversation. He saw the group from the parsonage making its way down the drive. Miss Bennet was wearing a very pretty yellow dress with a tan shawl. The days were remarkably warm, he reminded himself. Her hair was pulled back into a very pretty bun with a few tendrils loosely framing her face. Even from a distance, she was lovely.

"Richard, you must help me find a way to speak privately with her."

"Certainly, my young love-struck cousin."

Darcy was about to refute such a phrase, but he thought better of it. He did love her.

7: REJECTION

Darcy watched Elizabeth as she walked towards Rosings until the moment she disappeared. Even when she looked up at his window, he did not look away. Her slight smile at him sent his heart fluttering. He hoped the feeling never went away, such was his ecstasy. He said a small prayer in the hope that all would go well that evening.

When the door opened, admitting the Collinses, Elizabeth, and Miss Lucas, Darcy was standing behind a chair to hide his nerves. He felt support as he gripped the back of the chair. He smiled slightly as he bowed to them. Lady Catherine claimed the Collinses' attention from the off, wishing to speak of parish business. Richard, knowing his purpose, took Miss Lucas to a corner of the room to regale her with his old war stories. He was so used to these stories that he felt confident that he would be able to keep an eye and ear out for Darcy even as he told them. He would need all the help he could get.

Elizabeth accepted her fate of speaking with Darcy with alacrity. Darcy was relieved that he had a topic that would interest her. All he had to do was ask about the Bingleys, and she would carry the rest of the conversation. Her eyes sparkled as she thought of all that Jane had been through.

"She is so happy running her own home. Charles is

everything pleasing. In the month that they have been married, they have hosted 3 dinner parties. They are planning a ball when I return. Jane enjoys having the ability to run her own household. The only drawback is that I cannot visit every day. I have almost considered taking up horseback riding to shorten the time it takes me to travel to Netherfield."

"You do not ride?" Darcy asked, surprised.

"Not really. I know the basics, but I have never had the incentive to become more proficient."

"I could show you."

"I have no need to learn. My walks are suitable. The quiet calms my mind, and I like going at my own pace, even if that is slower than a horse's."

It took a great deal of effort for Darcy to divert his thoughts from a future of teaching Elizabeth to ride. He pictured her sitting astride in front of him, sharing a mount. This would never do. He needed to focus on the present. Undoubtedly, his mind would wander tonight.

"I heard the wedding was lovely."

"Yes, it was everything Jane deserved. I am ever so grateful to you for your assistance when Charles asked your opinion after the Netherfield Ball. If you had sided with his sisters, he probably would have listened to you."

Darcy shuddered. How close had he come that day to losing her regard forever! If he had prevented the wedding by giving his former opinion, she would never have forgiven him. "My only concern had been that she was simply following her mother's orders. Your words to me that day," he paused for strength, "gave me relief on that score. I believe they are very well suited for a happy future." If only my future were as bright, he added in his head.

"Yes. They are so compliant and generous that they will never argue. My father was quite certain they would be taken in by the servants because of this, but I know better. Jane is firm where she knows she is right. Charles hopes you will return to help him learn to run the estate over the harvest time. Have you thought about returning to Netherfield? I suppose you must see to matters at Pemberley first."

"I prefer to be at home, but my absence will not be detrimental to Pemberley. My steward is trusted to see to most matters. Through correspondence, we resolve any weightier issues that need my guidance. I should be glad to visit Hertfordshire again." In his head, he added that he would go wherever he needed to remain close to her.

"A good steward is invaluable. How long has yours been part of your estate?"

"For the last few years. Mr. Robson took over management of my estate when the elder Mr. Wickham passed away. So far, all has been going smoothly. They had been working together for a few years before Mr. Wickham passed, so he knew most of his duties before he had to officially begin."

Elizabeth nodded her appreciation. She wanted to ask about Mr. Wickham, but she remembered in time how much that had soured his mood before. She did not wish to surface an unhappy memory tonight. "I sometimes wish we had a steward. Papa likes seeing to matters himself, and he has taught Jane, Mary, and me to manage the accounts and care for the tenants. Kitty and Lydia were... not interested in learning estate management. The funds we saved from not hiring a steward have been put to use keeping our dresses up-to-date and smart. Of course, our estate is not so large as yours."

"That is true, and it could be said in your father's favor that I have only one lady to keep in fashion, while your father must keep six. It would be an insurmountable task in some of the richest estates. Your father should be commended for doing so well."

Elizabeth smiled, unsure of how to accept such praise from Mr. Darcy.

Darcy decided to change the subject. "Have you discovered any walks around Rosings to be to your liking?"

Elizabeth hesitated for a moment. "There are many walks with many enjoyable views. I cannot determine a favorite, although I tend to walk in the grove that borders the park."

Darcy released a small smile. With this information, he

could innocently meet her on these walks. Did she know she was giving him a chance to meet her privately? They continued the conversation of the various paths around Rosings until dinner was announced. Unfortunately, they were not placed at a convenient distance to talk. Darcy was between Anne and Lady Catherine. Elizabeth was at the foot of the table between Mr. Collins and Miss Lucas.

Darcy tried to watch Elizabeth converse from across the room, but Lady Catherine was very effective at drawing his attention back to Anne. She seemed determined to show her in a good light. For a short time, Darcy had been of the opinion that Lady Catherine would encourage Richard to offer for Anne, but it appeared that he was still considered the better catch. Unfortunately for her, Anne rarely said anything and never offered her own opinion. Instead, she nodded in agreement when Mrs. Jenkinson kept reminding her to eat or try a new dish. Darcy shuddered as he thought of passing the days listening to this. How could he have been seriously considering offering for her? Looking down the table, he enjoyed seeing Elizabeth. When she caught his eye, she lifted her eyebrow in challenge before returning to her conversation with Maria.

Lady Catherine saw a few of these exchanges, but she did not really believe Darcy could be in any danger from the penniless Bennet girl. Knowing Darcy's insistence on not marrying Anne had put a damper on her plans, but she was not without hope. After having a few hours to think things over, she realized that all was not lost. She simply needed to change tactics. If only Anne were more used to speaking and carrying conversations.

After the meal, Lady Catherine led the ladies to the drawing room, where she promptly asked Miss Bennet to play the pianoforte. She wanted her out of the way of stimulating conversation. Anne could certainly not hold her own like Miss Bennet could. But if such a comparison was not available, she could perhaps warm Darcy to her aim.

Elizabeth was pleased with the arrangement. She had not

played much since coming to Kent, and she did not need to converse with Mrs. Collins or Maria at Rosings. They could converse on their own terms better at the parsonage. From the pianoforte, she could play simple melodies and harmlessly watch the interactions. There were many intricate characters for her to analyze tonight, and the evening promised to be anything but dull.

Darcy was not so agreeably engaged. He was sitting with Richard, which would have been fine had it not been for the presence of Mr. Collins. Richard and Darcy sat quietly while they drank their port. Mr. Collins seldom drank as he was so busy speaking without either purpose or end. His audience barely paid attention unless Miss Bennet was mentioned. They received no interesting information yet knew better than to attempt to stop him. After half an hour and two glasses of port, Darcy felt he had listened long enough. He rose to signal the time to rejoin the ladies. Mr. Collins did not miss a beat as he continued the conversation all the way to the drawing room. He only paused to greet Lady Catherine and Miss de Bourgh with a bow before resuming his conversation, this time with a willing audience in Lady Catherine.

Richard chose to speak with Mrs. Collins and Miss Lucas, leaving Darcy to entertain Miss Bennet, which was entirely to his liking. He walked over to the instrument, pausing when he reached the point at which the music was louder than the conversations behind him. He did not wish to cause her to stop playing and converse with him yet. Her playing was lovely, and his mind jumped to future events, where she would play for him in the evening. The music moved him more than Georgiana's playing could do, probably because of how he felt for the performer.

Elizabeth smiled at Mr. Darcy when she looked up. He was watching her with unabashed adoration. She had never felt so much emotion from one look. The normally unperturbed Mr. Darcy was apparently capable of feeling great emotion. That it was her that had inspired such affection no longer surprised her. He had offered his love to her, and even though she had refused him at the time, she could not deny that he did still love her. She knew not what to think. She did not return his affections, and she became nervous that he would ask her to marry him again. How could she let him down gently a second time?

When Elizabeth finished the song, Darcy took his chance. "Your playing is as lovely as I remember from when you played at Lucas Lodge."

"I suppose that means I have not practiced enough to improve my performance."

"Your time has been better spent. No one who is privileged enough to listen to your playing could think anything wanting. May I turn the pages for you?"

"You may." Elizabeth watched as he stepped forward and claimed the seat beside her. To attempt a distraction from the warmth she felt emanating from where her body met with his, she changed the music sheet. Unsure as to how well she would be able to follow the sheet, she chose a piece she knew almost from memory. Invariably, her mind did wander from the notes on the page. It took all her focus to keep playing when her senses were being overtaken by Mr. Darcy. She had always thought him handsome. This close, she could hardly detect any flaws in his person. He smelled clean and enticing, although she could not name the scent. The warmth emanating from him was almost overpowering. When he turned the page, his arm brushed against hers, sending a nervous shiver down one side of her body.

When she finished playing, he asked, "Would you sing the next song?" He waited with anticipation.

"I do not believe I am ready to make such a fool of myself. I am certain you have heard more talented singers than myself. I believe I am tired." While the playing had not exhausted her, keeping her thoughts in check took more energy than she would have admitted to. Uncertain how to end the playing, she selected a very short children's tune.

Darcy used the music to give them some privacy. "While I have heard more talented women, none have moved me the way you have so effortlessly tonight, and on other occasions as well. I will not force you to sing, but I do not wish to share your company with the others just yet. I have something on my mind that I must discuss with you."

Elizabeth took a deep breath. Why would he return to this topic so soon after having seen her again? She had no wish to pain him again, but she could not let him continue. "Mr. Darcy, I cannot give you the answer I know you are seeking. I only wish to be your friend. You have proven a very valuable friend to Mr. Bingley. As Jane's sister, I imagine we will often be in each other's company in future. I do not wish for our meetings to be awkward or stilted. Please, tell me you will be my friend."

"I cannot deceive you and say that friendship is all I am looking for."

"I am not asking you to deceive me. I only ask for your friendship. That is all I can offer you. I do not wish to pain you again."

Darcy attempted to calm his breath. He knew it was too soon to ask for her hand, but he had been too overcome to resist. Now, he had to reign in his feelings. She had not rejected him. He nodded, as that was all the communication he was capable of.

Before the song came to a natural end, Lady Catherine interrupted them. "You play well enough, Miss Bennet, although you should practice more. Darcy, come and speak with Anne about your plans for the gardens at Pemberley. She is very interested in gardens. She is always going out in her phaeton to explore the verdure."

"Very well. Miss Bennet, may I escort you to your friends?"

Elizabeth nodded and accepted his hand as she rose from the seat. The walk was not far, but Elizabeth was not sorry to release his hand as she sat down beside Charlotte. While Charlotte talked of her plans for the week, Elizabeth glanced frequently at Mr. Darcy, but he never once returned her gaze. Instead, he focused all of his attention on Anne and Lady Catherine, glad for the separation. He needed to think over all that had been said before he interacted with Elizabeth again. All he knew now was that she had not completely dashed his hopes.

8: RHODODENDRONS

The following morning, Darcy left his horse alone in favor of searching out Elizabeth on her walk. If they truly were to become friends, then they must get to know each other. This idea was immensely favorable to him. Walking in one of his better suits, he watched the path leading from the parsonage. Surely, Elizabeth would be out soon. She never missed a walk unless the weather was inclement. He remembered her words from Hertfordshire very well. He assumed walking was the best way to avoid spending too much time with her family. He could not help thinking that he could prevent her from needing to avoid her family.

Darcy paced back and forth while he waited. His mind instantly wandered to potential future walks where he would not need to join her. Perhaps they would sneak down the servants' stairs together to avoid rousing the others. He could picture holding her hand as they moved down the passageways.

"Good morning, Mr. Darcy."

Elizabeth's voice made him whip around quickly. Apparently, she was returning from a walk rather than beginning one. It was a few moments before he was in control enough to be certain he would remember they were not married yet. "Good morning, Miss Bennet." He bowed stiffly, causing Elizabeth to giggle slightly. "Might I ask what amuses you so?"

"Forgive me, Mr. Darcy. It is just that you are so stiff. I cannot imagine that you have many friends you would be so reserved around."

"The proprieties must be observed."

Elizabeth nodded. "That does not mean you need to be so guarded." After watching him for another minute, she decided to change the subject. It was clear he needed the formality. "Will you walk with me back to the parsonage? I am searching for a way to ask you something important."

Darcy immediately offered her his arm. What she asked for was not unreasonable, but if he were to let down his guard, his emotions might overcome his rationality. He could only hope that in time he would be better at containing his ardor for her. Until then, he would be at her mercy. Every touch and smile sent his heart reeling. He barely registered her words. He matched her light step with his quick stride. They spoke of inconsequential matters while they walked to the parsonage. In that time, Elizabeth did not ask her big question. She was afraid of offending him. At least she had time; they would remain in the country for two more weeks.

As they reached the parsonage, Darcy asked one final, but important question. "What time do you usually leave for your walks?"

The question was anything but innocent. Elizabeth wondered whether to give him that information. In the end, she decided that their walks would be the best way to get to know him in privacy. If he called on her at the parsonage, there would be too many people watching, and too many questions that would need to be answered. They were just friends. "I wake to the dawn lights, and I leave for my walks as the first rays of sunshine hit the trees outside my window."

Darcy started at this answer. "Then you have been walking for two hours complete, perhaps more. Are you not tired?"

Elizabeth smiled in triumph. "Not at all. My body is accustomed to such exercise. You should see me on rainy days

- all I can do is pace the hallways."

Darcy nodded, hoping to be granted such a scene. He would be able to offer her many splendid hallways at Pemberley. "And remember, I am ready for your question whenever you are comfortable enough to ask. I am your friend. I hope you enjoy your day, Miss Bennet."

"Same to you, Mr. Darcy." On impulse, she held out her hand. "My friend."

Darcy claimed her hand, but he could not shake it. Instead, he raised it to his lips for a simple kiss.

"Is that how you say farewell to all your friends?"

"I must confess that I have no friends who are female. This is a new situation for me."

"No female friends? What about Miss Bingley?"

"She is my friend's sister. That is not the same."

"Yet you are comfortable in her presence."

"Then I have played my part well. I must leave now, or my aunt will wonder what has become of me. Good day."

With a final bow and curtsey, they parted. Elizabeth watched him until he had turned a corner and was out of sight. Twice he turned and smiled at her, waiting until she returned his smile to continue on.

Upon entering the house, she found Maria and Charlotte hovering, waiting for an explanation. They looked as though they had been watching through the curtains. "Yes, Charlotte. I know what you are going to say. You were right. He still holds affection for me, but we are content to be friends."

"How many gentlemen friends do you have, Lizzy?"

Elizabeth thought for a moment. "Two. Your brother and Thomas Hudson."

"They were playmates. It is one thing for you to grow up with those boys. It is another to try to be friends with a grown man who clearly admires you."

"What am I supposed to do, Charlotte? I do not want to disappoint the man who helped Charles chose Jane over his sisters, but I cannot marry him. I do not love him."

"Yet." Charlotte added.

"I am not very fond of him, as you well know. I will not say I completely dislike him as I used to freely say, but I am not likely to fall in love with him. He is too reserved."

Charlotte was about to respond when her husband returned with news from the village.

Darcy walked with a spring in his step the rest of the way to Rosings. Even his aunt could not dampen his mood, and he was willing to humor Anne, even though she rarely spoke. That evening, he instructed his valet to wake him an hour before dawn and have his best walking clothes ready again. His valet, though suspicious, wisely said nothing.

When Elizabeth spied him pacing at the gate from Rosings, she laughed merrily. "Good morning, Mr. Darcy. You look more prepared for a day at court than a simple walk through the country!"

"Good morning, Miss Bennet. I assure you this is not a jacket fit for a day at court."

Elizabeth smiled. "How are your family? Is everyone at Rosings well?"

"Yes, they are well. My aunt is still determined that I should marry her daughter, although I am just as determined that I will not. Richard loves observing our battles of wills, such as they may be called."

"I suppose they must be battles. I have seen her stubbornness and yours. You both can be quite formidable opponents."

"Am I really so formidable as she is?" Is that really what she thought of him?

"You are just as set in your ways as she is. Perhaps that does not make you formidable, but you do not like to admit when you are wrong."

"One could say you are the same way."

"On the contrary, I enjoy debating my point of view, knowing full well I might be wrong. Sometimes with my father, I will even change my point of view to challenge myself to be wrong."

"That explains how you have become such a great converser. I have always enjoyed our own battles of wits."

"And here I thought you had been looking for faults in my character."

Darcy had to bite his tongue to prevent a retort. She had misread him before, but acknowledging that now would not help. It would make her uncomfortable. Instead of responding, he smiled at her and kept walking.

"I remember you saying that you could not discuss books in a ballroom because your head is always filled with something else. Does such a problem exist in the great outdoors?"

Elizabeth thought back to that conversation. "I tend to spend my thoughts enjoying the view. There are so many more flower blooms now compared with when I arrived. Two weeks have made quite a difference."

"Which flower is your favorite?"

"I have not decided. To do so would damage the reputation of the others. Although, I must admit to becoming breathless when I see a rhododendron garden in bloom."

"Have you seen the rhododendron path behind Rosings?"

"No, I have not. I have seen a few sprinkled here and there around the grounds, though."

"Come then, you will be enchanted. Rosings hosts one of the largest rhododendron walks in the country. They are Lady Catherine's best accomplishment as mistress." He held out his arm to offer to lead her there, and he was pleased when she only slightly hesitated to accept his guidance.

"I wonder why Mr. Collins does not speak of it if it truly is her best accomplishment."

"He began his position in the autumn, and he has likely never seen it himself."

They walked in silence for a few minutes. Elizabeth observed his route as he guided them around the great house without actually coming into view. She wondered if he was purposely doing this to avoid being seen by his aunt, but she thought better than to mention in. As they emerged from the woody path, she looked in anticipation but was passing plain rose bushes that were only newly starting to grow after the cold winter. She looked ahead to see a large hedge obscuring her view.

"Miss Bennet, do you trust me not to lead you astray?"

Elizabeth looked at him quizzically.

"Close your eyes and trust me to guide you. Please."

After another odd stare, she decided to acquiesce. She closed her eyes and wrapped her arm more securely through his. He had to focus to remember to keep breathing. He led her to the path and walked her into it a few feet. He paused. "Do you smell anything?"

"Certainly. May I open my eyes now?"

"Yes." He stepped away as she opened her eyes. He wanted to see her response, and he was not disappointed.

"I do not know where to look!" Her mouth dropped open as she glanced this way and that. As she looked around, she noticed a pattern. At the entrance behind her, the bushes were covered with very dark purple flowers. As they progressed down the path, the color lightened and became more reddish before it finally turned out of sight. The fragrance was overpowering. She took a few steps, but then she stopped again and looked behind her. "Are you coming? Rhododendrons were not meant to be enjoyed alone."

Darcy nodded as he took his place at her side. "This used to be one of my favorite walks as a child. My mother loved the flowers, and we have a similar path at Pemberley, but it is not quite so long. We used to take naps in the shade together."

"Are the flowers a reminder of your mother?"

"Yes."

"She must have loved you very much. How old were you when she died?" To add to his comfort, she claimed his gloved hand and gave it a gentle squeeze.

"I was twelve. Georgiana was only two years old. She has no memories of her mother. Father wanted to have the rhododendrons removed, but I would not let him. The memory soothed me when it hurt him. As a compromise, he never looked out of the east-facing windows again. I used to walk Georgiana through the bushes when she was upset, and I told her to think of how her mother would wish to know what her daughter was feeling. It helped."

He looked up to see a small tear welling in her eye. He had not wanted to make her sad.

"You said this used to be your favorite path."

Offering her a handkerchief, he replied, "Yes. Lately, I have come to discover the grove that borders the park to be much more to my liking." He spoke in jest, hoping to introduce some levity. She responded with a light laugh as she dabbed her cheeks. He took her hand and placed it over his arm to encourage her to keep walking.

"How long is the path?"

"Roughly a quarter of a mile."

"Why is it bordered by a hedge so others cannot see it from the outside?"

"It is only bordered on that side. The hedge is actually a maze. I would offer to take you there, but I know the route too well. There are many more flowers inside the maze."

Elizabeth smiled. "Very well, then you shall learn to follow. I have never been inside a maze before. You may not direct my steps, sir, unless I have already asked for assistance five times and am truly lost." Her eyes glinted with mischief.

"You are saying that I must deny your request five times before I may be a gentleman and aid you. What would others think?"

"That you are following my directions, which is very gentlemanly indeed." Elizabeth watched the rhododendrons blossoms become a darker red as they neared the end of the path. At the very end, she paused to touch them. "I do not know why Mama has never planted these in her gardens. They are lovely and very easy to tend to, if I am not mistaken."

Darcy wisely said nothing. He pointed to the entrance of the maze as he looked around to see if anyone was near enough to see them. They were disobeying the strictures of propriety by being out together, but if she did not care, then he would follow their lead. Perhaps tomorrow he would ask a maid to come with him to ensure Elizabeth's reputation.

Before they entered the maze, he took a final look at the great house and was glad to see no one looking out the windows. "Which way will you go first?" He asked.

Elizabeth crinkled her mouth to one side in thought. "Right. Come on!" He allowed her to lead the way, chuckling a few times when she hit a dead end.

"This is a pleasant maze. I imagine most mazes do not contain amazing statues or flowers at the dead ends. I almost wish to remain lost!" She laughed to herself as she leaned into a lilac tree that was only just beginning to bud. It was too soon to smell the flowers, but she tried anyway.

As he had been told, Darcy refused her request for help, and her pout made him glad to do so. After just the one request, Elizabeth found the exit at the far end of the garden. Once again, she pouted. "I suppose that means it is well past time to return to the parsonage."

Darcy nodded, knowing the sense in her words but not wanting to relinquish this time with her. Once again, he offered her his arm and led her to the path that went through the woods. They had not been seen yet, and it would be good not to push their luck. Elizabeth enjoyed the bluebells that bordered the path and happily chatted about her childhood memories. After all, Darcy had shared his; it was only right that she do the same.

When they moved past the gate marking the edge of Rosings, Elizabeth paused. "I have really enjoyed our walk, Mr. Darcy. Would you care to join us at the parsonage to break your fast?"

She looked so innocent that he could tell she did not realize the import of what she asked. If Mr. Collins guessed correctly how much interest he held in Elizabeth, he would likely tell Lady Catherine. That would make things very difficult for the both of them. He was about to politely decline when his stomach rumbled fiercely.

Elizabeth laughed with delight. "There is my answer. You

will come."

"I should not. I would not wish for Mr. Collins to become suspicious."

Elizabeth shrugged. "He is not the most observant if Lady Catherine is not present. I cannot tell you how many times I had to refuse him, yet still he was certain I would have accepted him."

Darcy's memory went back to that fateful day. "That explains why you had no patience for me."

Elizabeth shrugged as her memory also sped back to that day. "No, it does not. I was short with you because of your manner. I had no reason to confide in you, and you thrust yourself upon my person without any thought to my reception."

They had begun walking, but Darcy stopped. "You are right. You cannot imagine how much I have berated myself for my poor choice of words. I have often wondered, had I worded my emotions better, if I would have been more successful."

Elizabeth stepped up to him. "No, you would not. I am determined that only the deepest love will persuade me into matrimony. I have seen too many unhappy couples forced into marriage. I wish for a marriage of affection and respect. I would rather spend the rest of my days tending to my nieces and nephews at Netherfield than in an unhappy marriage."

"I can only admire you more for that, but we are veering off topic. As you said the other night, we are friends. If you are certain Mr. Collins will not get the wrong idea, then I would be happy to join you to break your fast." He held out his arm.

Elizabeth watched him carefully, trying to ascertain if she had hurt him. His face was unreadable. "You are a very hard man to read. I am happy to be your friend. Come, Mrs. Collins has probably already eaten, but the others are usually not up at this hour. The coffee will still be warm."

Darcy took her arm and walked the rest of the way to the parsonage. He had so many questions to ask, but he knew better than to do so. At least he knew her much better now.

Her reason for rejecting him was very sound. Even before she had the security of her sister's marriage, she would not marry for convenience or security. He could only love her all the more for it.

Upon entering the house, they found Mrs. Collins in the parlor alone. She agreed to move to the dining table so that the three of them could eat; she could not break propriety by allowing the two to be alone.

While they ate, Elizabeth carried the conversation. True to her abilities, she managed to keep it flowing with topics that would please all three of them. By the end of it, Mr. Darcy felt he knew more about Mrs. Collins than he had ever known about anyone not related to him, besides Elizabeth. The party was not broken up until Mr. Collins entered the room. He was profuse in his thanks for it could not be anything other than great condescension that the nephew of Lady Catherine would sit and eat at his table.

Elizabeth winked at Mr. Darcy when she was certain no one would notice. He smiled and bowed before excusing himself from their company. In her room, Elizabeth watched him return to Rosings. She had never had such an engaging morning, and she suddenly realized that there would surely be many more such mornings to come.

9: SEASIDE HOLIDAY

Over the next few days, Elizabeth and Darcy met regularly for their walks. After a quick pass through the rhododendrons and maze, they would walk leisurely through other paths. True to Darcy's honor as a gentleman, he asked a maid to escort them. He had known her for many years and trusted her to reveal their walks only if it became necessary. The maid was glad to be able to leave the house for a few hours. A steady friendship was forming, even though Darcy was having to hide his passionate feelings. Occasionally, Colonel Fitzwilliam joined them, and the three of them chatted merrily about everything and nothing. Richard had been impossible, teasing him for his budding romance over their evening glasses of port.

Darcy prevented his aunt's curiosity by spending time with Anne and her in the afternoon. He would escort Anne around the village in the phaeton, occasionally stopping at the parsonage to speak with its residents. On other days, he would read to her from a book of her, or more likely Lady Catherine's, choosing. When Lady Catherine was not present, he hinted that his desires lay in another woman's direction, and Anne did not appear upset. In fact, she rarely responded to anything he said.

The following Sunday, Darcy went to church hoping for another chance to see Elizabeth. Where he sat the week before, he had been able to watch her without inviting suspicion. He was hoping for the same chance.

Upon entering the church, he looked for her. She met his gaze with a smile. He smiled in return before his attention was commanded by Lady Catherine. When he looked back, she was still smiling at him. He arched his brow, causing her to blush and look away. Maria then claimed her attention, and she did not look back until the service started.

It was halfway over when Darcy noted that it had been written for him. It was about doing one's duty to God and family. Darcy stole a sideways glance at his aunt to note her watching him with a satisfied demeanor. She must have planned the sermon with Mr. Collins. He attempted to hold in a discontented sigh. Changing the sermon was a new low for her. At least he would only be in the country for another week. He had originally planned to leave the following day, but he had postponed his itinerary to coincide with Elizabeth's departure.

He wished he could escort her to her uncle's house, but he knew that would be overstepping his bounds as a friend. Propriety would be risked if he were to arrive at her uncle's house without an invitation. He would not open her reputation up to scorn.

He was roused from his thoughts by the beginning of the final hymn. He pushed them aside as he watched Elizabeth sing quietly. He could not hear her, but her voice played through his mind as though she were sitting beside him. Once again, his mind wandered to a hopeful future. Such a future might be far away, but he no longer thought it impossible.

After the final notes played out, the parishioners began to leave. Darcy noted that Elizabeth lingered even after Maria moved to stand with her sister. He hoped she was waiting for him, but he dared not be too obvious. He remained with Richard while Lady Catherine moved to speak with a disappointing tenant who had evaded all her other attempts at intimidation. When he next chanced a glance at Elizabeth, she was speaking to someone he had never met. Most likely she was a neighbor of Mrs. Collins. She was at ease speaking with this near stranger. Undoubtedly, she knew precisely what to say. After a moment, they laughed and broke away, both happy with the encounter.

Richard watched Darcy and could tell that he was deliberately lingering longer than usual. He chuckled to himself as he tried to hold a conversation with his cousin. His attempts were only successful at making them seem less stiff and formal, for no conversation lasted more than three turns. With Darcy's normally dour countenance, no one dared interrupt them. Anyone except for Elizabeth, who slowly wandered their way with the remnants of her laugh still etched on her perfect face.

After exchanging pleasantries, she stated that she planned to walk home. As gentlemen, Richard and Darcy offered to escort her to the parsonage on the main road. With so many cottages in view, no one could think it improper for two men to escort a lady. The three chatted amiably about nothing in particular.

When they arrived at the parsonage, the gentlemen lingered at the door until the Collinses and Maria returned. Mr. Collins was outraged. "Oh, my dear sirs! What can my cousin have been thinking, keeping you out here? Please accept my apologies on her behalf!" He was tripping over his own feet in his haste.

Richard felt the indignation, but Darcy was too busy enjoying the light in Elizabeth's eye as she silently laughed at the absurdity.

"Mr. Collins," Richard began. "We could hardly enter the house until you returned. Miss Bennet has been nothing but amiable as we waited for you."

Mr. Collins seemed to realize the truth of the matter and let it drop. "You must come inside to partake of some refreshments. You must be famished. It is so good of you to escort my dear cousin to our humble home."

Darcy decided to interrupt him before he could go on

further. The man had irritated him at every turn, especially when he thought of how he had had the audacity to propose to his Elizabeth. "Then let us go inside. It is unseemly to wait at the door for so long." He did not mind being rude if it yielded the desired result.

Mr. Collins quickly opened the door and offered Mr. Darcy and Colonel Fitzwilliam entry to the house. The ladies followed. Mrs. Collins moved to the kitchen to alert the cook to the need to provide some extra servings for the gentlemen, before joining everyone in the parlor.

Elizabeth happily followed with Maria into the dining room and selected a seat beside Mr. Darcy. Maria and Colonel Fitzwilliam spoke quietly together on the other side.

Elizabeth began her conversation. "I hope Lady Catherine is not put out because you are not eating with her and her daughter."

"Certainly not. She is probably still fuming about the situation at the Matthews' residence. I doubt she will notice our absence for another few hours."

Mr. Collins stepped up before Elizabeth could speak. "Lady Catherine is so benevolent to tend to the care of all her tenants and the people in the village. No task is too small for her."

Mr. Darcy sighed. He would never understand either his aunt or her sniveling parson. Elizabeth giggled under her breath at his response. Thankfully, Mr. Collins was oblivious to the exchange as Mr. Darcy smiled slyly at Elizabeth.

"Lady Catherine has graciously invited our party for tea after dinner. Your aunt is the height of condescension and grace, to be always inviting my family to Rosings." He continued in the same vein for another ten minutes while Elizabeth and Mr. Darcy exchanged a few small smiles and a quiet conversation whenever they felt the least chance of being heard. Elizabeth checked her laugh to keep from discovery. The subterfuge was entertaining in itself. Mr. Collins continued unabated until his wife reminded him to eat.

When the cold meats and cheeses had been consumed, the gentlemen excused themselves. Elizabeth then paid her attention to her cousin, who had not forgotten that she had been walking alone with two unmarried gentlemen.

"You must use proper decorum, my dear cousin. You should have waited for us to walk you home. It is unseemly for the nephews of Lady Catherine to have to escort you home and wait at the door for us. We can only hope that Lady Catherine will not be too displeased when she learns of this." He continued for some time unabated. Elizabeth reminded herself that Charlotte's happiness depended on her listening quietly to her cousin. In fact, she barely listened, thinking instead over the various conversations she had shared with the gentlemen and regretting that her time with them was coming to an end.

Once she was free to pursue her own engagements, she sat at a table to write a letter to Jane. It was so pleasant to read her letters, as she was feeling many peaks of happiness in her marriage. Nothing seemed too dull to mention with glee, especially now that Elizabeth had begun to write about Charlotte's domestic tranquility. Of course, she also had much to relate from her conversations with Mr. Darcy and Colonel Fitzwilliam. Knowing of the willing listener she held in Jane, she was happy to relate that her opinion of Mr. Bingley's friend had improved so much. She knew this would be welcome intelligence.

That evening, Elizabeth walked to Rosings with the Collinses with a spring in her step. Her heart was light, and she was ready to be pleased. She even waved at Mr. Darcy when she noticed him from an upper window. Thankfully, Mr. Collins was too caught up in a conversation with Maria to notice.

After dinner, she played the pianoforte again for the company, while Colonel Fitzwilliam turned the pages for her. A few songs into the performance, Mr. Darcy found himself free of Lady Catherine and able to walk towards the instrument to hear his young friend. While he could detect a few errors in her fingering, the melody was light and pleasing. Her expression conveyed ease and familiarity. He could only hope that he would be granted more evenings in her company.

When Lady Catherine demanded they switch to cards, Elizabeth closed the instrument. Luckily for Darcy, his aunt insisted on playing with the Collinses and Anne, leaving Darcy to make a table with his cousin, Elizabeth, and Maria. At Maria's request, they did not play for any money. Darcy partnered with Elizabeth so that he could sit across from her and glance frequently at her without inviting any suspicion from the other table.

"Do you enjoy playing whist?" Colonel Fitzwilliam began the conversation, speaking primarily to Maria.

Maria shrugged. "I suppose so. I prefer lottery tickets, but I know that is not as acceptable at Rosings as it was at home."

"There is more concentration involved with whist to be sure," Mr. Darcy added, as he played his first card. The others played theirs and Maria claimed the first set. The group continued in silence for a few rounds as Darcy concentrated on the gentle tapping of Elizabeth's fingers as she considered her cards.

Colonel Fitzwilliam was the next to speak. "Have you made any plans for while you are in London?"

Elizabeth looked up. "We are to stay with my aunt and uncle. When we passed through on our way here, my uncle took us to the theater. I do not know if he plans any further excursions. They have a very quiet social life with a few true friends. My uncle's business does not give them access to many social functions."

Elizabeth's bold speech was directed at her partner, who had schooled his features to remain neutral. He wished Elizabeth's connections might have been better than they were, but from her conversations he had ascertained that she thought them wonderful people. He would accept them for her sake. Perhaps, he might even learn to enjoy their company.

"How long are you to remain in London with the Gardiners?" He noticed her eyes widen slightly, as she must have been surprised that he would recall their names from previous conversations.

"We will remain for only a fortnight. With the warmth of the spring, it is unpleasant to spend much time in London."

"Do you enjoy spending the summer in Hertfordshire?" Colonel Fitzwilliam chimed in.

"Yes, I do. However, most of my summer will be spent on a tour of the Lake District with my aunt and uncle. They have invited me to travel with them."

Darcy perked up once again. "Have you ever been to the Lakes before?"

"Never. I am very excited for the chance to travel. My father does not like to be away from his bookroom, and our funds are not such that many excursions have been made. I do not regret my time in Hertfordshire as the country is very lovely, but my eagerness cannot be well concealed." Elizabeth stopped as she realized she was rambling.

Darcy watched her intently. Should he ever win her favor, he would ensure she toured many other parts of the country. "You say you have rarely traveled. Have you ever been to the seaside?"

"No, but I have read of the waves in many books."

"We are quite close to the seaside here. I would say forty miles, which is less than half a day's journey. Would you be interested in an excursion? The sea air would be healthy for Anne, and it would be something to do."

Elizabeth did not dare speak. She had not intended to travel while visiting Charlotte. Could she rationally travel with a gentleman to the seaside? If Miss de Bourgh traveled with them, surely it would be proper.

While she thought about how to respond, Maria piped in joyfully. "What an idea! Oh, I should love such an excursion. I will persuade my sister to come with us. Surely she could spare a day of chores and duties to come."

"There is plenty of room in my carriage for your sister, but I doubt there would be room for Mr. Collins, unless he were to sit with the driver," Darcy said plainly, hoping the obsequious parson would not deign to come and ruin a perfectly pleasant day out.

In her distraction, Maria lost the remainder of the rounds, earning a scowl from the colonel which lasted for barely a second as he enjoyed her glee. Two games later, Darcy and Elizabeth won each round, and Lady Catherine had finally grown tired of cards. Servants came in to remove the tables to their proper places, and the group gathered around the comfortable sofas.

Elizabeth quietly moved Charlotte to the side to ask for her opinion.

"Dear Eliza. If Mr. Darcy wishes to take you to the seaside, then who am I to oppose him. I believe Wednesday would be the best day, for Mr. Collins will be busy with his sermons for the majority of the day. I will have time to see all my other duties before then, so I will not neglect a thing." She turned and nodded at Mr. Darcy, knowing he had been listening from his perch beside his cousin.

"Aunt Catherine, what do you say to a tour of the seaside at Whitstable? We could be there and back again in one day. The sea air would do Anne a great deal of good, I am certain. Miss Bennet, Miss Lucas, and Mrs. Collins would appreciate the trip as well, I am sure."

Maria's legs started shaking as she attempted to sit quietly.

Lady Catherine looked at her daughter for a moment, who sat quite unresponsive. "I suppose Colonel Fitzwilliam will insist on coming as well."

"I cannot let my cousin enjoy the company of four women on his own. I would not miss the excursion even if my commander insisted upon my speedy return."

"I do not doubt that," Lady Catherine harrumphed. "I suppose it would be a good outing. What day would be best? There will not be room enough for Mr. Collins or myself, and we have no interest in spending the day in a comfortable carriage. We will be busy on Wednesday. Mrs. Collins, do you think your husband could spare your company on that day?"

When Mrs. Collins agreed to the scheme, Mr. Collins began a speech on the amazing condescension of Lady Catherine and her great nephews. This speech lasted until the carriage was called for. Maria spent the time quietly speaking with Elizabeth about all that she hoped to see. Elizabeth was not so engrossed in her conversation as to notice Mr. Darcy sneak out of the room and return fifteen minutes later with a book at his side.

When it was time for the group to leave, Mr. Darcy approached Mrs. Collins with the book. "Mrs. Collins, I wish for you to borrow this book from the Rosings library. It is about the environment of Whitstable and other seaside locations in Kent. You and your guests might have an interest in learning about the place we are to visit. I have marked a couple of pertinent chapters."

Mrs. Collins thanked him for his generosity and handed the book to Elizabeth, knowing that she was the intended recipient.

Elizabeth held the book to her chest as the carriage moved along the drive. Mr. Collins attempted to instruct Elizabeth on the proper care of a book from Rosings. She barely heard a word of it, which might explain the reason she snuck out of the house in the morning with it, clearly against Mr. Collins' edicts.

Mr. Darcy paced along the grove in the morning, wondering why Elizabeth had not come. He tried to think of reasons for her rejection of him, but he could not bring anything to mind. Perhaps Mr. Collins was upset that he had been paying so much attention to Elizabeth. Or perhaps Mrs. Collins had asked for Elizabeth's help with her duties to the village. It was even possible that Mr. Collins had learned of his true interest in Elizabeth. Any number of circumstances could have occurred, and he was at a loss as to what he should do until he heard her tinkling laugh from behind a tree a few yards away.

Upon turning toward her, he noticed that she was barely visible to him. No wonder he had missed her presence. How long had she been here? Had she seen his pacing?

"I would wish you a good morning, sir, but I fear you are

quite distressed!" Elizabeth laughed again, seeing his relief.

"I assure you, madam, that is very far from the truth. I see you have made good work of the book I sent home with your friend."

"Certainly. How could you expect me to do any less? I have never thought about the smell of salt as being refreshing. In the kitchen, it always seems so bland and sour."

Darcy claimed a seat beside a small tree and motioned for the maid to take a seat farther away. "That is because the kitchen is usually so full of other, more enticing aromas. When you are by the sea, there are no other smells to distract you. The wind calls to you and beckons you to walk along the beach. The salt dances over your skin, and undoubtedly through your curls as well."

Elizabeth blushed at such speech, but she did not back down. "It sounds exhilarating. Thank you for suggesting this adventure."

Darcy nodded and moved the conversation to the book. They talked about some of the sights the book suggested. Darcy had been there before, so it was easy for him to recount his memories of them. Neither noticed the passing time until the maid timidly asked that she return to the house. Darcy agreed, knowing they needed to part for the day.

The following day passed similarly. Darcy knew to look for Elizabeth sitting and reading the book, and he found her right away. After talking about the book's recommendations, he shared stories of traveling to the seaside with his family, particularly his mother. The sincerity of his emotions moved Elizabeth, and she had to blink back a few tears as she thought of Darcy as a young boy, losing his caring mother. She began to wonder how she had ever thought him reserved and ill-suited to company.

On the day of the planned tour, everyone rose before dawn, so as to arrive at the seaside with time enough to spend a couple of hours before returning. Four hours in the carriage seemed like a very long time, but the six people fit very comfortably. Darcy had thought to bring blankets and cushions for those who wished to sleep and books for those who wished to read. For himself, he was content to hold a book and watch Elizabeth as she read quietly. Her foot tapped out the poems, and her lips danced as she silently mouthed the words. How he wished to know her thoughts on the poems, since the author was one of his favorites, but with the other passengers sleeping, it was impractical to ask.

The carriage stopped three times along the road to change horses. Miss de Bourgh did not wake, but the others stirred to relieve themselves and to walk around the villages. Mrs. Collins bought a few trinkets to send home with Maria for her brothers and sisters. Elizabeth eyed a few bonnets, but she did not wish to burden the carriage with extra hat boxes that were unnecessary. Darcy noted her interest but could not think of a reason to purchase them for her.

When they finally stopped at their destination, Elizabeth quickly noted that they had arrived at an inn. Miss de Bourgh and Mrs. Collins, not suited for walking along the beach, hired a phaeton to take them around the small fishing village. Elizabeth, Maria, Colonel Fitzwilliam, and Mr. Darcy chose instead to walk along the beach after a refreshing tea at the inn. They walked with the ladies in front and the gentlemen behind for the first half hour. Elizabeth enjoyed the feeling of the sand pushing against her feet as she walked. Maria found it exhausting because she was not as used to walking.

Darcy and Fitzwilliam watched the ladies walk ahead of them.

"How long are you going to pretend to be Miss Bennet's friend?" Fitzwilliam began the conversation.

"For as long as she will allow me to be," Darcy stated simply.

"She has warmed to you."

"I have eyes."

"I never said that your eyes were failing. I do believe, however, that you are too close to see that she has begun to admire you."

"This is not your concern."

"I only wish for your happiness."

"Then be silent on the matter. You do not know what it is like to be on the receiving end of her anger. I will not put myself in such a situation again. When... if I am ever certain of her affection, then I will bare my heart to her. Until then, I am content to be her friend."

Colonel Fitzwilliam was silent as he watched the ladies. He had grown fond of the two ladies before him. If he had not known of Darcy's interest, he might also have considered Elizabeth for a wife. He had never felt that way about a woman before. Miss Lucas was engaging, but he thought of her as a distant cousin or sister. She was young and refreshing. While some of his acquaintances would consider a sixteen-year-old woman for matrimony, he could not become intimate with someone almost half his age. It was also clear she held no affection for him. No hearts would be broken. He would show her what gentlemanly behavior was, so that in the future, she would be able to recognize a rake.

After half an hour, Maria was panting from the exercise. She did not wish to quit the stroll, so instead Colonel Fitzwilliam offered her his arm and they moved farther up the beach where the sand was easier to walk over. Elizabeth and Darcy walked in the tough sand together, finally free to have any conversation they desired. Instead though, they walked quietly and slowly through the sand. Elizabeth supported her weight by leaning into Darcy, and he was too thrilled to suggest any conversation.

They were shaken from their camaraderie by Colonel Fitzwilliam. "Maria is asking if we know the castle ahead."

Darcy looked to where the colonel had indicated. "That is Tankerton Tower. Mr. Pearson owns the house. He is a lucrative business man. He has been changing careers since the decline of his copperas works. The manor is built from the bricks of said works. It is impressive, if a little unclean."

"As you have been here before, do you know the family?"

"No," Darcy replied simply.

Elizabeth realized that she should have known that answer. Mr. Pearson was a businessman.

"We should probably turn back."

"Is there anything to eat here?" Maria piped in.

"Yes. The oysters here are known to be the best you can buy. If that does not suit your fancy, we should be able to find a tea house nearby. The village square is just over there." Darcy indicated a row of houses in the distance followed by a church steeple.

Colonel Fitzwilliam asked if they should join the others first.

"We will if we can. They could be just about anywhere. Anne loves driving the phaeton around. It might be hours before we see her. Hopefully she understands that we must return tonight."

"I do not wish to spend more time in your coach today, Mr. Darcy." Maria piped in.

"Maria!" Elizabeth scolded her. Maria had never been so bold before.

"Do not reprimand me. I am enjoying today. I wish for more time at the seaside. Do not pretend you feel different."

"That is beside the point, Maria. Your sister must return."

As they walked toward the village, they spotted the phaeton approaching. When it stopped in front of them, Elizabeth noticed the first smile she had ever seen on Anne de Bourgh's face. Charlotte was smiling breathlessly.

Charlotte calmed down first. "I have not had many rides so fast. Miss de Bourgh has been so kind as to show me the area. We came to find you for we are famished. There is a tea shop just over there. Come and join us."

"We were just contemplating finding a place to rest and eat. We will follow you at a more sedate pace." Darcy bowed in agreement.

After collecting an eager Maria, the phaeton rode off and the three followed it on foot for the quarter mile to the small shop. Elizabeth looked around at the seaside village with great appreciation. Instead of a quiet afternoon in the Meryton village she was used to, this village was teeming with workers as they moved their fare to its destinations. She knew this was where many oysters in London came from. It must be quite a business keeping Londoners well-supplied. She had never had a chance to eat a freshly caught oyster before and was brimming with excitement.

They entered the small shop and their clothing, particularly that of Mr. Darcy and Colonel Fitzwilliam, earned them first rate care from the owner of the establishment. They were given a cozy table beside the window. Elizabeth looked over her shoulder and could see the waves rolling up the beach. Birds were dancing along the shore, looking for critters in the sand. The sound was exhilarating, energizing, and calming all at once. She turned back. "I had no idea how wonderful the seaside could be."

Colonel Fitzwilliam smiled. "So, which do you prefer: Hertfordshire or Kent?"

Elizabeth did not need time to consider her answer. "I would not discount the beauty of Hertfordshire simply because I am enchanted with the seaside. Both are remarkable areas. I would not give up my home for Kent."

Charlotte chipped in. "I have not regretted my decision, Lizzy, but then again I have not been so adamant about the out-of-doors as you are." A small smile indicated she was not actually upset.

"Charlotte, you cannot think I am blaming your choice. I am happy for all you have gained by marriage, even though I would not trade places with you if given the chance."

"So then, are you planning to marry a gentleman of Hertfordshire?" Colonel Fitzwilliam brought the subject back. Darcy coughed, wishing he could discreetly kick his cousin under the table for beginning such a topic.

"I have no intentions to marry at present. I am happy visiting my friends and meeting new people. When the time comes, it will not be the location of the gentleman that encourages me to the altar."

Darcy was thankful when the owner returned to the table

with the tea and steamed oysters. This would easily change the topic. "We are all hungry. We should not stand on ceremony."

Elizabeth noted the danger this topic had touched upon, but she could not regret her response. A small smile directed at Darcy was returned with a half-smile before he turned his focus to his plate. A few minutes into the meal, Maria remembered her desire to remain for a day.

"Charlotte, would you be terribly upset if we chose to stay until tomorrow? The carriage ride was so long, and there are so many places I should like to visit."

Charlotte looked around the table. Everyone either shrugged or smiled, indicating agreement. "My husband would not be pleased if we did not keep to our original plan, but I can see no other reason not to remain. Is there a way to send a message to let Lady Catherine and Mr. Collins know our plans? I suppose we should travel back to the inn to determine if they have rooms for us. If they are booked, then it makes no difference if I should object or not."

Darcy nodded and motioned for assistance from the owner. Once he arrived, he asked for a messenger to be sent to the inn to acquire rooms. Elizabeth had never seen such efficiency. Mr. Darcy was sure of the responses before the owner could give them. The messenger returned with a promise of three rooms reserved. Then came the discussion of who would share with whom. The ladies were insistent they would all share a room, so the gentlemen could be comfortable. The gentlemen, though, could not conceive of forcing ladies to share a room. An hour later, the group had still not come to a conclusion.

"I believe there is no way to resolve this situation, and it is now too late to return to Rosings. There is merit in all of our arguments. Send a messenger to Rosings so as not to worry Lady Catherine." Elizabeth spoke up. "Then we shall devise some sort of challenge and the winning team will share the room." She waited while Mr. Darcy paid for an express messenger. "Very well. What would an impartial challenge be? Certainly not fencing or any such physical challenge. Ladies are not allowed to practice such arts."

Darcy noted a look in Elizabeth's eye that hinted to the contrary. He smiled. "What would you say to a game of billiards?"

"Do you know where we could find a billiard room that would allow women to play in a respectable manner?" Charlotte quipped.

"Only if Lord Holsgrath is home, which I doubt."

Elizabeth laughed. "What would you say to a game of wits? Perhaps a poetry recital. Or we could stage a singing contest."

Colonel Fitzwilliam coughed. "That would never do. There is no contest when it comes to your ability to sing, and I have no intention of losing. Why not flip a coin and be done with the matter?"

"There is no skill in flipping a coin, Colonel," Maria quipped.

"On the contrary, there is much skill." He pulled out a shilling and flipped it four times. Each and every time it landed with the face of the king up.

Maria quickly asked to learn his trick, to which he refused. This started another round of arguments. "I have found a solution to our problem; so simple that we cannot argue the point. There are six of us. There are three rooms. We must all share with one person. Obviously, you and your cousin shall share a room, Mr. Darcy. Charlotte and I can share a room, while the remaining room can be shared by Miss de Bourgh and Maria. What is your opinion?"

Everyone nodded, clearly unused to hearing Elizabeth speak so determinedly. Mr. Darcy took this moment to whisper to Elizabeth that they should probably continue their walk. Elizabeth agreed. "I am ready for another walk in the sand. Mr. Bulstrode must be eager to have this table for another party."

The others barely halted the conversation as they rose and quit the shop. Maria eagerly asked for a phaeton ride, so Charlotte gave her space to her sister. Colonel Fitzwilliam also declared an intent to ride, tired as he was of watching Darcy and Elizabeth. They rode away with Anne directing the ponies.

Elizabeth watched in awe.

"I am amazed at her energy. She seems so pale and sickly when in company. I rarely see her speak. It is a surprise to see her so vibrant, even if she is quiet."

Darcy smiled at his cousin's retreating form. "Anne has always overplayed her illness. She has been weak ever since she survived a terrible fever when she was twelve. The phaeton gives her better motion, which is why she chooses it for her exercise. By sitting very quietly at home, her mother does not bother her. When you get to know her, you will see how talkative she can be."

"That must be a Fitzwilliam trait. She is much like you, I imagine. You have said more today than I ever heard you say in Hertfordshire."

Darcy scowled. "I should have exerted myself more while in Hertfordshire. I was afraid of drawing attention to myself. I do not enjoy being the talk of the town."

Elizabeth laughed. "You were still the talk of the town. The talk was simply uncharitable. You have improved upon acquaintance." She moved away to run down along the beach.

Mr. Darcy and Charlotte followed behind. Charlotte knew more than to speak when Darcy was so clearly enjoying his view of Elizabeth. It warmed her heart to know her dearest friend would be so well-settled when she finally realized her good fortune.

They walked along the beach in the general direction of the inn. Elizabeth eventually returned to her companions. Her cheeks were red from the chilled wind, and her chest was heaving from the exercise. Darcy could not imagine a lovelier scene. It was with difficulty that he refrained from proposing to her again then and there, such was his desire to be able to claim her lips.

"Today has been such fun! I believe I am growing very fond of the seaside," Elizabeth stated. Darcy could not think of a response.

When they arrived at the inn, the rest of their party were enjoying hot chocolate and oysters. Elizabeth accepted some chocolate, but she had eaten her fill of oysters, so she requested some biscuits instead. They were a little stale since they had been cooked in the morning, but they tasted delightful when dipped in the chocolate. The meal was a perfect balm for the chill they had caught along the shore. It brought out Elizabeth's playful side, and she recounted many stories of going out in the cold with her sisters and the Lucases as children. When prompted, she learned a few stories of the gentlemen's youth. She enjoyed hearing of Colonel Fitzwilliam as a boy, coaxing Mr. Darcy out of his reserved nature to play in the snow. Colonel Fitzwilliam had been fearless. Many of his tales seemed fraught with danger. Only when Elizabeth watched Mr. Darcy could she tell he was exaggerating.

Long after the hot chocolate had disappeared, they remained in the warm dining parlor. It was not until Miss de Bourgh yawned that the group decided to retire. Darcy watched the ladies as they left the room. He and his cousin then ordered a brandy before retiring themselves.

Richard was the first to speak after nursing the drink for a few minutes. "Darcy. I have to admit, you have picked the perfect woman for you. I cannot imagine anyone better to keep you happy. She will challenge you every day to be even better than you are."

Darcy could not speak. He already knew this. He did not need convincing. If only he could win Elizabeth's heart. "It is not late, but I am rather tired. Goodnight, Richard."

"You must be tired from having to hold your tongue throughout the day. If you had declared your heart, she would have run away. I am starting to agree with your tactic. The only thing I am certain of is this: you cannot let her go."

Darcy nodded and left the room after placing a few coins on the table. Fitzwilliam joined him soon after.

Darcy woke the following morning to the horrendous snores coming from the other side of the bed. He sighed as he got up. There was no point trying to go back to sleep. He moved to the window and looked out at the crashing waves. While the inn was not anything particularly wonderful, the view was certainly worth every farthing. He opened the window to allow the cold, fresh air to wash over him. While he had not slept entirely well, he was nevertheless rested and ready to face the day.

The sound of a door closing caught his attention, and he watched as a woman slipped down the path, having just left through the door beneath him. He smiled as he recognized Elizabeth's small form covered in a shawl. He watched as she swayed gracefully over the path toward the shore. Once she reached the sand, he watched even closer as she lifted her skirts just a few inches to walk in the water. Once she was secure of her footing, she began to dance and twirl. The water splashed around her ankles as the waves washed up and trickled down the shore.

Suddenly his feet needed to move. Not wishing for his cousin to wake, he shut the window slowly, careful to not make any noise. A few minutes later, he was standing at the edge where the beach met the grassy shore by the inn. He no longer had a plan. He looked around the beach and noted it to be deserted, save for a few workers a long way away. He and Elizabeth were alone. She had not yet seen him, but it was only a matter of time. He moved to the side of the path and found a bench looking out over the ocean. He innocently claimed his place and resumed watching Elizabeth.

A few minutes later, she turned and noticed him. She waved and walked up to him. Instead of greeting him, she simply claimed the seat beside him. They sat in silence for a few moments before Elizabeth chose to speak. "How long have you been watching me dance?"

Darcy responded that he had only just sat down.

Elizabeth laughed. "Did my shrieks wake you up? I must confess to not acting quite as a lady ought."

"You did not wake me. My cousin snores. You cannot think me about to reprimand you for any un-ladylike behavior. In private, such displays are acceptable. Your energy and vivacity are commendable." He wanted to say so much more, but he knew better.

They descended into silence once again. A breeze rushed by, and Elizabeth shivered. "We should return inside," Darcy said.

"I have no wish to sit in the parlor as we wait for the others to rise. I am comfortable enough." Elizabeth brought the shawl closer around her. "It is my own fault for going in the water." Attempting to warm up, she buried her bare feet in the sand. In doing so, she brushed against Mr. Darcy's arm. The heat was instant. After her feet were safely covered, she leaned lightly against him, enjoying the warmth.

"Watch over there." Darcy pointed with his free arm.

Within minutes, the sun crested over the water in the East very near the shoreline. Elizabeth closed her eyes as the warm beams bathed her. Darcy enjoyed the glow of the light over her face. They remained this way for two hours. The others were unlikely to rise early in the morning, so they had no obligations to keep. When they heard the owner rouse in his small cottage to the West of the inn, Darcy rose and offered Elizabeth his arm. They walked back into the dining room, and Elizabeth slipped upstairs to change while Darcy requested some food and hot chocolate with their tea.

Once their meal was coming, he looked around. Realizing the lateness of the hour, he decided he should wake Richard. It took a glass of water splashed over his face to finally rouse him. The disgruntled colonel descended the stairs half an hour later. Seeing the rest of the party happily laughing around a table, he checked his ill humor. Instead, he quietly listened to the others as he sipped his coffee.

With the meal finished, they refreshed themselves quickly before climbing back into the carriage. This time, no one slept. Anne happily chatted with Maria as they formed a friendship of sorts. Elizabeth joined in occasionally, but she was just as happy watching the scenery outside. Charlotte began thinking of the duties ahead of her, the first being the need to change into a dress free of wrinkles when she returned home.

10: CONFESSIONS

Darcy sighed as he took one last glance at Elizabeth. He knew he must be more circumspect for the rest of this visit. He wondered when he would see her again after she left for London. He did not have an invitation to Netherfield. He would need to explain his actions to Bingley. Darcy could not fear that Bingley would be upset. Hardly anything ever upset him. Certainly, this would be no difficult matter, other than Darcy's own reluctance to share his intimate thoughts.

"Mr. Darcy." Elizabeth's voice shook him from his thoughts. "We have arrived."

Darcy looked around and noted that the others had already departed from the carriage. "Thank you." He smiled and nodded before he climbed out of the carriage, turning to aid Elizabeth as she followed him.

Mr. Collins had been waiting at Rosings for the carriage to return. By the time Darcy descended the carriage, he had already been talking for some time. He barely listened, except to acknowledge that refreshments had been served in the parlor for them. Darcy took the initiative to offer his arm to Elizabeth and then to his cousin, before climbing the steps and leading the way to the parlor.

Lady Catherine and Mrs. Jenkinson were waiting inside,

eager to hear that everything had gone according to plan. Lady Catherine was so glad to see Darcy escort Anne into the room that she did not even notice Elizabeth until they had all sat down. "It was good of you to act as chaperone, Miss Bennet. I hope you enjoyed your excursion to the seaside."

"I did, Ma'am. Thank you."

Mr. Collins made his grand entrance as he escorted his wife into the parlor, talking of every minute detail that Mrs. Collins had missed the previous day, as though she did not already know what had happened at the parsonage while she was away. Elizabeth smiled at this scene of domestic tranquility, as Mr. Collins would call it. Mrs. Collins listened attentively.

Darcy attempted to engage his cousin in conversation, but Miss de Bourgh had already reverted to her quiet self. Lady Catherine smiled at his attempts as she turned her attention to her other nephew, who was quietly talking to Maria. Once she was safely talking to Maria and the colonel, Darcy was able to shift his attention to Elizabeth once more.

"How well did the waves compare to what you had read in books, Miss Bennet?"

"That is an easy question. While books have the ability to transport you around the world and see new things, they cannot encompass all the senses the same way the real scene can. The waves laugh as they lap up the shore. The smell both tickles your nose and refreshes your mind. No book can compare."

Darcy smiled with the pride that came from having caused her to enjoy such a scene. Surely, he could show her much more as her husband. Quickly, he quelled that thought. He would not be caught dreaming of her again.

"It is refreshing. My sister loves trips to Ramsgate, where we have a cottage during the summer months." Suddenly his thoughts darkened as he remembered her last trip to Ramsgate. Would they ever go again? Ramsgate would never be the same.

"That must be delightful," Elizabeth replied. She could not tell why Darcy was suddenly troubled, but she knew that the conversation must end to save his spirits. "How similar is the seaside to the Lake District? Are the lakes large enough to mimic the sea?"

Darcy nodded. "The smell of salt is absent, but the lakes are large enough for you to experience some waves, though smaller than those you experienced this morning. It is the mountains and rugged terrain that captures the senses more than the water."

He continued for some time describing the various haunts he had visited with his family until Mrs. Collins interrupted to say that it was time to return home. Maria agreed, stating that she was tired, and Mrs. Jenkinson took the chance to steal her charge upstairs before any protests could be made.

Darcy watched as Elizabeth exchanged her goodbyes with Lady Catherine and Colonel Fitzwilliam. She moved with such grace that an unskilled observer would not have thought she had just traveled. It suddenly became important to Darcy that she visit his home over the summer. He would invite the Bingleys for a few months. Then it would be nothing to invite Elizabeth and the Gardiners to visit as they passed through.

The winter was more uncertain. He would invite the Bingleys to join him for the season, but then Elizabeth would not be able to accompany them. It would be unseemly for her to stay in a bachelor's home for so long, even if her married sister were present. It would be best for her to stay with them at the Hurst's home, although she would not get so many invitations to balls and dinners from the best of society. Perhaps he could use his leverage to bolster the Hursts' interest between now and then. He certainly held plenty of sway with members of the ton.

He watched her carriage ride away. She would leave in a few days. Their time of separation was coming. At least he knew he had a chance to win her heart and hand.

"Darcy, are you planning on leaving on Saturday, as we had planned?"

"No," he said, still watching the carriage.

"Good. I am enjoying the company immensely. You have made great successes on this trip. A letter came for you while we were away. Lady Kennilworth has invited us to her ball on Friday. We should attend. It would be good for Anne to be seen out in society. Perhaps someone will fall in love with her or her money."

"Do you suppose they would invite the clergy?"

"Most certainly not. They are as pompous as our aunt. You cannot refuse just because she will not be there. It would do for our aunt to see you interested in escorting Anne to the ball. Mrs. Jenkinson can attend her, so once we arrive we need not pay her any mind, as she would prefer. You know that she never attends any functions if you are not to be there."

"Perhaps we should have your mother invite her to London for the season."

"Only if she can survive a ball held here in the country."

Darcy nodded. He would prefer a ball with Elizabeth in attendance, but it would be better than staying at Rosings with his aunt for the evening. And Richard had a valid point. Getting Anne out into society would increase her chances of finding a husband. It was her only chance to leave the confines of her mother's own society. "How shall we convince our aunt of the scheme? She never attends, for she has certainly never received an invitation when we were not present."

"There is nothing so easy if you are escorting our cousin."

Richard's prediction came true. Lady Catherine was so delighted with the idea of Darcy and Anne attending a ball that she did not mind the slight of not having been invited before. Lady Catherine could never imagine staying awake for so long, especially since she would not be the highest member of society present. Being only the third or fourth highest rank did not please her. She released her daughter to attend with Mrs. Jenkinson, Darcy, and Richard.

With the matter settled, Darcy departed to inform his valet, who would surely need to send a messenger to town for suitable evening wear. Looking out of the window in his chambers, he spied Elizabeth walking through the rhododendrons. He smiled, thinking of meeting her there, especially since their time was coming to a close. A missive from the steward tore him from the possibility. He needed to finish going over the account books and preparations for the planting by the end of the week. With a final glance out of the window, he strode from the room, wishing for once that he were not such a hard-working estate master.

The next morning, Darcy woke early, even though he knew he would be awake late in the evening. He wished to see Elizabeth. He would risk being tired at the ball. He smiled as he prepared his toilette. He needed to savor these interactions. He could count the number of times he would see her here on his right hand. His smile vanished. He needed to return to Pemberley to see to various matters. He could not delay his departure any further.

Knowing he could do nothing to change this, he dashed downstairs and out of the door. The cold air hit his face as he braved the morning chill and breathed in the fresh air. Minutes later, he found Elizabeth waiting just beyond the gate. Her smile was infectious. This time, she took his arm before he could offer it to her. Would he see her before the season? Only if everything panned out.

He smiled at the thought that she welcomed his attentions. Surely, he could not be mistaken, even if she was only accounting his actions to friendship. "Shall we tour another part of Rosings' fine grounds today?" He asked.

"I am at your disposal, Sir." Elizabeth smiled in eager anticipation. He led her down the path leading east of the estate. After rambling through a well-traveled path, Darcy led them to the right and onto a narrower path that had many low branches to avoid. Twice, he helped Elizabeth and the maid over a fence to continue the journey. They did not say much, as the scene required. The birds had begun their morning calls, and it was pleasant to simply listen to them. "A few months ago, this would have dirtied our hems. I am glad the ground is so dry," Elizabeth remarked.

Darcy's memory returned to the time she had walked to

Netherfield through the mud to tend to her sister. Indeed, she had looked surprisingly lovely with her cheeks red and her hair disorganized. It had been a vision about which he had dreamed often. Now, she looked the same again, and her chest was beginning to heave from the exertion. He slowed their pace. Fifteen minutes later, they arrived at a small clearing where deer were quietly munching grass. He signaled to remain silent. Standing at the edge of the clearing, they could see six deer and four fawns meandering through the meadow. They watched with fascination until they were spotted, and the mothers escorted their young away.

Elizabeth let out a long breath. "I have never been so close before. They are magnificent. It is hard to imagine someone sporting for such a creature."

"It is a good meal for many if one can be caught. We do not hunt them until they are older and no longer need their mothers."

"I suppose that makes it more acceptable. This meadow is heavenly." Elizabeth walked out to where the sun could bathe her face in its warmth.

Darcy watched, wishing he could act on his impulses and embrace her with his warmth, but he had to be content. A few minutes later, the maid coughed. They should be returning. He claimed Elizabeth's arm for the walk back and relished in the small victory. When the parsonage came into view, Elizabeth made her farewells. "I shall see you tomorrow."

"That might not be possible, though I will try to be here." At Elizabeth's quizzical expression, Darcy elaborated. "I am escorting my cousin to a ball at a neighbor's residence."

"I am surprised you came this morning. How will you keep your eyes open tonight?" Elizabeth laughed.

"Such a cost will have been well worth it, Miss Bennet." On impulse, he kissed her hand as he bowed and bid her farewell.

The evening was a success. Darcy danced once with his cousin and found a few other ladies with whom he could dance as well. Conversations were stilted, either because Darcy kept thinking of another lady or because his demeanor was not suited to encouraging a conversation. Anne had a grand time, meeting many of her distinguished neighbors for almost the first time. As the colonel had hinted, a few of the second sons had paid her a good deal of attention.

The following morning, Darcy woke tiredly and made his morning ablutions. His steps felt like lead, but he could not forsake a chance to walk out with Elizabeth. His valet fared better than he, as he had been able to rest until Darcy's return. Consequently, Darcy's attire was impeccable, even if he did not feel equal to it.

They walked in silence for some time. Darcy realized she was agitated and so let her be. At first, he racked his memory, trying to determine if he could be the cause of her agitation. Her warm welcome quickly put that thought to one side. Ready to be a listening ear, he waited for her to begin.

"Mr. Darcy, I have a confession to make to you," she finally said.

His breath quickened. Only two thoughts came to the forefront of his mind. Either she was ready to finally reject him definitively, or she had warmed to him and was welcoming his suit. As it turned out, neither was the case.

"I was overly rude to you when we first met. My only excuse was that I overheard a remark that wounded my vanity at the assembly."

Darcy thought back to that night. "I thought you had heard me, but I was too self-absorbed to care. I did not wish to be there, and I wanted everyone to be as miserable as myself. I ought to thank you for showing me how wrong I was to assume my behavior was acceptable."

Darcy watched as Elizabeth brushed away the compliment. "Miss Bingley had no interest in checking your behavior, so someone else had to. My purpose today was not to discompose you or to ask for your thanks. I wanted to explain why I chose to dislike you so much in Hertfordshire. That is why I tried to argue with you at every turn. Then..." She paused. Darcy hesitated, and they stopped. They were enclosed by the heavy woods, alone but for the maid who trailed behind. "That is why I believed his lies, for that is what they must have been. Now that I have seen your true character for myself, there is no possibility that what he said could have been true. I was a fool."

"No." He paused, startled by his own vehemence. "You are not a fool. I had given you no reason to believe any good of me. Should I return...when I return to Hertfordshire, I will take further steps to correct the bad impression I have given."

Elizabeth looked at his eyes, suddenly unsurprised by his sincerity. "I need to know, however much it might pain you. I can no longer believe that you resented him without reason. For the protection of the people of Meryton, I must ask if we are... safe."

Darcy stopped in his tracks. He had not considered the question before. He could not have imagined telling the people of Hertfordshire his reasons against the lieutenant, but now it seemed necessary. Knowing he could trust her, he began, "I would certainly not be surprised to learn that he has run up debts with the merchants and debts of honor with his fellow officers."

After a few deep breaths, he looked her direction and noticed her expression, such that he knew he must continue. "What he has done is not suitable for a lady's ears. No, you are not safe when he is near. Women, particularly unprotected women, have perhaps more to fear than shopkeepers."

"He is engaged at present to a Miss King."

"Is she rich?"

"She has inherited a large fortune."

"He is unlikely to maintain his marriage vows past laying his hands on her money. I hope her father is good with his finances and protecting her money. Her only hope of a happy future is if he changes his mind before they are wed. It would be better to be jilted than to be stuck with him forever." He turned and began to pace. After a few minutes, he began again. "This is not his first engagement. I doubt it is even his second."

Elizabeth looked up in confusion. She could clearly see the anger lurking behind his eyes. It must have been someone close to him. "Do you mean your sister?"

Darcy closed his eyes. He had not meant to give away her identity, but he also knew he could trust her. "She was fifteen at the time. She has not fully recovered."

"We should continue walking, Mr. Darcy." She wrapped her arm around his, offering what comfort she could.

For a few minutes, he let her lead the way to the rhododendrons. He could not help thinking of how much he wanted her by his side always, not only for himself, but for Georgiana as well. "I wish you could meet her," he said, barely realizing he had spoken at all.

"I am certain I shall meet her eventually. Perhaps when we are in London for the season. Mama is hoping that Jane will host me in London, along with Lydia and Kitty, of course. I doubt Charles could survive so many Bennets in one house, so I shall simply have to claim seniority."

"There is another alternative," Darcy added, "I have been pondering the issue for some time. It is my desire to host the Bingleys at Pemberley over the summer. You would be welcome as a guest as well."

"I will be traveling with my aunt and uncle."

"I would invite them if I were acquainted with them. I do not wish to extend the invitation if your aunt or uncle would feel slighted because we have not been introduced."

"I doubt either my aunt or uncle would feel the slight, but if that worries you, then you could simply come to Netherfield at the time of my departure. I am certain we would come together at some function or other."

"Do you suppose the Bingleys would wish for a houseguest so soon after their marriage?"

Elizabeth laughed. "Charles and Jane are the least likely people to mind a houseguest, and even if they did, they would never admit to it. I shall confess that I am often at Netherfield when I reside in Hertfordshire. My sister is an excellent hostess, and I have encouraged Charles to purchase some books to improve his library. He has been able to procure some freshly-printed books from some of my favorite authors. My father does not have such connections."

Darcy nodded, and they continued the conversation for a few turns of the maze. Eventually, Elizabeth brought the conversation back to her initial query. "I promise to keep your sister's past to myself, but should I attempt to warn Miss King?"

"Are you much acquainted with her?" Darcy sobered immediately. His mind had been, once again, on his potential future.

"We do not meet often, although she has been at a few social functions where I have been present."

"Then there is not much you can do. Correspondence is not possible. I suppose you will be in his company when you return to Hertfordshire."

"I suppose so, but you cannot think me in any danger."

Darcy smiled. If Wickham knew how much Darcy admired her, she might be in some danger. "No, I do not believe you susceptible to his false charms. Perhaps you or your father could hint to the shops that they should be wary of his debts. He is so able to please that many do not even know how indebted they are. The credit pinch might make him flee."

"How can he have accrued so much debt in Hertfordshire? He has not even been there for a full year."

Darcy laughed. "Quite easily. He gambles and purchases without thought of money. His colonel might be able to check his behavior, if he is aware of the man Wickham is."

"Would you be able to speak with Colonel Forster?"

"Colonel Fitzwilliam could, and he would definitely enjoy Hertfordshire society in the process. This is supposing my cousin and I are invited to Netherfield."

"I suppose Colonel Fitzwilliam and Mr. Wickham are not on the best of terms."

This time Darcy roared with laughter. A few minutes passed before he could explain himself. "I doubt you recall the first time I saw Wickham in Meryton. Wickham nearly fled at the sight of me, but it was not me on his mind. Colonel Fitzwilliam promised to run him through if he ever caught him. He is Georgiana's guardian as well."

"I remember. I was brimming with curiosity. That was when I first believed his lies. I still cannot believe what a fool I was. Every piece of evidence now in my possession contradicts him."

"You cannot be too hard on yourself. No harm is done, and many have fallen prey to his charm and easy manner."

Elizabeth changed the topic, not comfortable with his forgiveness. Five minutes later, they were out of the maze and returning to the parsonage. As they entered the gates of the parsonage, Elizabeth said, "We have not been invited to Rosings tonight, sir, so I shall see you tomorrow morning in church."

"Goodbye." With a gallant bow and a kiss of her hand, he walked away.

11: MATCHMAKING

The following morning, Elizabeth dressed with more than the usual care for church. When Charlotte asked the reason for this, she slightly blushed as she evaded the question. She walked with the Collinses and Maria to church but opted to walk around the grave posts before going inside. This gave her a clear view of the carriages. When Lady Catherine's carriage was visible, she meandered towards the entrance of the church.

"Miss Bennet, your dress suits you very well. I am relieved to see you are finally taking my advice." Lady Catherine nodded her approval.

Elizabeth thanked her ladyship as she turned her eyes to the colonel, who was escorting Anne. This was the first time she had seen Anne since the trip to the seaside, and she was surprised to see how healthy she looked. "Good morning, Miss de Bourgh. I will pass on your mother's complement to you, for you look truly well this morning."

"Thank you, Miss Bennet." On impulse, she abandoned the colonel's arm for Elizabeth's. "I have had such a good time this past week. First the seaside, and then my first ball in ever so long. It has been such a dream!" She looked over her shoulder to ensure they were not overheard. "Lord Metcalf is bringing his family for dinner tonight. I hope my mother invites your party for the evening. I should dearly like to hear your and Maria's opinions of his son."

"If invited, I will ensure we pay close attention to him."

They walked to Lady Catherine's pew, and it became apparent that Anne had no intention of leaving Elizabeth. As a result, Elizabeth sat between Lady Catherine and Anne while Darcy and the Colonel sat on each end. Lady Catherine enjoyed watching Darcy stare at Anne, although the actual object of his fascination was the movements of Elizabeth's hands through the service.

When the service ended, Colonel Fitzwilliam ensured the Collinses were invited after dinner by boldly inviting them himself. Lady Catherine was prevented from offering a response by Darcy claiming her attention. After the colonel winked at Elizabeth, she understood this had been premeditated. She returned to her party with the issued invitation, stating that they would not be the only guests. Mr. Collins was overwhelmed at being invited while other illustrious people would be present, and he attributed such an event to his belief that his position as servant of God meant he was one of the highest ranks of society. His foolishness provided Elizabeth with merriment for the rest of the day.

Elizabeth walked with Maria, slightly behind Mr. and Mrs. Collins, using this time to relate what Miss de Bourgh had said. With this information, Maria smiled, glad to be of use to someone. This would give her a purpose, making her less timid of meeting superior people.

Once the introductions were out of the way, Elizabeth chose a seat away from the others to observe them better. Maria and Colonel Fitzwilliam joined her moments later. "What are your impressions of our neighbors?" He asked.

"They know their place in society," Elizabeth answered noncommittally. "It would appear that Miss de Bourgh has an admirer."

"She certainly does. He has just finished his studies, and marriage to her would mean he would not have to look for a position or worry about working a day in his life. He could do worse than Lady Catherine for a mother-in-law."

Elizabeth nodded, looking over to Mr. Darcy, who was talking with Anne and Mr. Willstone, the second son of Lord Metcalf, before looking around the room again. Lord Metcalf and his eldest son were speaking with Lady Catherine, while Lady Metcalf spoke with Mrs. Collins. Mr. Collins was without partner, looking at the others as though determining who would be the most likely listen to him. Lord Metcalf's two daughters were talking to themselves in another corner, clearly not interested in anything the room had to offer. Returning her glance to Mr. Darcy, he nodded at her and moved from his group to speak with Lady Catherine.

"Yes, Darcy that is a capital idea. We should have some music. Of course, my Anne would play very well, if her health had allowed her to learn. Lady Metcalf, do you believe your daughters would be willing to perform for us tonight?"

Lady Metcalf answered for her daughters in the affirmative, and they moved to the instrument. Everyone moved seats to be able to attend to the music. Elizabeth smiled at the memory of her musical abilities not having incited such a movement. The ladies played three duets. Their voices were clear, and their notes were fast and accurate. No observer could detect a fault in their performance. Elizabeth hoped no one asked her to play, for she could not compete with such excellence. When there was a pause in the music, Darcy moved to sit beside Elizabeth.

"I would ask you to perform, but I remember you attempting to decline at Lucas Lodge when you were in front of *people who were in the habit of hearing the very best performers*, though I must say I should dearly like to hear you play for us."

"I cannot tell if that is a compliment to my playing."

"I do not find your playing to be lacking in any way. I would prefer hearing you miss a few notes than listen to others play so effortlessly and without feeling. However, I would not wish to make you uncomfortable."

Elizabeth nodded. "Your aunt's criticisms are enough for me." She looked over to Anne, who was quietly talking to Mr.

Willstone. "Anne has asked me to give her my impression of her suitor, but I know nothing of him. He certainly seems to be a gentleman of fine caliber."

"I have already given her my opinion of the man, since I have known him for a very long time."

Elizabeth longed to know if his opinion was favorable or not, but it appeared he would give no hints. "I leave tomorrow morning for London."

Darcy took a deep breath and slowly released it. "Will you have time for one last walk through the rhododendrons?"

"I will, but only if I can wake very early."

Darcy nodded and became thoughtful. While he had known she was leaving, the realization was unpleasant. He knew he would not see her for some weeks at least, even if he did secure an invitation to Netherfield.

When the song ended, Elizabeth moved to join Anne's small group. Mr. Willstone was regaling the group with an anecdote from town. "When my sister came into the room, everyone grew so quiet you could hear a pin drop. It was not until later that she learned everyone had been talking about her fall the evening before. It was quite the scandal for her to trip on her partner's leg and fall onto someone else's betrothed. The ton can be very unforgiving."

"I have heard such things. My family would be quite the affront, I am sure of it. I am glad to reside in the country where we laugh and gaily dance about without such cares," Elizabeth stated.

Mr. Willstone nodded. "That is why I seek a country life instead of the life of a judge in town, though that is what my studies prepared me to be. I shall not be sad if I can find a woman who will appreciate living a quiet life in the country. Country balls are much pleasanter than balls in London."

Elizabeth offered a quick smile to Anne and watched as Mr. Willstone did the same. It seemed certain these two would be betrothed quickly if left to their own devices. Elizabeth changed the conversation and they talked of books until Elizabeth realized neither her companions were well-read. Half an hour later, she was bored. She looked to Mr. Darcy to see if he would rescue her.

By the time Mr. Darcy accepted the invitation to join Anne and Elizabeth, Lady Metcalf had announced her desire to return home. This brought an abrupt end to the evening. Everyone shuffled around to assemble their party and say farewell to their hosts. Darcy walked through the hall with Mr. Willstone while watching Elizabeth out of the corner of his eye. In the drive, Elizabeth, Maria, and the Collinses waited while Lord Metcalf and his family had climbed into their carriage. Once they were on their way, the carriage for the Collinses drew forward. Darcy interrupted the footman so that he could open the door. This allowed him to offer Elizabeth his assistance to help her climb into the carriage.

Once the carriage was on its way, there was no one to worry about the fact that Darcy was standing outside, watching it slowly move away. Returning inside, he immediately made his excuses and returned to his chambers for the evening.

In the morning, Darcy walked briskly to the parsonage. He was just a few minutes late and was afraid he might not get a chance to walk with Elizabeth. The maid trailed behind him in a near run. When they arrived at the gate, Elizabeth was nowhere to be found. They paused long enough for the maid to catch her breath. The pause allowed Darcy to think. Elizabeth had never been late. Perhaps she had already walked to the rhododendrons. With her leaving after breakfast, it would be her last chance to see them for some time. The other possibility was that she had remained inside the parsonage, but it seemed highly unlikely.

He walked on the shortest path that would lead him to the rhododendrons. He slowed his pace when he heard her gentle humming. Walking slowly and carefully, he entered the rhododendron walk and came up behind her. She was breathtakingly beautiful as she dipped her head into a bush, smelling the flowers and humming happily. She did not turn to look at him as she greeted him. "I knew you would find me here. I woke early, so I came here straight away. This is such a magical garden. I shall dream of it often."

Darcy walked the rest of the way to her. He wanted to share his dreams, but he knew better. "You will return. Longbourn is not so far away that you cannot visit your friend again."

"That is true, but I do not know when that will be. Traveling to the north in the summer and spending the season in London is a full schedule. I doubt I will be able to come here again for some time. The flowers have started to fade."

"They are sad you are leaving." ... and so am I, he added in his thoughts.

Elizabeth turned and considered Darcy for a moment, realizing where his thoughts must be. "I hope we have a chance to meet again soon. I have grown fond of our time together. You are a very valuable friend."

Darcy nodded, not trusting himself to speak.

"Do I make you uncomfortable?" She asked innocently.

He frowned at the thought. He was uncomfortable, but he would not have her know that. "No, I enjoy our time together very much. We are both learning the process of being friends." He offered her his arm, and they walked together in silence down the rhododendrons and through the maze. This time, Elizabeth walked straight through without making one wrong turn. Satisfied with her progress, she announced the need to return the parsonage. "I would not want to delay the carriage."

Darcy made small talk as they walked their last few steps to the parsonage. At the gate, he bid her farewell and kissed her hand. "Until we meet again, my friend."

Elizabeth curtseyed as she claimed her hand back. "Goodbye, my friend."

Darcy did not return to Rosings until after he had seen the carriage ride away an hour later. Colonel Fitzwilliam was waiting for him, and they finished preparations for their own journey to London the following day. Nothing could tempt them to remain at Rosings any longer.

12: PEMBERLEY

The next two weeks passed slowly for Mr. Darcy. On his return to London, he found he had plenty of business with his solicitor regarding his many investments. In the evenings, he attended to his sister and the colonel's family. Everyone was surprised at the change in his demeanor. The sulking gentleman had disappeared so quickly that twice he was asked if he had decided to marry Anne. His response was even more puzzling, as he replied that he would never do so and that he was simply delighted by a new friend he had acquired. It was up to Colonel Fitzwilliam to explain what he meant, after he had enjoyed their repeated inquiries for a few days.

About the time that Darcy thought Elizabeth had returned to Hertfordshire, he and his sister removed to Pemberley. Georgiana was delighted to have her jovial brother returned to her. They rode over the estate and spent time in the music room whenever Darcy was not busy managing tenant and farming matters. Darcy was so happy to see his sister so changed from the previous year, he decided it was time to set his plans into motion. He wrote to Bingley inviting his family to Pemberley for the summer months.

Georgiana spent her time walking along the summer flowers, while Darcy spent his time seeing to various estate matters. Within the first day, he could feel the change that hope had rung through his actions. Before, he had been meticulous and honorable in finding fair solutions. Now, he felt something akin to flights of fancy, trusting the assertions of his trustworthy tenants who wanted to attempt radical change for the better, implementing new farming techniques that could prove either disastrous or fortunate. He was still not being careless but gave more leeway to tenants with long histories of good behavior.

Two weeks later, he not only received a favorable response from Bingley as to the invitation; he also learned from Bingley that the Gardiners had accepted the invitation to stay at Pemberley as they would pass through Lambton for at least two nights. Far too eager for their arrival, he immediately rang for the housekeeper.

Mrs. Reynolds entered quickly. "How may I help you, sir?" It was not uncommon for her to respond to the master, since the acting mistress of the estate was so young.

"I have a large party coming. Mr. Bingley and his new wife will be staying for a month complete. It is also very probable that Miss Bingley and the Hursts will come as well. Mrs. Bingley's sister, aunt, and uncle will be staying for a few days as they pass through, and they are to have the best rooms in the guest wing. They should arrive sometime in early July. I will travel to London between now and then, but I might have Miss Darcy remain here. She prefers Pemberley to London, particularly in the summer."

"She will be well protected. Everything will be prepared for your guests. I suppose Mr. Bingley will not wish for his usual rooms. Does he still prefer the setting sun?"

"Yes, so please give the golden suite to them. The rose suite with its westerly windows will suit the Gardiners well, I am certain, and Miss Bennet must be placed near them, since they are her chaperones. Miss Bennet will also require a maid to assist her and escort her on walks about the estate. She can easily walk three or four miles of a morning, so if no one is able, they should start practicing now."

Mrs. Reynolds noted how her master's demeanor changed at the mention of Miss Bennet. "She must be a very singular lady."

"Indeed, she is very singular. See to it that Cook has the best pies and lemon tarts prepared for her arrival."

Mrs. Reynolds offered him reassurance and left the room to see that preparations began. For the first time, she wondered if the mistress suite might be reopened soon and smiled the rest of the day.

Mr. Darcy was also smiling, but it did not give him an enjoyable day. It seemed that the more he wanted to stop and think of Elizabeth, the more matters of great import were being put before him. He already had five tasks to send to his solicitor in London and multiple business meetings for his steward to arrange. A trip to London would take weeks, and it meant that he would not be able to travel to Netherfield before the Bingleys began their journey. He would have to content himself with the fact that he would see Elizabeth in a month, give or take a few days or weeks.

A week later, he was able to confirm from Mr. Bingley's splotchy note that the Hursts and Miss Bingley would be in attendance. He also found out that the Gardiner's trip had been delayed by a fortnight and shortened. Instead of going to the Lakes, they would only tour Derbyshire instead. To be certain they would remain at Pemberley when they came, Bingley announced he would remain with his wife for two months while his sisters traveled on to Scarborough to visit Hurst's relations. Darcy counted the days before he would see Elizabeth again; there were too many.

Darcy had become used to seeing Elizabeth each day and felt her absence keenly. Every time he engaged in an activity, he could hear her voice alongside him. Whether he was reading, talking to Georgiana, or even dealing with estate matters, her opinions were made known. He longed to know if his thoughts were in any way accurate. Any other lady's responses would have been guaranteed, but Elizabeth's had always been surprising. She could even argue the opposite side

Bingley as he watched them walk away. When he finally looked away, he turned to see Mr. Bingley watching him.

"Is there any brandy in your study?" Mr. Bingley asked.

Darcy blushed and nodded. How many would find out about his quest for Elizabeth's hand? He led the way, glad Mr. Gardiner had chosen to retire with his wife and Mr. Hurst had followed. He had not seen Mr. Bingley since he had given his approval for Bingley to marry Jane Bennet.

They entered the study, where Darcy poured two short drinks. Handing one to Bingley, he said, "Marriage seems to really agree with you, Bingley."

"It surely does. My Jane is an angel, but I wanted to talk about you. The last time I saw you before this trip was the day after the Netherfield ball. You had supported my attachment to Jane and gave me the courage to disagree with my sisters."

"Your courage has certainly grown."

"It has, and since we have been friends for so long, I feel that I must ask after your own welfare. I worried for you for most of the winter when you would not respond to my letters. Then in April I found out from my newest sister that you have become amiable and pleasing."

Darcy smiled reflexively. He had made a good impression on her.

"You told me to ensure never to speak of her in my letters. It was too odd a request to forget. As I said, you never responded. Miss Bennet spoke well of you in April, and for the past month you have been a better host to my family than you ever have been before, not that you were ever lacking. You have taken pains to get to know Jane and ensure our comforts. Today, you stare after Miss Bennet as though you are dying of thirst and she is water. What happened between the two of you? As my sister, I care about her."

Darcy moved to the window, uncomfortable with this necessary encounter. "I care about her as well. She has agreed to be my friend."

"But that is not what you want."

Silence reigned for a few minutes as Darcy calmed his heart.

"I am willing to accept her friendship until I can convince her to accept my suit."

"Convince her! How can you think she would refuse you?"

"Because she already has. Bingley, I should have told you sooner. I shall always regret what I said then. That is why I left so abruptly from Netherfield and never returned. I had believed my lot cast to be miserable forever, but then circumstances changed when I met her again in Kent. I spent my time showing her that I was not really the man she had met in Hertfordshire."

"You have succeeded. She speaks very highly of you. Now what are your intentions?"

"I have no intentions other than to be her friend. I am not ready to risk facing her rejection again."

"I doubt she would reject you again. She holds a regard for you and was clearly glad to see you today."

"Can you call that love?"

Bingley shook his head, considering the pain Darcy must feel.

"Then allow me to plan my own future. I am content to be her friend, nothing more."

"Will I need to chaperone you?"

"We will never be alone together. Her chaperones are here, and they are sleeping in the rooms beside hers. Not to mention that you and her sister are close to her as well. I have arranged for a maid to accompany her on walks, should she go out alone. Her reputation is safe."

Bingley hung his head. "I never doubted your intentions. Jane insisted that I speak to you. I did not find it necessary until I saw how you looked today."

"They are very close sisters. I hope for Georgiana to have such a sister someday. Come, we should return to the saloon. The ladies will be looking for us," Darcy said with all the finality he could muster. He was not used to laying out his private affairs for the viewing of others. He did not need Bingley, of all people, to counsel him. Then again, Bingley was married. Perhaps he did know a thing or two about being accepted. He paused. "What is your wife's opinion?"

"She is afraid you will hurt her sister, or she will break your heart. She wants both of you to be happy."

"As do I. Your wife is a very remarkable person. I do not believe I ever understood her good qualities before. And I can safely promise that neither you nor Mrs. Bingley will have any cause to worry for Miss Bennet regarding myself. I know how a gentleman must behave, and I would never willingly hurt her."

"Thank you." Bingley grinned and led the way to the saloon.

The rest of the party had already assembled in the saloon. Darcy addressed Mr. Gardiner and his wife. "Now that you are refreshed, allow me to welcome you to Pemberley. Would you care for a tour to stretch your legs?"

Mr. Gardiner accepted. His wife and Elizabeth followed them out of the room. Miss Bingley was not far behind. "Do let me come too. I enjoy hearing you describe your estate, where we have spent so many wonderful summers and winters together." She wrapped her hand around his arm and looked as though she were on top of the world.

Darcy wished to extricate her arm, until he saw Elizabeth suppressing a laugh. He would put up with Caroline Bingley if only for her amusement. He knew better than to encourage her, so he simply accepted her presence and moved on. He led them to the front of the house where any tour would normally begin. He quickly described the age of the house and explained for how many generations it had belonged to the Darcy family. He then turned into the front parlor and allowed the ladies to walk around.

The room was quaint, with a few chairs fitted around a perfectly trimmed table for a tea setting. The windows made the room very bright, aided by the light walls and yellow furniture coverings. Darcy watched as Elizabeth looked around. "This appears to be a room suited to impressing guests rather than entertaining friends."

Caroline tutted her disapproval, but Darcy nodded. "You are correct. My mother kept this room prepared for neighbors who were not intimately acquainted with our family. My sister learned how to use watercolors in this room a few years ago, as the light is so bright. Now, however, she prefers her private sitting room or the gallery hall for her paintings. Shall we continue?"

The ladies followed Darcy and Mr. Gardiner out of the room. Across the hall, they entered a secondary parlor which lead into a magnificent ballroom, which was easily twice the size of the Meryton assembly hall. "The decorations are a little old. My mother redecorated this room the year before I was born. I have not seen the need to redecorate as it has only been used for harvest celebrations."

Miss Bingley beamed. "It needs some new colors, but it is clear that your mother held excellent taste. The room only needs some new vases and a lighter wallpaper to be perfect."

Darcy cringed at the thought of Miss Bingley redecorating any rooms in this house. Thankfully for both, she did not notice Darcy's response.

"Mrs. Darcy will be a very lucky woman," Elizabeth said, almost too quietly for Darcy to hear. He had to convince himself that he had indeed heard her. The words made him feel giddy again.

"Follow me through here." He led the way through a passage along the far wall to a staircase. At the top of the stairs, he led them through a door which in turn led to a balcony surrounding the ballroom. "What do you think now?"

Elizabeth walked to the edge and looked around. "It is perfect. Your mother had excellent taste. Other than some repairs, the room should not be changed."

"You know nothing of society, Eliza," Caroline Bingley simpered. "You cannot allow an old fashion to remain. People expect change. These dark colors will not do at all anymore. The room was expertly featured twenty years ago, but Mr. Darcy will choose a wife who will keep with current fashions.

He will never lose his social standing because of his wife." To add to her words, she winked at Mr. Darcy.

"It would take substantially more than decorating or not decorating a ballroom for society to shun my wife." Darcy rose to his full height. "My wife will be respected because I will choose one who can navigate society with ease. She will know how to be respectful and witty. The London elite will not know what has happened, but she will be firmly ensconced in their midst before they can form an objection to her." It took all of his willpower not to look at Elizabeth as he spoke.

"Of course, because you will only select the perfect woman," Caroline simpered, hoping in vain that he meant her.

"We should continue," Darcy said, after noticing an odd expression on Mr. Gardiner's face. "Come this way." He led the way across the balcony and onto a ledge which bordered the hall in which they had originally been. On the first floor, he showed them the drawing room, music room, dining room, and gallery in turn. Each end of the gallery led to another wing of the house. Both ends led to guest wings, while the stairs on the north side led to the family wing on the second floor. He looked at Elizabeth longingly, hoping to one day show her those rooms, before announcing the end of the formal tour. "Would you care to see the gardens?"

Miss Bingley tutted. "Oh, Mr. Darcy! We are all tired after our ride, and the Gardiners are just in from their travels. You cannot expect us to be ready for a tour of your expansive gardens so quickly! We must rest."

Darcy said nothing more as Caroline led the way to the saloon to join the others. The Gardiners had begun to follow her but quickly stopped when they realized that Elizabeth and Mr. Darcy were not following. Darcy sighed as he realized he had finally rid himself of Caroline's presence. "Would you care for a tour, Miss Bennet? I am certain a small tour of the gardens would not fatigue you."

"No, indeed. I should like a stroll very much indeed."

She accepted his arm and they descended the main stairs to the ground floor with the Gardiners following behind, refraining from laughing at Miss Bingley until they were well out of earshot.

13: SISTERLY APPROVAL

Instead of going out through the front doors, however, Darcy astonished the party by turning at once to the back of the estate. They walked through a small parlor to the other side, where double doors led them to a small conservatory. Elizabeth gasped with delight as she looked around. "I did not know so many flowers could grow without direct sunlight!"

"These are orchids. They live amongst tall trees, so they do better in indirect light."

In every available space was a bit of bark or wire holding different orchids and bromeliads. Only about a quarter were in bloom, and there were easily over a hundred flowers in various colors. Elizabeth walked around a corner to find the glass house wrapped around the building. She also found a spiral staircase.

Mr. Darcy stood behind her, watching her with fascination. "My grandmother designed this room to feed her fascination with orchids. The morning light here heats the rest of the flowers every day. Through the winter, we light a fire if it gets too cold." He pointed to a fire pit. "The orange trees provide fruit all year long. They were my father's favorite."

"Where does the staircase lead?"

"It leads to Georgiana's favorite drawing room on the first

floor, and to the mistress' suite on the second floor. My grandmother could not stand to be far from her orchids."

"How is it that you have kept this from your guests?"

"They never ask to see it."

"I did not ask either."

Mr. Darcy laughed. "I knew you would appreciate this space. Come, we can access the gardens from here." He led them through a double door and into a garden full of daisies. "These were my mother's favorites."

"They are such happy flowers." Elizabeth sniffed a large clump of daisies.

"That path there leads to the ridge, should you wish to exercise."

"Not today, please, Lizzy," Mrs. Gardiner said.

Mr. Darcy agreed and led them to the front of the house to walk along the stream. Elizabeth noted the rhododendron bushes, even though they were no longer in bloom. Darcy walked with Mr. Gardiner and spoke of fishing possibilities as they entered a small wood. Elizabeth walked with delight as she took a small footbridge over the stream that followed the path. "I wish we could circle the park to see all its treasures."

"That would be difficult, for the park is 10 miles wide."

Mrs. Gardiner declared herself tired at the thought, so the four turned back. A few feet farther up the path, Mrs. Gardiner asked for her husband's support. In turn, Elizabeth gladly accepted Mr. Darcy's arm when it was offered. They quickly outstripped the others while Elizabeth recounted the places they had been traveling. Darcy enjoyed listening to her speak so much that he did not bother to tell her that he heard the majority of her accounts from the letters she had written to Jane.

The two were so engrossed in the conversation that they outstripped their companions by a quarter mile. Darcy recollected himself first and stopped to wait for them. "I hope this is a pleasant time for you."

"There is no way I could not enjoy my time at Pemberley. The grounds are magnificent and the company is delightful.

My host, especially, is turning out to be such a dear friend."

"I am relieved to hear it. There was a time I had feared we would never be able to meet with tranquility."

Darcy watched as Elizabeth grew pensive. She bit her lip, and he could sense her remorse even though she said nothing. He placed his free hand over the hand she had placed on his arm. "Do not worry about the past. The future is much brighter, Miss Bennet."

"Indeed it is, Mr. Darcy. I always say that one should think of the past only if its remembrance yields pleasure."

"You have no cause for concern there. I, on the other hand, must remember the more painful parts of our history, so that I can change for the better. There is not much of our past that does not reflect poorly on my part."

Elizabeth thought for a moment. "On the contrary, you were always honest to a fault, and I certainly admired your intellect when we were able to debate our differences. Besides, you proved to be very amiable when we met again in Kent."

Darcy smiled, "Thank you, Miss Bennet. You have given me something to think over. I am particularly suited to admonishing my behavior since I met you."

"You are... almost always a perfect gentleman." Darcy watched as she blushed, thinking of his botched proposal. Then she smiled again. "You only need a little liveliness to make you quite perfect now."

Darcy had to grip his hands to his sides to avoid crushing her with displays of his admiration. He could not believe what his ears had heard. Before he could speak again, the Gardiners caught up to them. Mr. Gardiner asked again about fishing prospects, causing him to abandon his scheme and entertain him.

That evening, Jane pulled her dearest sister aside to speak privately with her. The conversation began in the usual way, until Jane was comfortable enough to broach a delicate topic. "Dear Lizzy, you appear so happy here."

"Indeed I am, Jane. I had no idea the terrain could be so rugged and beautiful. I look forward to many hours out of doors tomorrow."

"The terrain is not what I was referring to. Lizzy; what is your opinion of the master of this estate?"

"He is my friend, and I look forward to seeing him more."

Jane paused, not wanting to pain her sister, but she had promised her husband that she would have this discussion. "You used to hate him with such vehemence."

"I was wrong, Jane. We mended our quarrel in April, as well you know. He is now one of the most amiable men of my acquaintance, after Charles, of course."

"Take care, Lizzy. I believe he is still in love with you. Would you break his heart so callously?"

"He does not act like a man in love."

"How many men in love have you seen?" Jane asked.

"One, but Charles' love for you was so easy to see. Why can Mr. Darcy not be the same?"

"His emotions are generally hidden."

"I do not believe that is the case. I did warn him in April that I was unlikely to fall in love with him. I do not love him, and you know I cannot agree to marry a man whom I do not love. I hope he does not ask me. I should hate to feel uncomfortable around him."

She would have said more, but a noise brought their attention to Mr. Darcy, who had dropped his book.

"Do you think he heard us?" Elizabeth asked in a quieter voice.

"I believe he did. Lizzy, please be careful."

"He is my friend. I will not hurt him if I can help it, but I cannot pretend to harbor a love which I simply do not feel."

Darcy held his breath. They were speaking so low that he could barely make out their words. If only Elizabeth knew what torture he was feeling. He had been about to propose again, with her words during their walk reinforcing his thoughts. Now, his heart had broken anew. Truly, she had not said anything she ought not to have. He had interpreted her words in the way he had wanted, and he was now paying for it.

Releasing his breath, he tried to think positively. She cared about him. That might be all she ever felt towards him. Patience had served him well in the past. He must endeavor to continue on that course. It was his own fault for listening to a conversation to which he should not have been privy. At least he had not made a fool of himself or made things worse, as she had hinted, by proposing too soon.

For a few minutes the room grew quiet, except for Miss Bingley, who was talking to her sister very loudly of the recent changes in London fashions. Georgiana was sitting with her but was clearly not interested in the discussion. The Gardiners had been talking quietly, but they seemed to have stopped and were observing their nieces intently. Mr. Bingley was standing by the fire, lost in thought.

Darcy counted his breaths as he regained his composure. It would not do to seem so out of sorts. When he felt master of his emotions once more, he asked if the party would enjoy a little music. Georgiana, Miss Bingley, and Elizabeth each agreed and perused the selection. By mutual agreement, Miss Bingley began with an Italian sonata. Her playing was spirited and quick. She rarely made any mistakes, despite the speed of her fingers over the pianoforte.

The second song she chose was an Italian love song. As her fingers moved fluently over the keys once again, she began to sing. Her voice was able to perfectly enunciate the words such that most in the room could understand her. They blushed, as is often the case with Italian love songs. Everyone tried to ignore how often she looked at Mr. Darcy, and he avoided her gaze entirely by watching Elizabeth throughout the song. Elizabeth quietly talked with Georgiana about their next performance.

When the song ended, Georgiana sat down to the pianoforte and Elizabeth stood behind her. Georgiana played while Elizabeth sang, and the performance moved more than just Mr. Darcy. When the song ended, Elizabeth laughed. "Georgiana, I have never been able to sing so well! It is rare that someone as talented as you will play with me. Perhaps you will be able to teach me a thing or two tomorrow. I know that my playing is flawed, although people are usually very kind."

Georgiana gasped. "But I have only heard your playing praised as some of the best music my brother has heard!"

Elizabeth laughed again. "Your brother has misjudged my abilities, no doubt for some mischievous reason. I believe it is my turn to play, however, so I will let you judge my performance yourself." Elizabeth joined Georgiana at the bench and rifled through the music, selecting a piece she had played before. The song was slow and steady, suiting her abilities perfectly. When the song ended, everyone applauded, including Miss Bingley, although she only half-heartedly appointed praise, adding at the end that she herself had stopped playing that song years ago.

"Thank you, Miss Bingley. There are so many songs here from which to choose. I might just have to spend some time in the morning going through the selection." She rifled through a few pages. "I notice some of the sheets are for a violin. Do you have a friend who plays?" Elizabeth looked pointedly at Mr. Darcy for an answer, but Georgiana responded first.

"My brother sometimes accompanies me on his violin."

Darcy nodded in agreement. Miss Bingley tittered, "Oh, Mr. Darcy, how can you have time to practice when you have so many matters to deal with on your estate? You are such an accomplished gentleman."

Elizabeth smiled. "It is rare to see a gentleman apply himself. Would you be opposed to performing? I believe I could play this one with you." She handed him *Canon in D* by Pachelbel.

Darcy looked at the music he had played in private before and then back at Elizabeth. He could not deny her request, although he preferred people not to believe he had such a talent. "Yes, I would be delighted to perform with you, Miss Bennet." He moved around the pianoforte to a small box where his violin had always been stored. The party watched as Elizabeth practiced a few notes to prepare and Darcy quietly tuned his violin. Once they were ready, the group listened quietly for half an hour. To say Darcy was accomplished was an understatement. His playing was superb, and he shocked his audience with his skill, except for Georgiana, who had heard him play many times. Elizabeth's part was simple enough that she played very well but was able to listen to Darcy.

After the performance, Miss Bingley announced that she was tired. No doubt, she was tired of not being the center of attention. Mrs. Gardiner agreed that it was late, effectively breaking up the party. Elizabeth followed her aunt and uncle with the others through the gallery to their wing. After bidding a good night to their hosts, the party left them at the stairwell to the second floor. Once the last guest was out of sight, Darcy led his sister up the stairs.

"I highly approve of Miss Bennet. She will be very good for you," Georgiana said once they were outside her door.

"I believe she will be a good friend for you as well, Georgiana. Thank you for being such a wonderful hostess today," Darcy said, after kissing her forehead. Now that the house was quiet, he thought over what had been said today. He was thankful that Elizabeth had said what she did. He knew where they stood. He knew it would take time. He would be her friend. She wished for as much and cared for him as a friend in turn. It would be enough for him; it had to be.

Once he fell asleep, his mind betrayed his true feelings by dreaming of Elizabeth touring the mistress' suite alone with him.

14: LYDIA

The following morning, Darcy rose from his bed and moved to the window. Looking out, he could see a small figure twirling about on top of the ridge above him. He smiled, knowing it could only be Elizabeth. She and her maid had probably awoken at sunrise to climb the ridge. He longed to join them but knew it would be improper. He needed to ready himself to break his fast with the others.

This was his chance to show Elizabeth how he had changed with regards to her family. He dressed with care, his valet wisely overseeing the process. His thoughts were still in turmoil from the previous evening. However, he knew he must not let it get the better of him. He thought of the Gardiners. If it were not for his knowledge of their profession, he would not have thought them to be in trade. Their conversations were rational and informed, their dress proper and elegant. He could find nothing wanting. Being a perfect host was no difficulty with them.

Darcy laughed at the thought of what Miss Bingley would say to him on the subject. He knew of her ready dislike to people in trade and how she ignored their remarks in conversation, almost pretending they were not present. Once again, his valet pretended not to notice his distraction. When he was finally ready to leave his chambers, he thanked his valet before rushing to the door.

Downstairs, he found Mr. and Mrs. Gardiner alone at the breakfast table. Sitting beside Mr. Gardiner, he enjoyed a lively conversation about the crises on the continent. He found them to be well-informed, thoughtful, and considerate of those who were on the front lines of battle. He could not be happier with his company, even more so when Elizabeth entered.

Her cheeks were rosy from the morning chill. Her hair had relaxed from the knot her maid had tied that morning, causing her curls to fall about her neck. Darcy rose to greet her and helped her to a seat across from him. She quickly joined their conversation, and they talked until their tea and coffee had turned cold.

After an hour or so of conversation, Mr. and Mrs. Bingley joined them. The conversation naturally moved to plans for the day. Mrs. Gardiner intended to visit with her old acquaintances. Jane and Elizabeth offered to go with her. Darcy hid his disappointment very well. He could not commandeer her time. Instead, he wished her a pleasant trip and offered them his finest carriage which, in addition to being very comfortable, had a convertible top which would increase their enjoyment of the ride. Mrs. Gardiner gratefully accepted the offer.

Darcy then offered Mr. Gardiner the opportunity to go fishing in the stream. Mr. Gardiner was very conflicted, not wishing to abandon his wife, but he had also been very much looking forward to the prospect of fishing. Mrs. Gardiner laughed as she released him from his obligation to her. "You have been very accommodating to us on our journey here. You may rest for a day in any way you feel best."

Mr. Gardiner was not too shy to kiss his wife's check in his relief and joy. Mrs. Gardiner laughed while Mr. Darcy blushed lightly.

The conversation was halted as a servant entered with an express for Jane. "It is from Mary." She read it quietly while the others looked on. Her usual smile disappeared about halfway through the letter. "They are all well, but there is a concern about Lydia. It appears that she has eloped from Brighton. We must hope that she will be happy with her choice. He must love her very much to elope when he must know my father cannot afford a dowry." Jane looked pale, but she clearly attempted to reason with herself that all would be well.

Elizabeth snatched the letter and began to read aloud when she found the beginning of Lydia's tale. "We received an express at twelve last night, just as we were all gone to bed, from Colonel Forster, to inform us that she was gone off to Scotland with... Mr. Wickham." Elizabeth stopped reading and looked up, immediately searching for Mr. Darcy.

Darcy's jaw tensed, and she wondered what he must be thinking. However, he was prevented from revealing as much by Mr. Gardiner. "Foolish girl! What other information do they have?"

Darcy interrupted the response. "We should adjourn to my study. We do not need Miss Bingley or Miss Darcy to walk in on this conversation."

Mr. Gardiner eyed Mr. Darcy carefully, wondering why he should be privy to the Bennets' concerns. When no one else seemed to mind, he let his concern go. The Bennets would need all the help they could get if the elopement did not take place. No one spoke as the six people made their way to the study. When the door was shut, Darcy motioned for Elizabeth to continue.

"There is no more information, other than to describe the turmoil at home. Our mother has taken to her rooms and is inconsolable. Kitty apparently knew something of this nature would happen. Papa is concerned, but he has no way to alter the circumstances. Colonel Forster has gone to look for them. I suppose we must wait to hear of their marriage."

"I doubt they will marry," Darcy said, after a moment's consideration.

"Why not? He had shown her much deference in Meryton. He must love her," Jane pleaded.

"From my understanding, he was engaged to a Miss King," Darcy stated.

"Miss King was whisked away by her uncle to protect her dowry in April, as I learned when I returned to Hertfordshire," Elizabeth explained.

Darcy scowled. "Is that when he showed a preference for Miss Lydia?"

"No, he first showed a preference for me, but I did not encourage him after our conversation." Elizabeth attempted a smile of thanks to Mr. Darcy, and he returned with a half-smile.

Mr. Gardiner was most interested in this discussion. "Mr. Darcy, you seem to have information that will help us understand this situation. Would you care to share? You can be certain of our discretion."

"Mr. Wickham loves money and nothing more. No doubt you heard his story that I denied him a living in the church. I only denied this after he refused it and was compensated accordingly. I hold many of the debts he left in Lambton when he departed. There were also a few maidens left with child, claiming the babes to be his." He paused when Jane gasped. "He also attempted to elope with Georgiana last summer when she was but fifteen, but I discovered the plot in time. She is only just returning from the melancholy that the experience caused her."

Elizabeth smiled reassuringly at him, once again feeling how much Mr. Wickham had pained him in the past.

Darcy continued. "He is probably only using her funds to escape new debts in Brighton and with the other officers. They will probably stop in London, where he will most likely abandon her. On what day did they elope?"

"Saturday," Elizabeth added after scanning the pages once more, "Two nights ago. With so much time having passed, we can only assume her virtue is gone. We must hope that Colonel Forster has found them early or that we can find them and make them marry."

"There might be another way," Darcy said, as he walked to

the window and stared out at the woods where he had walked with Elizabeth the day before.

Mr. Gardiner watched Mr. Darcy for a moment, hoping he would say more. When he did not, he decided to ask, "Would you care to elaborate?"

"We could put it out that Mrs. Bingley has sent for Miss Lydia to join her here at Pemberley, where I intend to hold a ball to announce my friend's marriage. Mrs. Bingley should write a letter from a few days ago that can be given to the Forsters with the invitation, even claiming to bring a maid and carriage to accompany her here. The Forsters have much to gain from this deceit, as it would not do for their lax supervision to become known. That would give us time to find her and bring her here, married or not, though I doubt we will find them so. They have not the funds."

Mr. Gardiner thought over the idea. "What if we do not find them?"

"We will look for her until we do," Mr. Darcy added. "I know some of his haunts in London, if that is where they are. I can send a search party to watch the road to Gretna Green. There are a few here who would do much to stop Wickham from harming another innocent soul with discretion. The express would have traveled faster than a carriage with a lady."

"We do not have the funds to force them to marry," Mr. Gardiner stated.

"If we can encourage them to marry, then we shall do so. If not, then we feed him to Colonel Forster. Desertion in a time of war is punishable by death, even for local militia. Lydia can be brought here for the ball, and then we can determine a future path."

Elizabeth moved to the window to stand beside Mr. Darcy. "You would risk partaking in our ruin if she comes here."

"That is a risk I will gladly take to protect my friends." He wanted to take her hand, but he wisely kept his own at his side. "Besides, if I had been more open in Hertfordshire, no one would have believed his lies, and your sister would have been safe. Do you agree with this plan?"

"Will you really hold a ball?"

"Yes, if you will remain here when the Gardiners leave. The Bingleys can chaperone you. You must be here to give the story credibility. Mrs. Reynolds is able to plan everything in a week, and there are enough neighbors to attend to make it remarkable. This country has at least four and twenty families of high distinction."

Elizabeth laughed as she remembered the conversation between Mr. Darcy and Mrs. Bennet at Netherfield so long ago.

"Then I agree. Uncle, will you help the search for Lydia?"

"Certainly, since I must return home tomorrow. Mrs. Gardiner can travel with me to Longbourn, and help your mother spread the new rumors. Mr. Bennet and I can search for Lydia in London, since you say that it is their most likely location." Mr. Gardiner bowed to Mr. Darcy.

"I will travel to London tomorrow, on the pretext of business. I will meet you there, after I begin the search. You cannot leave today, as that would raise speculation. You must go to visit your friends in Lambton and pretend that all is well. Mrs. Bingley, would you write letters to your sister to fit the story we have developed? I will write a note to Colonel Forster explaining the need for this farce. Tomorrow we shall depart at first light. I will also send riders to watch the road to Gretna Green immediately and alert Mrs. Reynolds to begin her preparations. The ball shall be on Friday, the day before the full moon. Miss Bingley and the Hursts leave in two days for Scotland. We should prevent their staying for the ball." Mr. Darcy opened the door to allow the others to precede him out.

Elizabeth and Jane left to write the letters together. Mrs. Gardiner went to her room to prepare for her visit to Lambton. Once the expresses were sent to Longbourn and Brighton, they joined Mrs. Gardiner on the trip. Mr. Darcy also wrote a letter to his cousin, Colonel Fitzwilliam. As he was stationed in London, he would be able to begin the search quickly. The servants knew better than to ask questions about three expresses being sent at the same time. In any case, the ball gave them too much to do to speculate.

15: PLANS MADE

With the letters written and plans set in motion, Elizabeth, Jane, and Mrs. Gardiner sat in the carriage watching Pemberley shrink as they made their way to Lambton. Not much was said for the entire ride. They looked around at the vistas, but nothing felt remarkable. They put on brave faces as they met Mrs. Gardiner's acquaintances. They were not afraid of the townsfolk, or indeed apprehensive of them. They were simply upset over knowing a secret that could ruin the family. They had a role to play, placing a burden on their time, which should have been dedicated to a joyous reunion.

They conversed easily with the townsfolk, Mrs. Gardiner recalling fond memories or explaining a local history to Jane or Elizabeth. Many times, they laughed so hard they began to cry. But not far away from their thoughts, the memory of Lydia's plight hung. Elizabeth had the easiest time faking enjoyment when these moments trespassed. Her education included defending positions that were not her own, which now seemed incredibly relevant. It seemed a delightful farce, and by the end of the morning, Elizabeth's mood had improved.

"What shall we do next?" She asked laughingly as they left the tea room "There is a dressmaker. Should we have new gowns for the ball?"

Mr. Holdston, the town's baker and an old friend of Mrs. Gardiner, stood behind her. "That is a grand idea. You must have a ball gown made new. Pemberley is known for its balls, even if it has not hosted one in many years. It brought back many fond memories to receive the order for cakes this morning. It tickled my feathers to rekindle the ovens at the thought of a Pemberley ball. Not that I was ever invited, but Miss Wolc... excuse me... Mrs. Gardiner, to think your niece is the guest of honor is definitely something this town will not forget for some time. Tell old Codsworth you were my guests, and he will give you a fair rate; you know how some folk raise their rates for visitors. Saved his hair a few times since he moved here two years ago. He owes me. Mrs. Gardiner, it was lovely to see you again. I hope you will mention my business plan to your husband when he is an agreeable mood."

"I will, Mr. Holdston. Thank you for the fine tea cakes." Mrs. Gardiner curtseyed gracefully as he bowed before shutting the door. "Lizzy, I think the dressmaker is a good idea, even though it is not my idea of a good time. We have the funds, since Mr. Darcy putting us up is saving us money. Your father will pay us back in good time. Have no fear, Jane."

"Thank you, Aunt Maggie," Jane said, amiably. "Surely Mr. Bingley will pay for my gown, and probably the rest of them, should I ask him to. It is no expense for us."

Elizabeth laughed. "No, expense, you say! Shall we wager on that? We should also buy a gown for Lydia. She is your height and build, and my skin color. Between the two of us, we should be able to arrange a gown to be made ready for her. I do not much like the idea of spending an hour in a dressmaker's shop on such a fine day, but I do see the necessity."

"You are the one who made the suggestion," Jane reminded her sister.

Elizabeth nodded as they made their way across the street. True to Elizabeth's estimate, they were ready to leave in one hour. The measurements had been made, the cloth purchased, and the styles selected. Three dresses would be ready for a final fitting two days before the ball. They only had to hope that Lydia would be at Pemberley by then. The trip to the dressmaker helped Jane feel better. It brought a sense of normalcy to this act of deception.

Returning to Pemberley, the three talked about more of Mrs. Gardiner's childhood time in Lambton. They felt easier knowing that the lie had begun to take form. When the horses stopped, they found Mr. Darcy waiting to help them down.

"Have you enjoyed your outing?"

Mrs. Gardiner answered, "We have enjoyed meeting so many old acquaintances and a few new ones as well. Everyone was delighted to receive orders for food, flowers, and decorations for the ball. You should have seen their faces as they reminisced over the idea of a Pemberley ball. We also purchased new gowns."

"Jane is the same size as Lydia, so measuring a dress for her was easy. Hopefully she will be here in time," Elizabeth added.

Darcy nodded and dismissed the carriage, ensuring there were no servants to overhear. "I am not comfortable deceiving so many people, but I believe we have one more angle we must cover." He paused, looking at Elizabeth for support. "Miss Bingley is dangerous to our lie. She feeds on gossip and would love to push someone down for ten minutes of attention. My sister knows everything we discussed, and she and Mrs. Reynolds have made a plan to keep the preparations for the ball private. I hope you will help as well. It is only two days."

Jane looked sad at the poor analysis of her new sister, but she could not refute the claim. Despite Caroline being everything friendly and proper, Jane could sense the conniving beast lurking within, not that she would ever admit such a thing. Caroline's interest only fit within what she thought would improve her status. "We shall do our best. Miss Bingley should continue on to Scotland on time. Her aunt is expecting their party by Saturday."

Elizabeth smiled. "Certainly, we can ensure she knows nothing of the ball, but she will suspect something when I remain here."

"No, she will believe that I need you by my side when I am not feeling myself. You are such a comfort to me," Jane stated simply.

"What do you mean you are not yourself?" Elizabeth asked, completely perplexed.

"I have been feeling... funny... in the morning. Nothing too out of the ordinary, but my stomach complains."

"Is Charles not by your side in the morning?"

"He is, but he is too solicitous of my needs. He gets distraught when he cannot take away my pain and discomfort. You have always been the perfect bedfellow, helpful when needed and caring when all I need is a companion."

Mr. Darcy moved to take Elizabeth's hand. "May I escort you inside? My sister is eager to practice the pianoforte with you, once you have refreshed. We should not remain on the steps for too long."

Elizabeth felt exasperated that she could not inquire further into Jane's illness. Instead, she resolved to watch her sister that evening. She accepted Mr. Darcy's arm and allowed him to lead the way to the music room from where Miss Darcy's magnificent playing drifted softly through.

They entered to find Miss Bingley turning pages for Miss Darcy. Mrs. Hurst sat over by the window, admiring her many bracelets. When Miss Bingley looked up, she smiled and greeted her host as though he was the only person who had entered. "Mr. Darcy, it feels as though we have been here an age. We are so comfortable and relaxed that we almost feel at home, with all our worries behind us. It is too bad that our aunt must command our attention, but we are pleased to be of service to our family when they are in need. As you know, Mrs. Campbell is getting on in years. There might not be very many summers remaining for us to visit her." She patted the seat beside her, clearly inviting him to join her.

Elizabeth smiled and claimed the offered seat first. "Can you tell me about Mrs. Campbell? I am eager to learn of all my new relations. Someday, perhaps I will travel to Scotland as well. I long to explore the country I have read about in books.

Where does she live?"

Mrs. Hurst looked Elizabeth up and down twice but could not detect any inauthenticity, so she began a pleasant conversation detailing her family in Scotland while Miss Bingley remained silent. Mr. Darcy claimed a seat where he could focus on his sister's playing and Elizabeth's conversation. If he had not known better, he would have assumed Elizabeth and Mrs. Hurst were becoming fast friends. When he turned a few minutes later to catch her eye, she winked at him. He smiled before turning back around to applaud his sister's performance.

Miss Darcy was succeeded at the pianoforte by Miss Bingley, who enjoyed displaying her talents, and her choice was based on her abilities alone rather than being considerate of what the group would wish to hear. Half an hour later, and at the request of Miss Darcy, tea was served with a wonderful display of fruit and cold meats. The party gathered around the small table and ate quietly. Only Mr. and Mrs. Bingley sat back from the group to share an orange and talk together.

When Elizabeth finished her peach, she wiped her face and asked if anyone cared to join her in a walk around the garden.

Miss Bingley tutted. "Miss Eliza, you cannot seriously envision going out in this heat. You will outdo even your spirits. You must wait until the sun is lower, or you will fall ill. This heat must be taken seriously."

With a laugh, Elizabeth laid her fears to rest. "The sun is almost behind the ridge, and as we are farther north, the heat is not so heavy as it is in Hertfordshire. I shall be quite well. Would anyone care to join me?" Elizabeth looked directly at Mr. Darcy, who accepted her challenge.

"I have been cooped up in my study for the majority of the morning; a good stretch of the legs would be enjoyable. I shall walk with you. Have no fear, Miss Bingley, I will ensure Miss Bennet returns safely." Darcy turned to his sister, who looked crestfallen that she would have to endure the Bingleys alone. Fortunately for her, Jane chose that moment to engage her in conversation.

Darcy and Elizabeth walked out the room, and the sound of Jane and Georgiana laughing followed them to the stairs. "Our sisters have formed quite the friendship."

"Indeed, Mr. Darcy. They both have such a pleasing disposition that they will always agree with each other. It is not my preference, but then I have no problem going about my friendships in my own way."

Darcy paused to send a servant to fetch Elizabeth's maid. Even if they were to remain close to the house, a chaperone would preserve decency and prevent Darcy from making a fool of himself should she inadvertently act too intimately.

Exiting the house, they walked to the rhododendrons. Without their blooms, they were simply large bushes, which provided plenty of shade. There was a breeze wafting through the branches, cooling their backs as they walked. They reached the end of the path in silence, each content simply to be together. As they moved toward the wood in front of the house, Elizabeth commented on his trip to London. "I am truly grateful that you will be part of the search for Lydia, although it really is too much to ask of you."

Darcy looked back and was glad to see the maid was out of earshot. "That is why you did not ask for my help. As I said, I share responsibility because I knew what he was and should have warned you and your family earlier."

"Only one man is responsible. You cannot blame yourself, so that you may absolve me of the gratitude which I should feel. My family are indebted to you."

"Not yet. Should I fail, your family will owe me nothing."

"And should you succeed, what would you ask for in payment?"

"I shall have to think over your offer. I will let you know when I think of something."

Elizabeth laughed, happy that they could be so easy together. She sighed and leaned closer to Darcy's shoulder, much as they had at the seaside. Darcy dared not speak, for fear that she might withdraw. He wanted the walk to continue forever.

"The townsfolk hold great respect for you and your family. It is clear that you are an excellent master of the estate."

Darcy nodded, not sure of an appropriate response.

"I had not thought about how many people are dependent on your care. No one here can say anything against you. You carry a heavy burden as most of the decisions you make will affect others. I doubt Bingley could be half the master you are. You started at a very young age, if I remember correctly."

"Yes. My father started grooming me on my breaks from school. It is good that he did, or I would have been lost when he died. I have been master of the estate these five years, with Mr. Robson as my steward."

Elizabeth nodded, not wishing to continue this conversation, worried that he would turn pensive from the grief. "What is your favorite part of the gardens?"

"I have not thought about it much. I suppose the rhododendrons are my favorite, as they remind me of my mother." *And you*, he added to himself. "Other than that, I suppose I prefer these woods. The stream is relaxing in its constant babbling."

"I must agree with you. Are there bluebells in the spring?"

"Yes."

"Then I might have to trespass on your hospitality this spring, so that I can see this wood in its blue splendor. I suppose the winters are harsh."

"Yes." Once again, Darcy could barely breathe, let alone speak.

Elizabeth imagined he would prefer silence, so she turned her attention to the creek and listened to the babbling. She wished she could dip her feet in the creek, but that would have to wait for another day. She did not want to distract Mr. Darcy any further.

That evening, the group played card games until it was time to retire. Very few slept that night as they wondered what the following day would bring. Darcy felt upset that he would leave while Elizabeth was in his home. Despite her feelings not changing, she was clearly warming to him. Patience.

The following morning, when everyone was settled around for breakfast, a servant brought an express from town. Darcy read the note quickly. "This is from Colonel Fitzwilliam. He asks for my assistance in a matter of importance."

"The colonel, how I long to see him. You should invite him here when your business is finished," Miss Bingley cooed.

Darcy wondered when she had ever met the colonel, but he knew better than to question her. "If I leave this morning, I should be there by tomorrow. Miss Bingley, and Mr. and Mrs. Hurst, I am sorry to say I will likely not return until after your departure. Miss Darcy will keep you company, as will Mrs. Bingley, Miss Bennet and your brother." Darcy bowed to the Hursts.

"Your absence will be keenly felt," Miss Bingley simpered. "I shall help dear Georgiana with her hostess duties. You know I keep a fine house."

Darcy avoided rolling his eyes, but Elizabeth did not. She smiled as she said, "I wish you a safe journey and a speedy return. Your carriage must be sent with you, even if you will not travel in it. You may return in comfort, knowing we will feel more assured of your safety in your carriage."

"Very well, Miss Bennet. I shall have my carriage ready to depart with me. If you will excuse me, I must see to the matter of my departure." He bowed to everyone in the room before leaving on the pretext of ordering the carriage that had, in fact, already been ordered.

Two hours later, the party gathered on the front steps to bid adieu to the Gardiners and Mr. Darcy. Miss Bingley was distraught that Miss Bennet was to remain, but she reserved her tears for her adieu with Mr. Darcy, who barely even waved her goodbye.

Miss Bingley remained with Miss Darcy for the rest of the day. Elizabeth, Jane, and Charles were left to their own pursuits if they did not wish to join the two ladies in the music room. Elizabeth and Mr. Bingley worked hard to keep the atmosphere cheerful. Jane disclosed that she believed herself to be with child, although it was too early to tell for sure. As such, she felt unwell most mornings and barely ate more than crackers and fruit the rest of the day. Elizabeth was overjoyed at the idea. It was a welcome distraction from waiting for word from London or Gretna Green.

An express arrived in the evening from Mary with very few details. Elizabeth and Jane retired for the evening to read the letter in privacy. It was as they feared. Colonel Forster believed them to be in London and could not continue searching for them. The rest was up to Darcy. They were about to fall asleep together when there was a knock at the door. Elizabeth opened the door to find Georgiana with a letter of her own.

The three made themselves comfortable in the dressing room while Georgiana described her news. "My brother was sent an express from my cousin, Colonel Fitzwilliam, this morning. He thinks he has found Mrs. Younge and believes he will have Wickham's address by morning. There is reason to hope for your sister."

"There is reason to hope, but we must also hope that Lydia will agree to come away from Wickham. My father has never convinced Lydia to do anything she did not wish to. If she is dead set on marrying Wickham, what will become of her?"

Jane intervened. "Then they will marry. Surely something can be worked out. Perhaps he is in love with her."

Elizabeth sighed, but she did not wish to contradict her sister in her fragile state.

"She will have no choice if… when… Wickham abandons her. He cannot love. He only takes what he wants from women." Georgiana looked crestfallen.

"Georgiana, you really cannot be too hard on yourself. You were taken in by a confirmed rake. We must praise God that your folly did not become your undoing, but instead became the making of you."

"What do you mean?" Georgiana was thoroughly confused.

"You have grown into a remarkable young lady in the wake of his abuse of you. You may now enjoy your season, knowing how to tell the rakes from honest suitors when your time comes. You will know to be on your guard. No one can fool you more than he did."

Georgiana nodded thoughtfully. "I should retire. Perhaps we will learn more tomorrow."

Georgiana's prediction came true. As they were bidding farewell to Miss Bingley and the Hursts, an express came for Jane from her father. She waited for the carriage to begin its route down the drive to open the letter. "We should go inside first," she said, her hands shaking.

Mr. Bingley took her arm and guided her up the stairs. They walked quickly to the music room, and Georgiana asked for refreshments to be brought up half an hour later. Everyone sat around Jane while she read the letter with trembling fingers. She read aloud, "My wildest child has returned to me. Just when I had begun to despair of ever seeing my daughter again, Mr. Darcy and Colonel Fitzwilliam showed up on Mr. Gardiner's doorstep with a plan to find Lydia. They had already spoken with her but needed myself to bring her away with me. We used Mr. Darcy's home to avoid servant gossip. Suffice to say, she was not well when we rescued her. She was tearful and could not breathe for shaking so hard. It was not until she fell asleep crying that I was able to learn from the colonel that Wickham had refused to marry her and so was returned to his commanding officer to await punishment for desertion.

"Mr. Darcy was able to tell me of the plan he concocted with you and Lizzy, and I agree that it is for the best. I will escort her to Pemberley, where she will remain for some time if necessary."

"Poor, foolish Lydia." Elizabeth interrupted. "At least they were found." Everyone sighed in relief. "She will not have to be tied to such a man, even if that is her desire now. In time, she will learn that this is best. She will be tough to handle when she arrives. She has never been denied anything in her life."

The four of them sat in silence until the tea tray arrived. When the servants were out of earshot, Jane attempted to change the conversation. "This makes the ball that much more important. Georgiana, what has been done to prepare? There is not much time left. We can help if there is more work to be done."

Miss Darcy accepted the help, and the next two days passed in busy preparation. Mostly, the servants did the work, directed either by Miss Darcy or the Bingleys. Elizabeth walked the paths often and brought in flowers for the bouquets in the ballroom. The townsfolk began delivering their supplies for the feast. They were busy enough that they almost forgot that Lydia was to come.

16: REVELATIONS

Elizabeth was out walking by the daisies, when a sound drew her attention to the drive. She turned in time to see the Darcy carriage slow as it passed in front of the house and out of sight. Excited to see her friend, father, and sister again, she ran around the house to join the others, a smile plastered across her face.

A footman stepped forward to open the carriage door. Darcy emerged first and turned to welcome his guests. Mr. Bennet followed him and then helped his youngest daughter out. Mr. Bennet's pale complexion showed how hard these few days had been. Lydia was Lydia still. She huffed as she looked around her, displaying her anger at the events that had unfolded. When her eyes took in the vastness of the estate, however, she quieted and blushed. For the first time, she thought Mr. Darcy might have some good qualities.

Darcy, who had not enjoyed the days spent in London, smiled at the sight of Elizabeth and Georgiana standing side by side to welcome him. He gave his sister a warm embrace, and although he longed to embrace Elizabeth as well, he kept his arms to his side and bowed to her. He then turned to Mr. and Mrs. Bingley and greeted them cordially, before introducing Lydia and Mr. Bennet to Georgiana. Elizabeth greeted her father with a curtsey followed by swooping her arms around her father and embracing him fervently. She shared no such warmth with her sister though; a short curtsey was all that Lydia was due, even in front of the servants. Jane was more forgiving.

The introductions and greetings completed, Mr. Darcy invited everyone inside to refresh themselves and meet for tea an hour hence. Mrs. Reynolds stood at the top of the stairs to guide her guests to their rooms and give a small tour as she went. Jane and Georgiana returned to the saloon to wait for the others, leaving Mr. Bingley, Mr. Darcy, and Elizabeth standing in the hallway. Elizabeth wondered whether she ought to leave with the other ladies, but she greatly wished to hear about the happenings in London. Mr. Darcy noticed her indecision and invited her to the study.

The three walked to the study quietly, with Darcy escorting Elizabeth, glad for the opportunity to be so close. He could smell her lavender scent, to which he always wished to come home. His trip had been very trying.

Charles began the conversation as soon as they entered the study. The door was left partially open for propriety, even though Charles was a married man. "You returned faster than I had expected! Can we assume all went well?"

"Not exactly." Darcy poured two decanters of whiskey before realizing Elizabeth might enjoy a drink. He looked at her expectantly and waited for her to nod. He then poured a small glass, such that she might experience the drink with no ill effects. As he handed her the glass, he gave her a warning to sip very slowly. She smiled as she accepted the glass but made no attempt to drink while he was hovering over her.

After a few moments of silence, Charles asked for an explanation.

"Colonel Fitzwilliam had found them before I even arrived."

"That seems remarkable," Elizabeth stated. "How did he even know where to look?"

"Mrs. Younge is a woman of mean understanding who

worked for us, and she has ties with Wickham. For a price, she will divulge almost any secret. She has a boarding house now with rooms to let, so she was easy enough to find."

"They were staying with her, then."

"No. She had no rooms available, but luckily for us, she recommended a place where they were found the next day. The place was not..." Darcy paused, wondering how to explain properly to Elizabeth while not lying. "reputable."

"You need not spare my sensibilities. I once told my father that this was a likely outcome of Lydia's rash behavior. At least with how miserable the accommodations must have been, she will have been more willing to leave. Whenever we have been at an inn, Lydia complains something dreadful at the smallest lump in a bed or seat."

"Not in the slightest. She did not even seem to notice they were in a brothel." Darcy turned away to hide his anger. He could not blame Elizabeth for her silly relations, especially when his own sister had almost eloped with the same man. "She refused to talk to Richard, but his talk with Wickham was enough. Richard walked away, knowing Wickham would not marry Lydia without a sizeable dowry. Richard did not promise one, and he insisted that no dowry would be forthcoming if Wickham left in the night. It was the best plan to ensure that they did not leave before Mr. Bennet, Mr. Gardiner, and I would arrive the next day."

"It would not have been proper for Lydia to go off with Colonel Fitzwilliam either, so I suppose that one more day would hardly matter." Elizabeth shrugged. She could not help but feel the weight of her sister's actions on her own shoulders. Mr. Darcy had been right to criticize her family when he had proposed.

"Richard met us at my home that evening. We traveled through Cheapside to collect your father and uncle who had only just arrived there. He told us of his conversation with Wickham." Once again, Darcy paused to look at Elizabeth. "Your father was ready to cut her off. He was not certain he would be able to welcome her back into the family. Sharing our plan to fight the rumors helped him calm down. He was able to meet with Wickham the next day. Richard and I waited outside, in case Wickham should attempt to flee. We did not want him to think he could bribe or taunt us. We could still hear their conversation. Men from Colonel Forster's unit were with us to apprehend him.

"Your father spoke with Miss Lydia first. She was certain they would marry, and she did not care how long they had to wait for it to happen." Darcy sighed as he poured himself another drink. "Wickham was called downstairs to sit with Lydia. When Mr. Bennet claimed to have no intention of giving any dowry, Wickham laughed and said he had nothing more to say. He rose and attempted to leave."

"Attempted?" Elizabeth prompted when he paused.

"Lydia ran after him, exclaiming that he loved her. Even Richard felt bad for her when he laughed in her face. Devastated and heartbroken, she fell to the ground as he left. Colonel Forster's men took him after a bit of a fight outside. Richard's sword helped Wickham stop fighting and accept his fate. It was only after he was bound that he saw me. He looked so helpless."

It was difficult for Elizabeth to watch the emotions convey themselves over Darcy's face one by one. She rose and claimed his glass, pouring him another drink. Darcy hardly registered her assistance as he took another drink. "We grew up as friends. I cannot help but think that I have somehow failed him. If I had cared more about his upbringing and behavior, he might have changed his ways. Instead I shut him out. Now his fate is sealed."

Elizabeth pressed her hand against his arm to get his attention. "He sealed his own fate. It was his own doing. You cannot blame yourself for his demise. He was given a chance few could have squandered. He was perfectly equipped with the ability to ruin his own life."

Darcy looked into her eyes, which were so full of concern for him. He placed his hand over hers and gave her a very small smile. "Thank you, Elizabeth."

Her eyes widened as she realized he had used her Christian name, but she smiled gently and let it pass. "As your friend, I could not have you berating yourself over something that you cannot change." She smiled and pulled her hand away. "It appears that Lydia recovered from her disappointment."

"Yes and no." Darcy escorted Elizabeth back to her seat before setting his glass down. "Your father and uncle had to pull her up from the ground and carry her to the carriage. She cried the entire way to my home."

Bingley finally spoke up. "Why did she not go to her uncle's home?"

"Because she is not known in my section of town. We used fake names for your family while they were there. I doubt my staff would remember your sister or father should they ever see them again. It was a measure to prevent scandal, which Mr. Gardiner had suggested. Remember, according to our plan, she was slowly on her way with a maid to Pemberley. She could not appear in London at this time."

Elizabeth nodded. "I cannot imagine what is going through her mind. She is still a child in essence. A child fooled by a common rake."

"There is nothing common about Wickham, but it is in the past now. I do not blame Georgiana for her near elopement, I shall not blame Miss Lydia for her foolishness."

Elizabeth interrupted him. "And you shall not blame yourself for whatever you are likely to consider your duty to have been."

Darcy sighed. "If I had warned the people of Meryton of his duplicity, this…"

"Would have still happened." Elizabeth huffed. "The people of Meryton would not have listened to you. We are a stubborn lot. We must move forward now. You prevented any scandal with Georgiana. We must do so again with Lydia. We shall go to Lambton for a final fitting for the dresses soon, and then we will expose ourselves as well as we can at your ball. Perhaps Lydia will learn that men cannot be trusted with our reputation."

"Your father asked us not to say we were holding a ball. He did not want her to think that she was being rewarded so soon."

Bingley laughed. "It was hard keeping the ball from Caroline when we were in the initial planning stage. How do you propose we keep it from Miss Lydia, now that the ballroom is being decorated profusely?"

"Keep her busy in other areas of the house," Elizabeth suggested. "If any house is big enough, Pemberley is. So long as Georgiana plays her music, Lydia will be with her dancing until she has blisters. She is not one to suspect secrets."

"Her innocence is refreshing," Darcy admitted.

Their conversation was interrupted by a scoff from Mr. Bennet as he entered the room. He looked around and selected the seat beside his favorite daughter. "I am so relieved this business can be put behind us. Mr. Darcy, I owe you and your cousin a great debt. I am afraid I will never be able to repay you."

"Think nothing of it. I am glad to be of service to a friend."

"Then you have my friendship, Mr. Darcy. Lizzy, I will admit that you were right to caution me about Lydia's behavior. I will be a reformed father, starting from now. Lydia will be taught to comport herself as a lady, as will my other daughters. Lizzy, will you teach them?"

Elizabeth laughed. "They have never listened to me!" She tried to match her father's unconcerned temperament.

"Oh, I would not worry about that. I threatened her with a governess and even got a name from Mr. Darcy in the carriage. Lydia convinced me to allow you to teach her instead. Whenever she steps out of line, we can threaten her with a governess. I do not foresee much difficulty."

"And if she is with child?"

While a few had chuckled at Mr. Bennet's threat, this question silenced the room for a few minutes.

"We will cross that bridge only if we come to it. I cannot think of such a possibility at present," Mr. Bennet finally said.

Elizabeth nodded, tucking the thought away in her mind. If

her father were not worried, it would do her no favors to worry herself.

The group sat quietly for a few moments before Darcy suggested they move to the music room, where refreshments would be served. As they walked through the house, they attempted to shift their moods to lighter topics, although only Bingley was sufficiently able to laugh and be merry without effort.

Entering the music room, they found Jane, Lydia, and Georgiana silently drinking tea. Jane's face brightened upon seeing her husband. The others remained fairly somber, although Georgiana smiled at her brother. Lydia refused to look at them, either from embarrassment or annoyance. No one could ascertain which was correct.

Knowing her duties, Georgiana served tea to everyone. The room then threatened to fall into silence. Lydia was the first to break it, even though she did not look up from her tea. "You have a lovely home, Mr. Darcy. Thank you for inviting me to stay for the summer."

Mr. Darcy accepted her thanks with grace, and the room fell silent. Elizabeth was the next to think of something to say. "Lydia, now that you are here, I will be able to show you the grounds around Pemberley if you wish. Some of your favorite flowers are in bloom. We can ride around the estate, walk through the gardens, take a carriage around some of the roads, and even search the woods for deer."

Lydia nodded and thanked Elizabeth for the suggestion. Jane was now able to carry the conversation as she expanded on how lovely the paths around Pemberley were for riding. Mr. Bingley and Mr. Darcy added the occasional word, but the rest were willing to let the talking flow around them. Elizabeth scarcely contributed, but she spent more time observing Lydia and Georgiana, as did Mr. Darcy. They noticed the two ladies sharing glances every so often. Neither would look at the other directly, rather they would both look down whenever one caught the other's eye. This was a very odd predicament. Both ladies had been wronged by Wickham. Their youth and their connection with him was the only thing the two had in common.

Mr. Darcy was unsure how to continue. He wished to know why his sister was so affected but could not discover the cause in current company. Hoping for help, he turned to Elizabeth, who looked up at the same time. She was apparently just as confused as he, but he could tell she had come up with an idea. "Have you no work to complete in your study?" Was all she said. He was hurt that she would ask him to leave, but he acquiesced. As he rose from his seat, Elizabeth added, "If you finish your business early, then we can take a stroll in the garden later." She smiled at him, lightening his mood considerably.

While in the hall, he paused. Part of him wished to remain, but he knew he could not eavesdrop. It would be wrong. Would Elizabeth tell him what she learned? He had to hope she would as he made his way to the study. Rifling through the mail that waited for him, he could not bring himself to work. Instead, he paced in front of the fireplace, even though it was not lit.

Realizing he would not hear from anyone for some time, he moved to the window where he saw the Bingleys walking together. They looked so happy strolling along the path, surrounded by daisies and coneflowers. He was glad nothing kept them apart; they suited each other perfectly. Seeing them so easy together made him smile. Elizabeth must have contrived this to get them out of the room as well. No doubt, he would find Mr. Bennet in the library if he cared to look. How long would it be before he would see Elizabeth again?

Certain he would not see her for an hour at least, he returned to his desk to read his correspondence. Opening the first letter, he read through a dispute between two tenants. Apparently, one was accusing the other of ruining their shared well. There was no evidence to support either claim. The well was damaged but could be repaired. Both tenants were current on their rents and had never had a dispute before. Both were very well-respected in the community and their families had owned the land for generations. He could simply fix the well and watch to see if anything else happened that might indicate malintent. He was just about to write his response when Elizabeth burst into the room.

"I am ready for our walk now," she said as she walked directly through his study and out of the doors behind his desk leading to the gardens. He barely had time to rise before she was already down the walkway. He walked quickly, but it was not until he had jogged a few feet that he caught up with her. She did not slow down until they had walked for a quarter of an hour and were well out of sight of the house.

Darcy wisely kept silent as they walked. When they approached a stream, Elizabeth sat upon a rock to remove her shoes and stockings. Darcy turned away to give her privacy, but she did not even register his presence. Once her toes were safely under the water, she breathed a sigh of relief.

Darcy was curious about her agitation. "I suppose your conference with our sisters did not go as planned."

"No, it did not." She grabbed a stick and swished it through the water, splashing Mr. Darcy and herself in the process. The cool water was a balm against the heat. Eventually, she elaborated. "Our sisters had an argument."

"What was their argument about?"

"Who loved Wickham more."

Darcy exclaimed, "But I thought Georgiana knew Wickham did not love her."

"That does not change her feelings for him."

It was Darcy's turn to take up a stick and attack the water.

Elizabeth's laughter made him turn back to her. "You have no need to berate yourself!"

"If I had been more open with my sister, she would not have fallen for his charms."

"Yes she would, if her words today were anything to go by. She looks up to you and would never cross you if it could be helped, but she was determined to love Wickham, and to receive his love. She would not have listened to the truth about his nature from you, or anyone else. Lydia and Georgiana were taking it in turns defending him to me, even after he broke both their hearts. He had told Lydia that he was only using her when he walked out on her in London. I hope the military does not spare him from being punished for deserting."

"Colonel Fitzwilliam traveled with Wickham to Brighton to ensure his fate was known. Should I go and speak with my sister?"

"No. She and Lydia left devastated. They are both heartbroken, but in time they will be normal again. It helps that they are heartbroken over the same person. I was able to prove to them that Wickham did not care for either of them without much difficulty. This is the tipping point for their recovery, I believe."

"Will they be able to attend the ball?"

"Yes. I have told Lydia that if anyone were to learn that she had run away with a rake, she would never marry. She tried to tell me that was untrue, but Georgiana was able to tell her some of the gossip Miss Bingley had talked about. Society is not forgiving to women."

Darcy chuckled under his breath. "I am glad Miss Bingley was able to help in her own way. Did you tell Lydia about the ball? Your father had said not to."

"Yes. Georgiana mentioned it before I could stop her. So, I told Lydia that if she does not behave between now and then, she will be locked in her room for the ball. I have done so twice already, so she believes me."

"Then we have no need for secrets on that score. That is a relief." Darcy looked at his pocket clock. "We should return to the house. The others will be looking for us soon."

"Jane knows that when I set out for a walk, I do not return for hours. But I suppose we should not be out together for so long, so I will return with you, but you must promise to speak of pleasanter things."

"Agreed." Darcy turned around to allow her to don her stockings and shoes. Once she stepped beside him and took his arm, they began walking. Then, he followed her edict and changed the subject. "Have you found anything in my library to your liking?"

"Yes. Your library is so enjoyable, it is difficult to choose what to read." She then began describing an early history of Britain and the Viking invaders as they walked back to the house.

17: WATERFALL

The following morning, Mr. Darcy woke with apprehension. Both Lydia and Georgiana had not returned downstairs for dinner the previous evening. How were they faring? His valet stood ready in his dressing room, and he made his way downstairs without much ado. He was pleased to find Elizabeth and her father debating animatedly over which of the past kings had done the most damage to the kingdom. After pausing to greet their host, they explained that each had been reading different histories they had found in the Pemberley library.

Darcy laughed and pointed them towards one of his favorite books comparing the monarchs and surprised his listeners with his own understanding of history, which was much more detailed than theirs had ever been. Mr. Bennet resolved to spend the rest of the day in the library partaking of said book. Elizabeth rolled her eyes and asked if today would be a good day to go riding.

"Certainly. I have no immediate business matters waiting for me in my study. Did you have a chance to ride in my absence?"

"No. We were busy shopping. I have no wish to buy another dress for another fortnight at least. It always tires me more than any other activity."

"Then we should take the horses over the ridge. There is a splendid waterfall on the other side, but the path winds around the difficult terrain. I doubt even your ability to walk long distances could get you there on foot."

"That sounds like a challenge."

"Will you feel comfortable riding? I know you said you had not had much training beyond the basics."

Elizabeth was about to answer when Lydia barged in. "She may have not had much training or any practice in recent years, but do not let her fool you. When she was ten, out of sheer luck she remained on her horse when it was frightened by a snake. She has not been riding since, but I doubt she has forgotten anything."

"Lydia! Were you listening at the door?" Elizabeth admonished her sister in the strictest tone she could muster.

"Of course I was!" Lydia replied. "I wanted to know that you were not talking about me, and that was my only way of ensuring honesty. Now, Mr. Darcy, do you have a horse who will not startle for my darling sister?"

"I have a very gentle mare who does not startle easily," Mr. Darcy said, glad to have this information about Elizabeth's past. "Is that why you do not ride?"

"Perhaps. I will not admit to being scared of horses or riding, but I do prefer to keep my feet on the ground. However, with the incentive of a waterfall, I should gladly accept a gentle mare. I doubt I would miss it even if all you had for me was a wild stallion."

Darcy enjoyed the intense look of excitement in her eyes. He smiled at her enthusiasm.

Elizabeth chose to change the subject. "Lydia, after we return, we shall retire to the music room. It is high time you practiced your music."

Lydia was about to complain, but a look from her father stopped her as she opened her mouth. She closed it again and agreed with a small nod.

Elizabeth smiled in triumph. "After we have been playing,

then we must practice our dances. We cannot disgrace Mr. Darcy at the ball, after all."

This was exactly what Lydia wanted to hear, and they changed their conversation to the current fashionable dances in the ton. Darcy, unfortunately for him, was the only expert on the subject. Thankfully though, his sister came downstairs after a few minutes and offered her knowledge from her friends who had sisters out in society.

The Bingleys were the last to come downstairs. After they finished eating, the party dispersed to change into riding attire with the promise to meet half an hour later at the stables. Mr. Bennet said his farewells and returned to the library once more.

Darcy entered the stables to find Elizabeth and Lydia brushing a horse. More accurately, Elizabeth was brushing the horse while Lydia was feeding it a carrot and cooing at the gentle beast. Elizabeth looked up first and greeted Mr. Darcy warmly, explaining that the stable hand had pointed her in the direction of this horse. "He was quite frightened when I insisted that I ought to brush the horse myself. I wanted the time to get to know her before our outing."

"Finnigan is used to Miss Bingley insisting someone prepare her horses for her. He will recover from his shock soon enough. Spare him not a moment. Do you approve of Athena? She truly is a gentle horse."

"Very much. I believe we will be friends if my sister ever stops bribing her."

The Bingleys arrived shortly, and the group headed off without further ado. The path was wide at the onset, so Mr. and Mrs. Bingley let the others ride ahead of them as they meandered sedately and enjoyed the solitude. Mr. Darcy rode ahead with Lydia while Georgiana and Elizabeth followed right behind them. He wished he could hear their conversation behind him, but Lydia could definitely hold her own, even with his short responses. He listened and responded in time as she flitted from one conversation to another with astonishing speed. The only other person he had met that could converse so quickly was Mr. Collins. He had to admit that Lydia's conversations were much more pleasing by comparison.

As they neared the waterfall, she surprised him by thanking him for rescuing her. "I am beginning to see that my behavior was lacking. My life would have been miserable in time if left to his care. Thank you for helping when you did not have to."

"You are certainly welcome. I would never leave anyone to his care if I had the ability to stop him. I have known him for many years and had seen first-hand how unchangeable he is." He paused as he contemplated the fact that Wickham was likely dead by now. "I wish there had been a way to make him see the error of his ways before."

"As you said, you could not have done more for him," Lydia stated.

"Then perhaps I should have done less. If he had less, he would have been forced to remain in his sphere and would not have attempted to rise to gentility by ruining ladies."

"You were not the one to raise him to think himself a gentleman, but that is in the past. We must all move on." She patted her stomach as if she felt sick but ignored the strange feeling. "What is that noise?"

Darcy looked ahead. They could not see the waterfall, but he could definitely hear its gentle roar. "We are close. We should tie the horses here." He stopped and dismounted, tying his horse to a tree with the reigns before moving to help Lydia dismount. Lydia then took her horse to another tree while Darcy tended to Georgiana and Elizabeth.

The foursome waited patiently for the Bingleys to catch up. Darcy had not realized how far ahead they were. Bingley's laughter was heard before they rounded the corner and into view. Jane was laughing as well, but she was more sedate in her enjoyment. Darcy noted Elizabeth's patience was nearing its end when she began to walk ahead alone. He could not allow her to view the waterfall alone, so he urged Georgiana and Lydia onward. The Bingleys would catch up in their time.

The path was so narrow that he could not catch up to

Elizabeth, except for when she needed to climb over rocks. He then had to stop to aid Lydia and Georgiana. Bingley and Jane caught up to them, but Bingley did not have the inclination to assist the other ladies as well as his wife. He was perfectly content to focus on Jane alone. Darcy laughed to himself and decided he would never become so lovesick with Elizabeth.

At last, they were looking up at the grand waterfall. The scene was remarkable. Bordered by boulders and trees traveling up the steep slope, a small trickling stream fell about forty feet down, pooling at the bottom. The sun shining through the trees made the water almost golden. Everyone was delighted, including Georgiana, who had seen the waterfall before.

They stood there, watching the water crash into the pond. Darcy was the first to look away; he turned to watch Elizabeth. Her face was radiant with joy. The golden rays highlighted the ringlets in her hair. Unexpectedly, she turned to him with a bright smile, indicating her appreciation of the scene. He walked closer to her. "Do you still believe that you would have mounted a wild stallion to see this waterfall?"

"I would have balanced between two stallions without a second thought. Can we go closer?" Elizabeth did not wait for a reply as she returned her thoughts to what was left of the trail. Sitting on a boulder ahead, she reached for her shoes as if to remove them again, but a glance at Lydia reminded her of her duty to show proper decorum.

Lydia and Georgiana sat on the rock with Elizabeth, while Darcy leaned against a tree. Jane sat with her husband, but she turned to Elizabeth, and they talked of how pleasant the view was.

Elizabeth smiled as she said, "This would be a favorite haunt of mine if we had such a path at home. The water is so loud that it cannot help but soothe your spirits. I believe I could even withstand Mother's nerves in a place like this. Mr. Darcy, you are tremendously lucky to live in such a place as Derbyshire."

"Hertfordshire has its own share of beauty."

"You are being polite. I agree with you when you said you prefer Pemberley to town. Pemberley has everything one could want and so much more."

Darcy wanted to offer to give her the house, but he refrained. Instead, he suggested they return. "The horses will grow restless with the sound of the water so loud, and we should not be out too long. Mrs. Reynolds will wish to discuss details of the ball with you, Georgiana."

The group reluctantly agreed on condition that they would return another day with supplies for a picnic. Once they were back at Pemberley, the group dispersed. Bingley and Jane retired to their rooms to rest. Elizabeth, Georgiana, and Lydia headed for the music room. Darcy decided to check on Mr. Bennet, who had indeed been reading the history book the whole while and was very happy to discuss it.

An hour later, Darcy walked towards the music room to see how the lessons were coming. He paused in the doorframe with the door mostly closed, hoping to not disturb the trio. Georgiana and Elizabeth were patiently explaining fingering to a bewildered Lydia. He watched from the door as she practiced the new fingering. She played a children's song that he recognized. It was a simple tune that allowed her to feel confident in her improvements. When she finished, she looked up and saw him.

"Mr. Darcy! We were waiting for you. Lizzy, you promised when he came by, we could switch to dancing. You cannot go back on your word now."

Elizabeth laughed lightly. "I made no promise, but I believe now is as good a time as any to stop. Mr. Darcy, do come in and dance with us. You know these new dances better than we do."

Darcy could not resist the invitation. "I should be delighted." He paused to summon a footman to come and move the furniture before entering the room.

Elizabeth gave him an arch look, but it was Lydia who responded. "I thought you despised dancing. What has changed?"

Darcy blushed as he remembered the night he first met the Bennets in Meryton. "I do not despise dancing. Rather, I only enjoy dancing when I am acquainted with my partners, as is the case here. Georgiana, would you play for us?"

After shuffling the music sheets around, she began a new song. Despite a few small fingering errors, her playing was well-executed. Darcy offered Lydia his hand first. Elizabeth watched him walk through the steps, and then she followed him with an imaginary partner of her own. The song ended when they had repeated the steps twice. It would not do to complete each song if they wished to practice so many different dances.

After an hour, Elizabeth took her turn at the pianoforte. Her execution was not anywhere nearly so good, but the dancers did not mind. Bingley and Jane joined them, and they all twirled around the room in time to the music. Darcy was not happy to be so far from Elizabeth, but he could see she was enjoying watching them. It was a relief to see Lydia keeping her excitement in check as she twirled sedately. He took comfort in seeing her becoming a lady. Georgiana took this time to sneak off and speak with Mrs. Reynolds about the ball.

For dinner, they sat in the formal drawing room, which had been enlarged to accommodate the people coming for the ball. Instead of Georgiana taking the foot of the table as the mistress of the house, the group sat around Mr. Darcy's place at the head of the table. The Bingleys sat to his right with Mr. Bennet. Georgiana sat between Lydia and Elizabeth to his left. The conversation flowed freely as Mr. Darcy discussed the guests who were coming for the ball. He expected Colonel Fitzwilliam to return from Brighton in time. His nearest neighbors had all agreed to come. His family would come from Matlock and be housed in the family wing. Some of his London acquaintances were coming and staying in the guest wing. He listed their names with a warmth that indicated he approved of them. He answered questions about their characters as Elizabeth asked him to describe them.

Before anyone even realized, it was time for the ladies to depart. Darcy watched with longing as Georgiana led the others away. Instead of thinking too long on what they would discuss, he returned his attention to Mr. Bennet, who seemed to be eyeing him carefully. Darcy fidgeted in his seat, suddenly feeling as if he were about to be admonished. He looked at Bingley, who was staring at his port and not paying any attention to his company. He would receive no help from his friend. He returned his gaze to Mr. Bennet, who was now ready to speak.

"You have proven your worth. If you asked me for my daughter's hand, I would give it to you with delight. What holds you back?"

"I will not ask for her hand until she has given me her heart," Darcy stated simply.

Mr. Bennet nodded and returned to his drink. Apparently, that was the only answer he required. Darcy sighed and studied his own drink. When they rose to leave the table, Mr. Bennet held Darcy back a moment. "You are a good man; one of the best I have ever met. It is only a matter of time before she sees that. No other would treat her as an equal. Many are too ignorant to even see when she is laughing at them. Others insist she is wrong simply because she is a female. It speaks well of you that you have chosen such a woman. I shall be sorry to lose her when the time comes."

Darcy nodded, glad to have Mr. Bennet's approval.

The following day passed similarly, but the day after, the ladies took the carriage into town for the final fitting of their dresses. Lydia nearly squealed in delight when she saw the latest fashion in one of the finest fabrics she had ever seen, but she caught herself after a sharp look from her sister. A few deep breaths kept her excitement in check, and she happily twirled in her dress in front of a mirror while the others similarly tested theirs, before purchasing matching shoe roses. Once everything was settled, they stopped for tea before returning home. The four ladies talked loudly, showing how comfortable they were together to the local populace in case rumors of Lydia's flight should travel there. To any casual observer, they looked like family members who had come together for the ball. Lydia certainly did not act or look ruined.

That evening, the group assembled in the drawing room, determined to remain awake longer so as to prepare their bodies for sleeping late in the morning. The ball the next evening would mean they would all be awake until dawn, or at least all the young people would. Mr. Bennet promptly retired at midnight, content to let the others have their fun. The groups played cards, read some poetry, and even attempted charades, much to everyone's merriment. It was certainly best played when everyone was tired and feeling ridiculous.

When Jane began to roll her head in sleep, her husband insisted they retire. Lydia and Georgiana soon followed, with Elizabeth intending to do the same, but Darcy held her back quietly. She stood looking at him, perplexed. When the others were a safe distance away, he declared he was not tired.

"Would you care for a stroll in the moonlight? The heat will have died down by now."

Elizabeth noted that he still held her hand by the wrist, but she was not bothered by it. She agreed, and they walked to the conservatory together. From there, they walked out over the lawn. Darcy wanted to avoid any prying eyes that might see them leave the house together without a chaperone. The moon was so bright that barely any stars could be seen. Its light reflected off the white daisies and the stone steps. The brightness was astounding, and Darcy delighted in the perfection of Elizabeth's face as it was reflected.

"Is there anywhere in particular that you wish to walk?" Elizabeth asked.

"No, I simply enjoy spending time with you." He turned them towards the front of the house where the open grass was easy to walk through. Once their feet were safely softened by the grass, Darcy released her hand and she began running down the gentle slope. He began running after her, staying close but enjoying her free spirit and laughing as she sped down the slope. Just as he was about to lose his breath, she tripped. He saw her begin to fall and he jumped the last distance to catch her and spin her around so that she landed on him. They fell hard to the ground and did not stop laughing for some time.

"Have I hurt you?" Elizabeth asked, as she finally calmed down.

"No, I am not injured, Elizabeth." He looked up into her face. Even in the moonlight, he could see her blush. It was only then that he realized what he had said.

"I like the way you say my name," Elizabeth admitted, recovering from her blush.

"We are friends. Miss Bennet seems too formal. Do you think you could call me Fitzwilliam?"

"No, I do not think I could. I would think of your cousin. Perhaps I could call you 'Darcy' when we are alone."

Darcy smiled. "Very well. I had not even realized I was calling you Elizabeth. I am so used to thinking of you as such." He cupped her hand with his cheek, but she shied away from him. Sighing, he assisted her in standing. They walked back to the house quietly. Elizabeth held his arm for support, and Darcy noted she appeared comfortable. He had not wanted to startle her with his desires, but she had looked receptive. At least, this was an improvement. Tomorrow, he would dance with her at the ball. He would introduce her to all of his best acquaintances.

He considered himself very lucky that she was warming to him so well. He remembered her coldness in Hertfordshire. His situation could be much worse.

18: PEMBERLEY BALL

Mr. Darcy watched as Colonel Fitzwilliam walked into the breakfast room the following morning, his clothing still dusty from the ride. Darcy shook his hand and offered to have a servant show him to his room, but to Elizabeth's amusement and Darcy's mortification, he took a seat at the table, unperturbed by his lack of cleanliness. "Miss Bennet, how thrilled I am to be here in time for the ball!"

"I am likewise thrilled to be here. How far did you need to travel to arrive today?"

"The ride is four days from Brighton, so I pushed to get here in three. Once my purpose in Brighton was completed, I started off for Pemberley."

Elizabeth frowned as she thought of his purpose in going to Brighton. "Is it over then?"

Colonel Fitzwilliam sighed. "Yes, it is over. We should not talk about it. Tell me, how is your sister faring?"

After a pause, Elizabeth described the past few days. "Georgiana and Lydia were at odds for the first day or so, but they are grieving together and have become friends. The benefit to Lydia is beyond compare. Her behavior is much improved; even more so than I could have inspired in her by threatening to have my father hire a governess. The peacefulness of Pemberley is also likely responsible for her new behavior. I could not have imagined a more perfect home or a better part of the country. I am thoroughly delighted with the place." She then proceeded to tell of her excursions to the waterfall.

Darcy could barely contain his glee at hearing such praise from Elizabeth. He knew better than to think her feelings had changed toward him of course, but it was a welcome sight.

With the topic of Lydia and Wickham completely behind them, the colonel took command of the conversation to regale war stories until Georgiana entered the room, thrilled to see her cousin. Once the entire party had assembled around the table, the talk turned to who was expected to arrive and remain at Pemberley.

After breakfast, the party retired to the music room, where Georgiana, Lydia, and Elizabeth practiced some of their new songs while Colonel Fitzwilliam freshened up. Lydia's capabilities had certainly grown in the short time. She would not be ready to display for the ball, for she was still playing children's songs, but it was clear she would become a proficient, and even better, she was clearly enjoying the practice. She might still become an accomplished lady.

The first guest to arrive was Mr. Williams from London. Darcy performed the introductions as Mr. Bingley sidled up beside his old friend and greeted him warmly. The hardest part of the introductions was the fact that Darcy wanted to single out Elizabeth as though they already had an understanding. He then watched as Elizabeth and Lydia warmly greeted Mr. Williams and learned of his extensive land holdings across the country. Mr. Williams had warm, friendly manners, which greatly appealed to Elizabeth, Georgiana, and Lydia, who spent the next hour making small talk with the amiable gentleman, almost to the exclusion of Mr. Darcy, who could not think of much to say.

Mrs. Reynolds entered a few times to ask for an opinion

from Georgiana, only once needing her to supervise the finishing touches to the decorations. The group chatted amiably as they waited for more guests to arrive. Colonel Fitzwilliam's family were shown into the music room at length. He stepped up to make the introductions. Lord Matlock and his wife stood proud and aloof as they met the Bennets.

Mr. Darcy watched them closely for any signs of affection or displeasure, but much like himself, they gave little away. With the introductions completed, the party returned to their seats. Lady Matlock selected the seat beside Jane and began to smother her with questions about her family. The questions were all polite, however, seemingly asked in order to understand the family better. Unlike the way in which Lady Catherine had questioned Elizabeth about her relations, Lady Matlock seemed interested in actually getting to know the Bennets. Whether or not she would welcome them into her circle in London remained to be seen, but she was polite and unmoving.

Refreshments were served half an hour later, and the group ate in silence as Darcy watched Elizabeth while eyeing Lady Matlock. He was curious as to what she would think of Elizabeth. She had always been discontented with his friendship with Mr. Bingley, even when she acknowledged how well Darcy's manners had improved during his time spent with him. At least she seemed to be giving the Bennets the chance to prove their worth. When the group dispersed to change for dinner, Lady Matlock gave Darcy her opinion.

"Mrs. Bingley seems a very gentle woman. She will be a good influence on him. He could not have picked a better wife. You, on the other hand, would be miserable with a woman like her. I hope you are not considering her sisters; Miss Lydia and Miss Elizabeth are much too young for the likes of you."

"I shall take that into advisement."

"Make certain to dance with all the ladies in attendance tonight only once. You must ignore the married ladies so as to not slight any of your esteemed neighbors. While this is not so large a ball as one would be met with in London, it is good for you to take this chance to get to know the daughters of your neighbors. There are a few women from which I wish for you to choose. Lady Harlow's daughter would do well for you. Lady Julie is too bookish to be of interest to others of our station, but that is more to your favor. Her dowry alone would keep Pemberley secure, but..."

"I do not need a dowry to keep Pemberley secure. I will choose a wife who makes me happy. A woman who is not only well-read, but likes adventure, is compassionate and kind, and enjoys spending time quietly at home as much as attending balls."

"Your standards are too high. If you are not more careful, it will be too late for you to find a woman who will have you. Dance with Lady Julie tomorrow and consider her qualities; that is all I ask for."

"Very well, Aunt." Darcy smiled as he agreed with her, although he knew Lady Julie held no charm for him. He would not raise suspicions about Elizabeth until he was more secure of her. He did not wish for his aunt to become disagreeable towards her, although he suspected that she would warm to her when she got to know her. She had barely spoken to Elizabeth, as she had no reason to consider the possibility of a match with him.

Sighing with relief that the day was going as well as could be hoped, Darcy went upstairs to change. His valet was prepared with the change of clothes, and he was ready to return downstairs within a quarter of an hour. He looked out of the window before leaving his room and smiled as he noticed Elizabeth in a simple evening gown walking amongst the daisies below him. He smiled again at the thought of one more chance alone with her before the ball. He dismissed his valet before heading into the mistress suite to take the stairs to the lower part of the conservatory.

Stepping out through the door, he watched as Elizabeth looked in his direction and smiled, inviting him to join her. He returned the smile as he took his place beside her. They walked a few steps in silence as they took in the scene around them.

154

Eventually, Elizabeth spoke.

"I am very pleased to be here. Your home is like a dream come true. The future Mrs. Darcy will be a very lucky woman."

"Thank you. It is pleasant to hear you praise my home. However, I am in no rush to find a mistress for my estate."

Elizabeth smiled. "I can see why Miss Bingley tried so hard to capture your fancy."

"Did she?"

"You cannot have been blind to her attempts to garner your attention."

"I am not blind, but I have no interest in her. My heart lies... elsewhere."

Elizabeth lost her smile for a few minutes, making Darcy uncomfortable. Taking a deep breath, she admitted, "I am very happy as your friend, Fitzwilliam." Elizabeth paused to test the name out and found it suited him better than his cousin. "Jane has invited me to join her at Mr. Hurst's home this winter to enjoy the season. I look forward to it only because I will not only have her with me, but I know you will be near as well. I would be daunted by the echelons of society if you were not to be there by my side, at least some of the time."

"I will strive to remain your good friend. I do not normally attend many functions during the season, but your companionship may make me change my mind. You have already encouraged me to hold this ball in my own home."

Elizabeth thought of the real reason for the ball. "I am nervous about Lydia. I do not think she should return to Longbourn with me. We do not know if there will be repercussions from her staying with Wickham for so long."

"We will likely not know for some time. Miss Lydia would be welcome to stay here. She and Georgiana are becoming friends."

"They would not be appropriate friends should Lydia be with child."

Darcy thought about this for a moment. If Lydia were with child, he would not want it known around Pemberley that a Miss Bennet had had a baby out of wedlock. It would not help him win over his aunt to accepting Elizabeth. "The Bingleys are to travel to family in Scarborough. She could go with them and remain there for the winter should it be necessary. Mr. Bingley's aunt is in poor health, and it would be fine for her to remain to keep her company. She could have the baby, if there is one, and send it to a family in need. Once the babe has a home and she has recovered, she could return to society here. Bingley might need to gift her with a dowry to make up for her loss of virtue when it comes time for her to marry, but it could be done. Do you know if the gossip has died down in Brighton and Hertfordshire?"

"Yes, Mary wrote the other day that they have been going out with friends as though Lydia had not eloped. That danger, at least, has passed. If she is gone some time, there might be speculation as to why she was gone, but I suppose it cannot be helped. Her going to care for an old relation of the Bingleys might help fix that gossip as well. I will suggest this idea to Jane. I am relieved you have been able to create such a good plan, despite your abhorrence of deceit."

He wanted to say that Lydia was almost family to him but checked himself in time. "It is time to go into dinner. We have delayed long enough that we should be able to remain awake throughout the evening with ease. Will you join your sister in the receiving line?"

"Yes, Lydia and I will be there to accept congratulations on our sister's marriage. It is reasonable to present the next women in line for matrimony now that the eldest is married, but like you, I am in no hurry to marry at present."

Darcy wanted to exclaim that he would marry tomorrow if she would only accept him, but he shook his head to clear his thoughts. He began to worry that he would never change her mind.

The receiving line was longer than Elizabeth had ever seen, and she admitted to being exhausted at the end of it as Darcy escorted her into the ballroom. "I thought Meryton was large with four and twenty families to attend balls with, but Derbyshire is promising to be much grander. How do you keep all of the names straight?"

"Practice, my friend. I have been practicing ever since I was a child on my mother's lap. Society here is varied, but other than that, you will find it is much like society in Hertfordshire."

"But with more lords and ladies than all of Hertfordshire could boast."

"Some of the lords here tonight traveled some distance to show off their daughters to my cousin and me. I would not call Hertfordshire lacking because this ball is larger than the Netherfield ball. Here is my cousin now, ready to take your hand for this dance."

They parted with a laugh, and Darcy found Lady Julie waiting for him to ask her to dance. He made certain his aunt was watching him give her the preference of selecting her for the first dance. She beamed at him. The dance was almost completed in silence, but Darcy remembered his manners in time to ask her about her opinion on books, and he was rewarded with a long discourse on those which she had read. It was a satisfying conversation for one dance, but he could not claim it would satisfy him through the long years ahead of him. Only Elizabeth's conversations would do that.

He shook his head at his aunt after each dance, telling her that he was not to be so easily moved. He kept an eye on Elizabeth and was pleased to see her having so much fun in his home. The hours passed quickly, and soon the supper set had come. He was thrilled that he had thought to secure Elizabeth for his partner for this dance, as it meant he would enjoy her conversation through supper as well. He took her hand and led her to the front of the dance.

As had been happening already, Darcy and his partner were of principle interest to the older ladies in the room. Elizabeth laughed at the curiosity displayed over their features. "If I had not seen them eyeing each and every one of your partners with displeasure, I would have been afraid of them."

Darcy laughed at this evaluation. "I cannot imagine you

would be truly afraid of anything! What is your opinion of my neighbors and friends?"

Elizabeth outlined her thoughts on everyone she had danced or conversed with. Her insights were delightful to him as she described her partners' conversations, so much that he had not even realized that supper was over, and the dancing had recommenced in the other room. His aunt had to retrieve him so as not to offend his partner. Lady Matlock then took a seat beside Elizabeth and grilled her politely about her relations. It seemed that she had finally discovered Mr. Darcy's interest. The half hour passed, and Darcy joined them, eager to find out how the two ladies had comported themselves. He had not needed to worry, however, for Elizabeth was clearly at ease, not sensing the purpose of Lady Matlock's inquiries.

They could not speak for very long though, because Elizabeth's partner came to claim her. Lady Matlock took her nephew's hand as he watched her walk away with Mr. Williams. "Is she everything you wish for in a wife?" She asked.

"I believe so."

"Be certain before you engage your heart."

"It is too late for that, Aunt. I hope you will learn to accept my choice."

"She comports herself well. I might have been wrong to say that the woman you desire does not exist. Miss Bennet is quite remarkable. She must be seen in the best circles so that she can be judged on her own merits. If she is introduced to them as your bride, they will doubt her abilities."

"She will attend the season with the Bingleys and the Hursts this winter in London."

"They are not often invited to the best circles. I suppose I shall contact some of my friends and see what I can do."

"Thank you, Aunt."

"Do not thank me yet, Fitzwilliam. You have an uphill battle ahead of you."

"I have discovered this already. That is why I will be grateful for your support."

Lady Fitzwilliam nodded in agreement before walking away.

Darcy then turned his attention to Elizabeth once more. He had not promised any dances after dinner, so he was free to watch her conspicuously. Mr. Williams was a very skilled dancer with easy manners. Watching someone flirt with his Elizabeth was hard to bear, but her own manners showed she was unaffected. Just that afternoon, she had stated she was in no hurry to marry. What would it take to make her change her mind?

At the precise moment the thought crossed his mind, Elizabeth turned her head to look at him and smiled. Darcy startled at being caught staring. He noticed Mr. Williams had even turned around to see what had amused his partner. Darcy bowed before turning away. He engaged a neighbor of his for a few minutes before turning back. Elizabeth was laughing with Mr. Williams as they walked to the edge of the dance. Darcy attempted to halt his conversation with his neighbor, but it was of no use.

Next, Elizabeth was led back onto the dance floor by Colonel Fitzwilliam. This was their second dance, which made a few heads turn. At least the music was quick, not allowing for conversation as they jumped and skipped through the rows of people. Darcy noted how comfortable they were together and wondered if they would have formed an attachment if the colonel had the means to marry where he wished. The more he watched, the more he became concerned. He would need to confirm his suspicions with the colonel later, but a surge of jealousy coursed through his veins. It pained him to think of another winning her heart, but he had to be practical. If she chose someone else, he would have to let her go. Her friendship would then have to be enough.

With these thoughts, he scowled his way throughout the second half of the ball. Elizabeth only sat out one dance, while Lydia sat out three. Darcy only danced twice more at the behest of his aunt. At last, the party began to disperse. Those with farther to travel had departed early. Now the closer families were beginning to take their leave. It was all Darcy could do to be polite and courteous.

19: DEPARTURES

The following morning, Darcy attempted to concentrate on estate matters in his study. However, the morning breeze was blowing over his desk, carrying with it a conversation that must have been taking place in the garden.

"Miss Bennet, I hoped to find you alone." The voice was easily recognizable as belonging to his friend, and he also recognized the quiet longing in the tone, for he had used it himself many times. He forgot about estate matters as his heart started pounding. He moved to the window to better hear the conversation, although he knew he ought not to listen.

"Good morning, Mr. Williams. I am surprised to see you about so early. Living in town, I would have expected you to keep late hours, especially considering how late we remained at the ball." Darcy also noted the hesitancy in Elizabeth's voice, although she was being very polite. She did not wish for him to continue. He wondered how he had missed that tone when he had last proposed to her.

"As I said, I hoped to find you here alone. Rising early was my best option. I am sure the majority of the guests will not yet have risen. You told me that you were fond of early morning walks through the garden."

"Indeed." A very short, off-putting answer, Darcy thought.

He smiled as Mr. Williams continued as though she had encouraged him.

"I thought we had a connection yesterday. You are very easy to speak to. Not to mention your kindness, gentility, and intelligence."

"You are very kind to notice such things. I hope we may be friends."

"Friends?" Mr. Williams hesitated. "You mistake my meaning. I know we have not been acquainted long, but I am enamored of you. I think we are very compatible. I wish to court you."

"You barely know me, and you know almost nothing of my family."

"I will get to know you, if you will allow it."

"Courtships are only for those wishing to marry."

"I wish to marry you once we are better acquainted. I intend to visit Bingley at Netherfield, I think he called it, so that I may spend more time in your presence."

"Mr. Bingley is not traveling to Netherfield for some time. He is going North tomorrow and will remain there until it is time for the London season. You cannot move into his empty home, for it would incite too much gossip."

"Is this your way of declining my offer?"

"I do not wish to pain you, but I have no intentions of marrying at present. I do not believe we would suit."

"I am very eligible. We could live either in the country or in town. We could travel around the world. You would want for nothing."

"I would want for happiness, which is everything to me."

"You need not decide today."

"Thank you for the offer of courtship, but I cannot accept you. If you will excuse me, I believe my sister will be looking for me soon."

Darcy barely made it to his desk when Elizabeth opened the door and strode through the room, not even noticing that she was intruding on his private space. He smiled at how much she belonged to this house. At least he did not need to worry about someone else stealing her affections when she departed. From her own mouth, she had no intentions of marrying soon.

A few minutes later, Mr. Williams walked into the room, surprised to find Darcy watching the door to the hallway with a smile on his face. "You have my apologies for intruding on your solitude. I thought the room would be empty. Actually, I thought this door would lead to a hallway and not to your study."

"You are welcome to come through at any time. Would you care for a brandy?" Darcy knew it was too early, but after being refused, it seemed likely that it would be a good time.

Mr. Williams nodded, wondering how much of the conversation his friend had heard. He blushed at the thought.

"What are your plans for the duration of the summer?" Darcy asked innocently.

He watched as Mr. Williams studied his drink for a few moments before speaking. "I will return to my estate in Sussex. The harvest will be here soon, and I enjoy helping my father manage it at this time of year."

Darcy nodded. He certainly should not travel to Hertfordshire at this time of year. His steward could manage without him, but being here made his tenants more comfortable. They switched to trivial matters for the next half hour. When Mrs. Reynolds entered to announce that tea was being served in the saloon, they joined the ladies. Darcy claimed the seat beside Elizabeth and watched as Mr. Williams moved to the window, thoroughly ignoring the rest of the room, or at least pretending to. Elizabeth did not even seem to notice him.

She quickly began a conversation with Jane, Charles, and Darcy about future plans.

"Jane, I do not wish to follow you North. My father has stated that he longs for my company. I must return home with him, although he did not bring his carriage."

"Do you miss your home and the surrounding walking paths?" Darcy asked.

"I will first admit to quite enjoying the paths around your

home, but, yes, I also miss the Hertfordshire countryside. Nothing can really compare to home."

"Hertfordshire will not always be your home," Mr. Williams said, coming closer to the group without taking a seat.

"That is true. One day I will leave my home for another. That is the lot of women."

Darcy watched as Elizabeth kept her gaze on her hands folded in her lap. He could not let her be embarrassed. "When that day comes, I doubt it will feel like a burden to you. Besides, your husband will undoubtedly allow you to visit Longbourn as often as you wish."

Other than a shy glance from Jane, no one suspected any hidden meaning from this statement. Jane then took the initiative to return the conversation to important topics once more.

"We should look at our plans once again. We depart tomorrow, and we cannot take you with us as we are traveling in the opposite direction. Will you return to Longbourn with our father by post?"

"I am traveling today, and I will go through London. It would be my pleasure to escort you and your father home," Mr. Williams responded.

Elizabeth politely declined by saying that she could not leave today.

Darcy wondered if Mr. Williams were upset by this or not. Had he decided to attempt to court her anyway, or was he leaving to nurse his wounded pride? "After you leave tomorrow, Mrs. Bingley, I will travel to London to see to some business with my solicitor. If Georgiana is willing to come with me, Mr. and Miss Bennet may travel with us in my carriage. Mrs. Annesley will accompany us as well. The ride should be easy enough to manage."

Georgiana agreed that she liked the idea of the trip. "I should like to go shopping with Lady Isabel."

Elizabeth was intrigued. "Who is Lady Isabel?"

"Lord Templeton's family has a long-standing relationship with ours. Lady Isabel is my age. Her family live in Devon, so we are rarely able to spend time together. We meet whenever our families are together in London."

"Do you know she is in London?" Elizabeth asked.

"Yes, she wrote me a letter a week ago."

Darcy noted she was hesitating. "Miss Bennet, would you let my sister and I transport you to Longbourn?"

"My only other options are to travel post or travel today. I am not ready to leave today. Having ridden in your carriage once before, I feel certain your carriage and your company will be preferable to traveling post. I accept your offer, and I am certain my father will do so as well. If you'll excuse me, I should go and prepare my trunks after I speak with him."

The party broke up as everyone realized they also needed to prepare. Darcy simply needed to alert his valet of his plans, and the remainder of his morning was free. He returned downstairs to see his friend off before returning to his study to think.

At least his competition would not be courting her in his absence. Would absence make her interest in him grow fonder? They had the London season ahead of them. How many other suitors would she have then? Would he be able to live if she were to prefer someone else? He had no choice but to wait and find out. He had heard her words to his friend: *I have no intentions of marrying at present*. He could not move forward now.

He smiled at the thought that he still had hope. These thoughts were interrupted when Elizabeth strode in, asking to go for a walk. "I want to enjoy my last day at Pemberley."

Darcy rose from his chair and offered her his arm. This would be their last walk through the grounds of Pemberley, at least until they married, if they ever did. He tried to act carefree, but his heart never once stopped racing. At least twice, he stumbled on his words, but Elizabeth was there and happy to catch his slips. They discussed flowers, books, streams, balls, and many other subjects. He never once alluded to his attraction to her, and she gaily walked with him by her side.

That evening, the air was easy in the dining and music rooms. Mr. Williams had departed a few hours earlier, and with him had gone all of Elizabeth's worries. She had not meant to engage his affection, not that she even believed she had done so. It had made her worry that her impertinence was at fault.

The three-day journey to Longbourn passed pleasantly, although everyone was tired of it after the first day. Elizabeth, Mrs. Annesley, and Georgiana sat together in the carriage, occasionally with Darcy on the opposite bench. Mr. Darcy chose to spend the majority of the time riding his horse alongside the carriage with Mr. Bennet, though. When they were in the carriage together, Darcy would read to the ladies. Mr. Bennet rarely entered the carriage, stating a preference for solitude to the conversation of three ladies.

When he was outside, they would talk of the coming season. Georgiana would be coming out in society, as would Elizabeth, although she would not be presented at court or expect a string of suitors after her non-existent dowry. Elizabeth, having already come out in Hertfordshire society, was able to soothe Georgiana's fears, even though Hertfordshire society could barely compare with the London elites. At each of the coaching inns, Darcy would find a secluded room for their party away from the other travelers. Each night, the girls roomed together to preserve propriety while Darcy slept with Mr. Bennet, wondering how he would survive after he left Elizabeth in Hertfordshire.

Elizabeth had never traveled with such style. Her every whim was attended to immediately. She was never allowed to tire overmuch, especially since Georgiana had a more difficult time traveling and was more likely to need aid. No expense was spared by Darcy if it would provide comfort or entertainment for Georgiana or Elizabeth.

Arriving at Longbourn, Mrs. Bennet welcomed her guests with aplomb. She insisted the Darcys accept her invitation to rest in her guest rooms. They most certainly could not depart that evening. Mr. Darcy, who had planned to remain at Netherfield, was happy to accept Mrs. Bennet's offer to remain with Elizabeth for one more night. He had a note sent to Netherfield to inform the housekeeper that she would not need to prepare rooms for him or his sister.

At dinner, Mrs. Bennet explained how the rumors had all but disappeared in Meryton. "Mr. Wickham is considered to be a very vile man. His debts are more than he would have made in two years had he remained here and worked hard not to spend a penny more. Many of the shop owners struggled to survive after the militia departed with their debts. Their disapprobation of the officers made it very easy for me to suggest Lydia had not gone off with Wickham and had instead sought Mr. Darcy's fine ball. No one even remembers that it had even been in their minds. Lydia is very lucky to have such a friend as you, Mr. Darcy."

"Where is Lydia?" Her mother asked. "I expected her to return with you, Lizzy."

"She chose to attend Jane and the Bingleys," Elizabeth asserted, with a sly glance at Mr. Darcy. "Jane was not feeling her best and decided that having a sister with her would greatly improve matters."

"Then they will both be in London for the season!" Mrs. Bennet squealed with delight. "No doubt she will catch a wealthy husband. I was surprised that she did not find one in Brighton, but surely the officers are all too poor for her."

Georgiana focused on her plate in an attempt to ignore the profusions that came from Mrs. Bennet. She could not imagine a more vulgar discussion. She looked to her brother many times, but his apparent easiness meant that she was on her own in her opinion.

Thankfully for Georgiana, Elizabeth noted her distress and claimed her hand under the table. She then whispered into her ear, "My mother does not know everything that happened to Lydia, or if she does, she has conveniently forgotten the worst. It is to our benefit, for she is the biggest gossip in Meryton. In time, I have learned to tune her out, as has your brother, it would seem. She will change topic easily enough. Watch and learn from me." With a wink, Elizabeth turned to her mother and asked if Meryton had had any new fabrics delivered.

The following conversation lasted for another hour before Mr. Bennet declared his resolution to retire to his library. He was not without manners, and he invited Mr. Darcy to join him in a game of chess. With the men out of the way, Mrs. Bennet talked of fabric and produced fashion plates in the drawing room. Georgiana, more comfortable with this discussion, engaged with her and Kitty for the remainder of the evening while Mary, Mrs. Annesley, and Elizabeth discussed music in another corner of the room.

When Mr. Darcy rejoined the ladies, without Mr. Bennet, Elizabeth offered to play for the party. Mr. Darcy turned the pages first for her, then for Georgiana, followed by Mary. Elizabeth then played duets with both Georgiana and Mary until Mrs. Bennet declared the evening too long. Despite having extra guest rooms available, Georgiana had chosen to share a bed with Elizabeth. The two talked late into the night about their future season, and Georgiana begged Elizabeth to remain at her home throughout, even though she knew it would be improper.

20: TRAVEL TO LONDON

The Darcys resumed their journey the following day, parting with the Bennets shortly after breakfast. Georgiana was saddened to part with her new friends, but it was nothing compared to the pain in Darcy's chest. The Bennets had assembled at the entrance to Longbourn as he bade his farewells, so he could not kiss Elizabeth's hand as he wished. He could not risk the idea of a courtship entering Mrs. Bennet's mind or Elizabeth would not know a moment's peace. He would not put her through that torment if it could be helped. Instead, he was the one tormented by the knowledge that he would not see her again until January. His only consolation was that Georgiana would write to her new friends, and he would hopefully hear about her through her correspondence.

He watched Longbourn shrink into the distance behind the carriage, watching the trees pass. He knew that Elizabeth would walk under them when she traveled to Meryton. When he could no longer reasonably pretend he could still see either Elizabeth or Longbourn, he returned his attention to his companions to find Georgiana looking at him with a thoughtful expression. Other than a small flush of color at being caught, Darcy's mien remained unaltered. Instead of reacting, which he knew Georgiana would like as she wished to hear his thoughts, he decided to begin reading to pass the time. He read a book of poetry aloud, so Georgiana's unspoken questions had to remain unasked.

The Darcys remained in London for a fortnight before deciding they had had enough. The smell was offensive, and the only reason they had planned to travel was Darcy's desire to escort Elizabeth himself. They had shopped for new clothes and books and were now ready to return to Pemberley. The next difficulty was to plan the route. Both Georgiana and Darcy wished to travel to Longbourn to see Elizabeth, but neither was willing to say so openly. Therefore, their normal route was selected, thoroughly bypassing Longbourn and Meryton.

This development delayed Elizabeth's first letter to Georgiana, for it had to be redirected to Pemberley. When it finally came, it was with great resolve that Darcy handed it still sealed to his sister at breakfast. He could not ask her to show him the letter, although he desperately wanted to claim it as his and open it himself. Georgiana said nothing of her brother's impatience and instead pocketed it to read when she was alone. Mr. Darcy could not help visiting his sister every half hour, but she never once revealed the contents. A sly smile was all he would receive. It was nearly dinner time when he finally gave in and asked her.

Instead of answering directly though, Georgiana decided to tease him. "Oh, I had not realized you would be interested. She writes of her various social engagements. She has purchased some new ribbon to update her bonnet. Her mother has encouraged her to remake her dresses as well. They have asked me for some fashion plates, if I would be good enough to find any that I am willing to spare."

"I can send to London for a copy of La Belle Assemblée. It is the reputed best."

Georgiana nodded. "My copies are older than they would like, I am sure. Will you purchase one for me as well? Then she and I can compare pages. If I am to come out this year, I should like to prepare my wardrobe with my own selections."

Darcy agreed to send a letter to his housekeeper in London to procure two copies before he left. He would need to have Georgiana write a short note to go with the periodical on its way to Longbourn. They could not know that he was the instigator.

With that finished, Darcy shifted into a slow and easy lifestyle. He kept himself busy to avoid letting his thoughts wander too far. He could not help it that he pictured her sitting beside him almost every moment. He could not let his mind prevent him from being a thorough and charitable landlord. As the months passed, the weather began to turn. With the cold, it seemed that Elizabeth was kept indoors more often, allowing her to write more frequently. Instead of receiving a letter every few weeks, she was regularly sending letters to arrive on Mondays.

In them, she claimed that her walks were shorter but not forgotten. Darcy enjoyed Georgiana's recital of her friend's letters. They were witty and encouraging to Georgiana, and Darcy steadily saw her sister become more engaging, thanks to Elizabeth's fine example. Occasionally, Elizabeth would write her curiosity as to how Mr. Darcy would respond to some event in Hertfordshire, requiring him to hear every detail of the assembly so that he could form an opinion. Darcy enjoyed hearing about her excursions, and he was becoming very skilled at thinking of witty rejoinders at which he hoped she would laugh.

With the constant contact between the Bennets and Darcys, the time passed very pleasantly. Although Darcy itched to be in Elizabeth's presence, he was content to know of her comings and goings. In October, however, her letter took a serious turn. Georgiana came to her brother's study where she found him mulling over a tenant dispute.

"Brother, may I come in?" She asked pleasantly.

"Certainly, you may. What is troubling you?" He said as he put his letters aside.

"I have a letter from Miss Bennet." She lifted the letter

above her head, knowing he would wish to read it himself, such had become his custom.

"Is she ill?" Darcy leapt up from his seat to snatch it and begin reading. He almost did not hear his sister's response.

"No, she is not ill. Her sister, Miss Lydia has decided to remain with the Bingleys for the winter. Apparently, she has become a favorite with Mr. Bingley's aunt, who is very ill. She seems upset about this development, although I had not thought her close to her younger sister. Another problem is that the Hursts have decided to spend the season in Bath. This means that the Bingleys will not have a home in London for the season. I was so looking forward to spending my first season with Lizzy and Jane. I shall be mortified if I must go alone."

Darcy put down the letter, having read through it once quickly, to respond to his sister's concerns. "You are not alone. Your aunt has already agreed to sponsor you at Almacks, and her two daughters will be by your side."

"They are known and respected by the Ton already."

"The Ton will respect you from the onset because you are a Darcy."

"Yes, but they will not know my character, and I will not know whom to trust."

"Then do not trust any of them but your cousins."

"I would still prefer a friend who was coming out with me. Lizzy was so warm and kind."

Darcy moved to the window, wondering how to fix this problem. He could understand why Lydia would remain secluded in the north. She must be with child. The Hursts were another problem. How could he get Elizabeth to London for the season without them?

He could not imagine going through the season without Elizabeth either. He could not court her if she were not in London. He wanted to invite her to remain in his home, but he could not convince himself of the propriety of the suggestion. He was distracted from his thoughts by the entrance of Lady Matlock and her son.

Greetings were dispensed with quickly, and Georgiana ordered refreshments.

Lady Matlock began the conversation. "We only have one month to prepare for the season, and you must have a new wardrobe, my dear." She looked at Georgiana's dress disapprovingly.

"This gown is new as of this summer."

"Then it is too old for London."

"Georgiana, you love to shop. A new wardrobe should not distress you," Colonel Fitzwilliam added.

When she did not respond, Darcy took it upon himself to do so. "You must forgive Georgiana. She has just learned her friend will not be enjoying the season with her."

"Who is this friend of yours?" Lady Matlock inquired.

"Miss Bennet has sent me a letter this morning. She was to stay with the Hursts, but Mr. Hurst has decided to go to Bath for his health." She kept her head down.

"Ah, now I remember her. She seemed a very pleasant sort of girl. I should like to know more of her. Georgiana, why don't you invite her and her sisters to stay at your home in London?"

Darcy kept silent as his mind raced through the possibilities. If his aunt approved it, then it would not be improper. He could not invite her to remain with him, even with the Bingleys to act as chaperone, but Georgiana inviting her was more appropriate. How had he not thought of this before? "I believe you should write to her immediately. I will invite the Bingleys to stay as well. She will be properly looked after with her married sister by her side."

"She can stay with us!" Georgiana squealed. "I thought she could not since you are unmarried."

"There will be enough chaperones and servants here that it would be proper," Lady Matlock explained. "Your brother is one of the few gentlemen who can be counted on to maintain strict propriety. Besides, she would not be invited by a bachelor. She will be invited by you, my dear. There is a very distinct difference between the two. It would not be proper for him to invite a maiden, even if it were for your sake. If you like, I can also live with you for the season. Your home is more comfortable than my husband's, although I would never tell him so. Go and write your letter to her now, extending the invitation."

Georgiana hugged her aunt before bounding out of the room.

"You will have to speak to her about her comportment tonight," Lady Matlock added, though she did not sound as though she were scolding her niece.

Darcy only nodded, and they then changed the subject to planning the next month of travels. Lady Matlock would stay at Pemberley for a fortnight before they would all travel to London together. From there, they would begin shopping for what seemed like the most interesting season for their family in a long time. Lady Matlock had despaired of Darcy ever finding a wife, but now the flame had been rekindled.

A week later, they had their response from Elizabeth. She gladly accepted their invitation to enjoy the London season with the Darcys and the Bingleys. Her letter was full of exuberance and anticipation, which thoroughly delighted Georgiana.

The Bingleys had already accepted their invitation a few days earlier and were planning to be driving down from their northern relatives in mid-October. With Jane feeling uneasy, they expected the trip to be very long. They wanted to have enough time to rest frequently. They would stop at Netherfield on their way down and pick up Elizabeth for the final leg of the journey to London.

Darcy sighed. It seemed as if everything was falling into place. Indeed, they were sitting in a carriage, making the long trip to London in next to no time. Darcy could not help smiling as Georgiana conversed with whomever would listen about her excitement for the season. She felt that there would be no problems with Elizabeth beside her. Darcy thought her ridiculous for needing Elizabeth when she had not only himself but also his cousins, aunt, and Mrs. Annesley to support her. However, he agreed that her presence would make the season so much more enjoyable.

Once in London, the party spent the majority of each day shopping and frequenting tea shops with acquaintances they had met while there. Georgiana was establishing a good footing in society by meeting people in very small groups. By the time the Bingleys arrived a fortnight later, the season was beginning, and Georgiana had a small band of fifteen ladies whom she felt were friends.

Mr. Bingley was given his old room, and his wife was given the room which shared a sitting room with his. Elizabeth was placed in the room beside her sister. Lady Matlock decided to place herself in the room across the hall, so as to hear any possible noises in the hallway. She had to be a good chaperone, as the newlyweds were unlikely to pay much attention to their charge. At dinner, Lady Matlock politely inquired after Bingley's family.

"My sisters and Mr. Hurst are in Bath. While the season is not so great there, Mr. Hurst's health is improving greatly, so they will remain at least for some time."

Mr. Darcy could not help feeling grateful that Miss Bingley would not be present. However, he attempted to show proper feelings as he said, "I hope Mr. Hurst's health improves. I know how much he and his wife enjoy the season."

"I have no doubt of that. They will enjoy the social gatherings of Bath well enough though. Perhaps Miss Bingley will be able to find a husband," Mr. Bingley stated.

Darcy carefully hid a smile. Miss Bingley would never encourage a man who was not a Darcy. Hopefully, this season would be the last time he would have to endure bachelorhood. He was tired of Miss Bingley and the rest of the desperate women of the ton. The only difference between previous years and this one would be that Elizabeth would be included in nearly all of his engagements. She could not be presented at court without a sponsor, so some of their engagements would not include her. He wondered if he even needed to attend those events. They certainly held no appeal. Unfortunately, he had to attend for Georgiana's sake. She needed to be seen by the right people with him.

Elizabeth smiled. "I wish her well. It must not be easy needing to secure a husband. I am glad that I have no such inclinations at present. Someday I might feel like Miss Bingley, but for now I may simply enjoy studying the characters I find at these balls. I am sure to meet some interesting people."

Georgiana took this as an opportunity to begin describing the people that Elizabeth was sure to meet.

21: SETTLING IN

The days fell into routine for the party. Elizabeth and Darcy were the first to wake and would sit in the library sipping coffee and tea while waiting for the others to rise. Their conversations thrived as Elizabeth had access to more reading materials than before. She enjoyed listening to Darcy's insights, and she found that they frequently held shared tastes in literature. Almost every book he suggested intrigued her.

When others began to rise, they shifted to the dining room where the sidebar was laden with delicious biscuits and fruits for their enjoyment, along with the strong aromas of coffee, tea, and chocolate ready for them. They would remain at the table for an hour or two as the rest of the party joined them. Elizabeth enjoyed reading Mr. Darcy's newspapers after she finished eating and talking about the current events in the nation. She enjoyed the fact she had access to so much information, and Mr. Darcy would share his insights which were learned from the people he knew to add to the information in the papers. At home, her father purchased only one newspaper, and rarely did she have time to peruse it as the noise level in the house would encourage her to spend most of her morning out of doors, not to mention that her father did not know anyone in the House of Lords to give context to the information in the paper.

After dinner, the group would depart for the day, either on a shopping expedition or to visit a museum, zoo, or park. As the day wore on, they would take a break at a tea shop, where they frequently met friends. Lady Matlock had so many acquaintances, and all were eager to meet Georgiana and her friends. If they had single women in their party, they were more interested in meeting Mr. Darcy again, and Elizabeth enjoyed laughing at their antics as they returned to the house in Darcy's carriages.

After dinner, the group would generally dress for going out. The season had not quite begun, but there were so many plays, soirées, and operas being held to pass the time that they rarely spent the evening at home. If they did stay in, the group would gather together and listen to Mrs. Annesley, Georgiana, and Elizabeth take turns playing the pianoforte while the others danced about the room or simply watched the performance.

As the weeks passed, the time came for the first balls of the season. Elizabeth and Jane stayed home as Georgiana was presented at Almack's Assembly Rooms by her aunt and brother. After this momentous event, which Elizabeth was pleased to forego, the season opened up and many balls were added to their evening outings. Georgiana's presentation was much talked of in the house, and Darcy began to feel slighted that Elizabeth spent all of her time with Georgiana, Jane, and Lady Matlock. At least he still had his morning chats in the library with her.

"Are you excited for tonight?" He asked on the morning of the first ball Elizabeth would attend.

"I must confess that I am. I have already secured partners for the first five sets and I expect more will come when I actually arrive. Being part of your aunt's party has certainly increased my standing in society. I expect to be hardly able to walk tomorrow, but it will be enjoyable to see new people."

"With so many dances, you will not have as much time to observe people."

"I shall observe enough to be content."

"My aunt does not often include people outside of other families in her parties, so the Ton will be quite interested in you, as you have seen happening already."

"I am starting to understand your reticence about always being looked at and talked of. I shall endure it with fortitude, but are you really looking forward to the ball tonight?" She looked at him earnestly.

"While balls in general do not entice me, I am looking forward to tonight. As I have said before, when I am well acquainted with my partners, a dance can be very enjoyable. My first three partners are very agreeable to me."

Elizabeth laughed. "Yes, it was quite ingenious of you to solicit myself, Jane, and your cousin for the first three dances. No one will be surprised when you sit the rest of the night out. The matchmaking mamas will have moved on to more susceptible bachelors by the time you are available."

"That would be the goal. However, it would be ungentlemanly of me to remain out the rest of the night."

"Yes, it would, but I do not believe that you always care for being a gentleman other than when it suits you."

"You are referring to the assembly at which we first met."

"I shall never forget it."

"I wish you would. I was not at my best that night, as we have discussed. In general, I dance with many of my acquaintances. As the master of a profitable estate, I am a desirable match, even though I am not titled. I have rarely had to work to find dance partners. However, I hope you are right that I will not be harassed by those who only see my estate and wealth. It will not come to pass, however much we might wish it. Those matchmaking mamas have their hearts set on a match, and they will not tire after three dances. I will dance with many of the daughters of my aunt's friends. There shall be nothing for it."

"If you scowl enough, perhaps there will be fewer daughters who allow their mothers to force a dance with you." Elizabeth laughed as Darcy scowled for her enjoyment. "Yes, that is the look I mean. You are so handsome when you smile, so be sure to use your scowl as often as possible or you will encourage the daughters."

Darcy's laugh died when a servant entered to announce that the dining room had been prepared.

"Come, we must eat to preserve our strength for the trials ahead."

"Only you could consider a ball to be a trial, even when you stated you are looking forward to it." Elizabeth laughed as she slipped into the hall.

Darcy watched the doorway for a few moments before responding, "Yes, Elizabeth. It will be a trial to watch you laugh and dance with eligible young men who might just capture your heart as I have been unable to do." Despite the early hour, Darcy drank a quick brandy before following Elizabeth to the dining room. Almost all of his guests were assembled, and Darcy was able to claim a seat at the head of the table. With the conversation about dresses and dances flowing around the table, he needed only to listen while his heart clambered in his chest.

"Darcy! We ought to make ourselves scarce today with all the preparations that are bound to happen today. Shall we have a fencing match at White's?"

Darcy turned to see Bingley addressing him. "That is an excellent plan." He turned to speak to a footman standing just out of the way.

The fencing match was enough to get Darcy's emotions back in check. The rigorous exercise and immense thought required to win the match put his own thoughts behind him. When he was changing for the ball, however, these thoughts returned with full force, albeit this time more ordered. Tonight would be his first test at controlling his feelings for Elizabeth Bennet with a crowd observing his every move. He had to control his feelings. He could not always observe her, as was always his wont. He had to remain neutral, as her friend, not her betrothed. She had to be allowed to dance with other eligible men. His cousins he could count on to not flirt excessively with her. His friends, some of whom she had already met on their walks in the park or at dinner parties, he could not entirely trust not to flirt or fall in love with her, however. Would he survive if she chose someone else?

Darcy shuddered. He could not let that happen, nor could he prevent it.

"You are ready, sir," his valet announced as he finished brushing lint off Darcy's grey coat.

"Thank you." Darcy looked in the mirror and sighed. He could no longer count his nerves as inconsequential. Indeed, it felt like he had snakes slithering around in his gut. He only hoped that others could not see his anxiety.

Descending the stairs, he found himself relying on the rail, its stability helping to prepare him for the sight of the ladies waiting at the bottom. Elizabeth's light green dress was cut lower than her previous ones had been, and he needed to swallow a few times to remember his place as her friend. After a warm greeting, he turned to his sister, who was also attired in a low-cut dress with short sleeves, as was the fashion. He nearly growled when thinking of other men staring at his sister in the way he had just done with Elizabeth. Within a few minutes, the party found themselves in two carriages heading for the ball.

Darcy was glad his carriage arrived first. He was ready to take Georgiana and Elizabeth's arms to escort them into the hall. The Darcys were expected to be part of the receiving line, so they bade Elizabeth and the Bingleys farewell for the time being. After a small wait, families began to enter. Darcy was introduced to many young women, daughters of lords and dukes, or at least rich men of no title. Darcy offered his hand to a few for a dance, but he kept some free so that he would be able to observe Elizabeth.

An hour later, the receiving line dwindled, and the dancing was about to commence. Darcy claimed his aunt's arm and walked into the ballroom. His eyes darted around, finally resting on Elizabeth, who was speaking with the young Lord

Helmsford. They had met a week earlier at a dinner party with his aunt. He wished to join their conversation, but he could not. The musicians were tuning their instruments in anticipation of the first song. He needed to find his first partner, Jane Bingley.

As they took their place a few places down from the head of the line, Darcy was relieved to see Elizabeth standing up with Colonel Fitzwilliam, as Lord Helmsford had a partner of his own down the line. Lord Matlock announced the music and the dance, and he began to move with Lord Grimsby's new bride.

Lord Matlock began the dance with gusto, and the dancers fell in line quickly. Jane made small talk with Darcy, but for the most part, he was able to watch Elizabeth's graceful moves. Twice, Colonel Fitzwilliam had made her laugh, although no sound so unladylike as a laugh had actually escaped her lips. Instead, her eyes danced in merriment. When the music stopped, Darcy handed Jane to her husband and moved to collect Elizabeth. His heart soared as he claimed her gloved hand, and he smiled at her.

The first few movements of the dance were completed in silence. Darcy enjoyed the slight pressure of her hand when the dance brought them together, but he also remembered how she enjoyed conversation and had preferred it when dancing at Netherfield. After a deep breath which allowed him to inhale her scent, he began with, "The musicians are very lively."

Elizabeth smiled. "Indeed they are."

After a turn, Darcy continued. "It is your turn to say something now, Miss Bennet. I remarked on the music, and you ought to remark on the dance."

"You are learning the social norms of speaking while dancing. Very well done. I will take my part as well and say I do believe I have never seen so many couples in one set before. London truly is a social oasis."

They continued to remark on the dance. In a lull in the conversation, Elizabeth turned to see Lord Helmsford watching them. "Your friend is very amiable."

Darcy turned to see the man smiling at Elizabeth. "He is, although I do not consider him to be a close acquaintance. His family are very close to my family. We met as children every winter, for his family house is but a few blocks from here. He is a good man and would make a very good husband whenever he chooses to take a wife."

"No, your aunt's schemes are bad enough. You must not choose a husband for me too."

Darcy scowled as he attempted to repress a laugh. "You must not accuse me of securing a husband for you," *unless said husband were myself*, he added to himself. The dance separated the couple for a few turns. When they reunited, Elizabeth chose to describe the people she had spoken to while Darcy had been in the reception line. Darcy listened and smiled at her characterizations. It seemed that his earlier comment had not changed anything between them. He was relieved.

When the dance ended, he escorted Elizabeth to Mr. Bingley, her next dance partner. He then sought out his cousin, Lord Matlock's youngest child, with haste, so that he could be as close to Elizabeth as possible. His cousin was not of the same mind, however, and delayed returning to the dance for some minutes, ensuring that they were not anywhere on the same side of the room. She enjoyed his frustration and made fun of him as often as possible.

Darcy cheered internally when the music stopped, but his cousin had ideas of her own. "You must take me to see my father. He wishes to speak to us about our mutual friend, Lord Helmsford. There is a vote coming in the House of Lords, and my father needs his support."

Reluctantly, Darcy agreed. They found Lord Matlock sitting in the card room, and they remained there discussing the pending vote until it was time for the next dance. Returning to the ballroom, Darcy had only time to collect his partner, Lady Eleanor, the Duke of Comsworth's daughter. He had known her for some time and enjoyed speaking with her, although her company could not compare to Elizabeth's. As he lined up, he searched for Elizabeth, but he could not find her. He was halfway through the dance before he heard her laugh. It was a small laugh, but it could not be mistaken. He turned towards the sound and found her with Lord Helmsford.

Darcy nearly growled with jealousy. He turned back to his partner, but he found himself unable to speak to her for the rest of the dance. Indeed, when he escorted her back to her parents, she was quite relieved. He then shifted his attention to Elizabeth. He could not stand another minute without her. Thankfully, he found her a few feet away speaking to a man he only knew by reputation as a rake. As he walked up to them, he heard him ask for her hand for a dance. She was about to accept when Darcy reached them and interrupted them. "Miss Bennet, this is our song. Mr. Fergus, if you will excuse us."

He reached out his hand towards Elizabeth, and although she looked confused, she accepted him. They took their place in the set, but Darcy did not release her hand as the music began. The familiar tones of a waltz drifted down from the music balcony above. Elizabeth stepped into Darcy's arms and placed her hand on his shoulder. As they prepared to step, she quirked her eyebrow at him.

Darcy smiled mischievously. "Yes, I know I took this liberty, but you must trust me. Mr. Fergus is not so honorable as he appears. In a normal dance, I would not have intervened, but this is a most inappropriate dance for one such as he. Besides, I have looked forward to a waltz with you since I was not allowed to dance with you during our practice sessions."

Elizabeth laughed at the memory of the afternoons with Georgiana's dancing master. "I see. With that being the case, I approve of your tactics. This means we cannot dance again tonight, but I do not suppose that will matter anyway. All of the next few dances are already reserved. You are safe from me."

Darcy thought that entirely unlikely, but he chuckled in response. The music began in earnest, and soon they were swirling around with the other couples. The dance was new and complicated enough that Elizabeth could not attempt conversation for the first few minutes. In fact, it was Darcy who began it again, asking after her impressions of the ball. Elizabeth smiled radiantly as she began discussing her partners. She mentioned each gentleman equally, so Darcy felt no one stuck out in her mind. They all amused her, so he had no cause to feel jealous. At least, he tried to tell himself as much.

The dancing lasted a few hours longer after the waltz, and Elizabeth had the fortune to be partnered for every dance. Thankfully, her shoes were of such high quality that she did not develop blisters. In the carriage ride home, Elizabeth and Darcy spoke about the ball while Georgiana, Charles, and Jane all attempted to rest. Dawn was not far away, but Elizabeth was energetic enough, and Darcy was thrilled to have her conversation to herself. Most days he could not get her alone any more, apart from their morning chats in the library.

"Who was your favorite partner, Elizabeth?" Georgiana asked over the dining table the next morning.

"Why should I have a favorite, Georgiana?" Elizabeth thwarted her question.

Georgiana laughed. "Of course, you have a favorite! We all have favorites. I liked…" but she was cut off by her brother choking on his coffee. They were sitting at the dining table breaking their fast. Lady Matlock entered at the same time that her sons had arrived to discuss the ball.

Lady Matlock laughed. "Georgiana, I do not know what your brother will do when you actually begin to take a real interest in a gentleman."

Georgiana sighed at the thought.

"There is time for that," Elizabeth interrupted. "If you must know, I believe my favorite was the colonel. He is so very amusing."

"I thought you preferred Lord Helmsford. He seemed to look at you a great deal and engage you in conversation as well. He would be an excellent match for you."

Elizabeth smiled. "He is very amiable and a superb dancer."

"You must also add that he is rich and titled. Just think

what your mama would say." Jane smiled serenely. "She would be so happy to hear about the men who have taken an interest in you."

"Which is precisely why I will not be telling her about him or any other young man at the ball. I have no reason to give her hope when there is none. Lord Helmsford is not for me. While he is certainly very amiable, I would be bored being pleased every day. I wish for a true partner who will not always agree with me. I was able to argue in circles around him, and he did not even notice. He is smart, but he lacks enough true conviction in his thoughts. He is too eager to please for me."

Darcy could not help smiling as his aunt looked at him after hearing this speech.

Georgiana did not completely understand Elizabeth. "Why would you want to argue with your future partner? I would think it would be extremely tiring."

"True discord would be tiring and unhealthy. However, a lively debate now and again keeps our minds active. Just think how dull it would be to forever hear your praises sung with no criticism. I should be bored within a week."

Georgiana hummed to herself as she thought of this, but Lady Matlock expertly changed the subject. "Our next outing is tomorrow. We are to go to the opera. Do you know what the play is about?"

Elizabeth leaned forward as Colonel Fitzwilliam described the gruesome details. Having never experienced an opera before, she had no means of comparison. However, she had read as much as she could about a great many operas, and they all sounded exciting.

22: LONDON SEASON

"I could not believe how expressive the music was! I could practically hear them walking. Each step was pronounced in the music. The words were unintelligible, but I knew exactly what they were saying. I did not believe that could be possible!" Elizabeth was almost crying in her excitement.

It was late, but Elizabeth and Darcy were sitting in the library discussing the opera. Once she had said she could not sleep, he could not let her sit alone. He poured two glasses of port and joined her by the fireplace, which was roaring with life. Having seen many opera performances over the years, he had grown accustomed to them. He could not even remember his first. Seeing the play through Elizabeth's eyes was both refreshing and delightful. He wondered if she would lose that light over time, but he highly doubted it.

His thoughts were pushed aside as Elizabeth described how the heroine found her inner strength to save herself from her attacker, even though she ultimately died in her escape. The topic made her animated; he loved seeing her like this. When the clock on the mantle chimed three in the morning, Darcy startled. Had they really been there that long? He had barely said anything, but he had responded enough. He knew he ought to bid her goodnight, but he could not. Instead, he shut his eyes to better listen to her voice.

"Mr. Darcy! Mr. Darcy!"

Shuddering as he awoke suddenly, Darcy looked up into his housekeeper's eyes. How long had he been asleep? He leaned forward in his chair, noticing his body had been covered by a blanket. He shook his head to clear the last vestiges of sleep. He moved to stand and noticed his shoes had been removed. Looking at his housekeeper, he wondered if she had been the one to take care of him.

She sensed his puzzlement and responded, "I was not the one who gave you the blanket. You startled the maid who came in to stoke the fire. She had not been expecting to see you, and she came to me, frightened. I thought I should wake you before the others rise for the day. Mr. Davies is expecting you in your room when you are ready."

Darcy nodded and followed her out of the room. When he reached the first floor, he paused at the stairs. If his housekeeper and maid had not given him the blanket, then it must have been Elizabeth. He looked up towards the second floor, where Elizabeth's room was. She had thought to care for him. He smiled. Surely, this was a sign of her improved regard for him.

A maid distracted him from his thoughts as she entered the hallway after stoking a fire in Georgiana's room. He shook his head and moved to his room. He would not be the mooncalf who stood at the stairs helplessly. He would be the perfect gentleman.

Two weeks later, Darcy was standing in front of his mirror. His valet had long disappeared, but he was still standing there. His clothes were perfect, but he did not look at himself. He was picturing a lovely brunette with fiery eyes standing beside him. This morning, he had finally brought up falling asleep that evening. She had blushed as she described how hard it had been to remove his shoes. She had been worried about his comfort in his big shoes, and she had taken the time to remove them before covering him with the blanket.

A scurry of laughter outside his room roused him from his reverie. He could hear Georgiana laughing with Elizabeth, probably about something Elizabeth had said. She had spent so long in his house that imagining her as his wife was easy. He could not imagine a future without her by his side every day. He wondered how much longer he could give her to choose him. In time, he felt she would love him, but every time she smiled at or laughed with him, he wanted to kiss her. He wanted to propose to her. It was only his fear of rejection that kept him from begging her to put him out of his misery.

But was he really miserable? This time with her had been the best of his life. It was only his thoughts had been plaguing him, and his aunt with her hints and looks. He took a deep breath and walked out into the hallway. His sister and Elizabeth had already disappeared down the stairs, but he could hear their laughter lingering. When he reached the foyer where they were waiting for him, Georgiana took his hand to express her excitement.

"Elizabeth has invited me to live with her in Hertfordshire for the spring. Please tell me you will allow me to go! I have always wanted a sister, and she is willing to let me live with three. May I go?"

Darcy laughed at her excitement. "Certainly, if Mr. and Mrs. Bennet approve the scheme, I cannot deny you such fun. Perhaps I will visit Mr. Bingley while you are at Longbourn."

Georgiana squealed with delight.

Elizabeth laughed as she put her coat on. "I hope you are that excited after spending so much time with Kitty and Mary. It is fortunate that Lydia is still with Bingley's family."

Georgiana stepped back and sighed. She remembered meeting Lydia. "You should remember that we were on our way to becoming friends before she left Pemberley. You cannot pick your sisters. If she had been at Longbourn, I would have enjoyed getting to know her better also."

"I know you would have," Elizabeth said, chagrined at being caught thinking ill of her family. She took Georgiana's arm and escorted her outside and into the carriage. Once they were settled with blankets over their dresses, she said, "How many guests are supposed to be at the Duchess of Comsworth's ball tonight?"

"More than any dance we have been to so far by about half. Their ballroom is twice the size of ours, and since she is married to a duke, there will be no end to the invitations which are accepted. Families would have to be in very dire needs to decline them."

"Is there anyone I have not met?" Georgiana asked.

"I doubt it. However, there may be a few people whom you have not seen since you were very small. I have heard that the Hermans will be in attendance. After his wife's death, he retired to his country estate and has not been seen since. He returned to London just last week after a 15-year absence. His three sons are using tonight for their debut into society. I have no idea what they are like, but their father was a very honorable gentleman. His estate is very profitable, if the reports are true. The family have been friends with ours for generations."

Georgiana scrunched her eyebrows as she tried to remember the name, but nothing came of it. She had simply been too young. "I look forward to making their acquaintance. Are you looking forward to dancing with Lady Eleanor tonight?"

"I am looking forward to dancing with many ladies, including you, Miss Bennet." Darcy continued to describe a few of the other families Elizabeth had not yet met. Elizabeth only half listened in her excitement. Georgiana responded with what she knew of each of the families. When the carriage stopped, Darcy escorted his two favorite ladies up the stairs of the Duke's house. Greeting the Duke and his family, Darcy was able to pass through without offering a dance to Lady Eleanor. Since his sister had noted their interactions a few weeks ago, he needed to make sure that the lady did not have any hopes with him.

They entered the ballroom to find a small crowd mulling around. Moving to the refreshment table, Darcy introduced his sister and Elizabeth to a few acquaintances. He managed to bite his tongue when nearly every gentleman asked for Elizabeth's hand, even though they were mostly being polite and asking both Georgiana and Elizabeth for dances. When they finally reached the refreshments table, Elizabeth was laughing at Darcy's sour face. She hid it beneath her gleeful eyes until she caught Darcy's gaze.

"You worry too much, Mr. Darcy. Smile!"

While he attempted to remain stoic, the corners of his lips turned up, and she declared her triumph. Her teasing had worked, and by the time the music started, Darcy was feeling calm and happy. It lasted for a whole fifteen seconds until Elizabeth and Georgiana were whisked away by their first dance partners.

Standing alone, Darcy watched the dancing commence. He knew that he could not stare at Elizabeth the entire time, so he turned away, looking for a familiar face. A few paces away, he found Mr. Herman standing alone. When Mr. Herman noticed him, he smiled and easily began a conversation. Having been close to Darcy's father, he had many stories of their early university years to share. A few minutes into the conversation, Darcy realized the relationship had been very similar to that of Mr. Bingley and himself. Mr. Herman's outgoing personality would have complimented Mr. Darcy senior's reserved nature.

Darcy only remained with Mr. Herman through one dance, then he searched for a dance partner for himself. He could not respectfully decline to dance for the entire evening, when he knew that ladies were sitting out without partners. He only hoped that soon he would be able to find Elizabeth again.

Three partners later, he was able to choose a partner in time to stand close to Elizabeth, who was now dancing with Mr. Herman's youngest son. He could not hear their conversations, but he noted Elizabeth's smile as she bounced around with the reel. Her flushed cheeks were driving Darcy insane. He struggled to keep up with the steps every time he glanced at her. When the dance ended, he quickly returned his partner to her family and turned towards Elizabeth. He saw as she slipped out of the room and onto the balcony. He thought about joining her and began to move in that direction. However, he was waylaid by a few conversations until he saw Elizabeth's previous dance partner following her out of the door.

Not trusting the young man, he curtailed his conversation and hurried after him. When he stepped outside, his fears were confirmed. He could hear Elizabeth struggling at the end of the balcony. He rushed to her and pulled the man off. Acting on his instincts, he threw his fist at the man's face. He fell instantly. Darcy turned to find Elizabeth had already walked down the balcony toward the small garden. He followed her to make sure she was well after he was certain that he was the only one on the balcony to have observed the events.

"Elizabeth, tell me he did not harm you," he blurted as he reached her. He could hardly breathe after having run so fast.

Elizabeth was leaning over the garden bench. She was not crying, but she was clearly upset. He stood by her, waiting for her to catch her breath, while barely breathing himself. Once she was master enough of herself to look and see his fearful expression, she explained what had happened. "He kissed me. I tried to push him away, but he held me so tightly... I feel like my entire face is covered in slime."

Darcy walked up to her closely and saw that her chin was shining in the moonlight. He pulled out a handkerchief as he asked, "Did he... lick you?"

"Yes." She shivered in disgust at the memory. "I shall never marry."

Darcy looked at her as he wiped her face. "Why would you say that?"

"Women become the property of their husbands when they marry. They have to allow their husbands... certain liberties. I thought it was supposed to be nice. I never want someone to get that close to me again. Marriage must be terrible."

Darcy stopped and looked into her eyes. She appeared

determined. "Not all men are alike."

Elizabeth closed her eyes as she tried to calm her emotions. Darcy waited for her to say something, but she seemed to be guarded.

What more could he say? Would she ever want to be with him? There was only one way to find out. Gently, he cupped her chin gently in his hands and tilted her face towards his. He smiled affectionately as he leaned forward and gently kissed her lips. He felt Elizabeth shiver, and he moved his hands to support her back. He could feel every part of her that was touching him, and he noted that she was not pulling away or indicating in any other way that he should stop. Very gently, he closed his eyes and moved to kiss her cheeks, her nose, her forehead, and her lips once again before pulling back.

"That was not so bad," Elizabeth said as she shivered again.

"We are not all the same. Don't give up on finding a husband. When someone does capture your heart, they will be very lucky." He stepped back, removing his arms from her person. She faltered a little, so he grabbed her arms to steady her. Once she was steady, he led her back to the party before anyone could discover them to be missing. She followed him without speaking.

They paused when they reached the balcony. Mr. Herman was sitting up, rubbing his jaw. Elizabeth took a deep breath as she watched him. Darcy noted her renewed distress, so he led her almost to the door. He turned to her to inspect her dress for any tears or stains. "You look well. Now you must act the part. You were out here catching some air. You must return to the ballroom as though nothing has happened. You excel at expressing opinions that are not your own, so I have no doubt you will do very well. Mr. Herman and I will enter in a few minutes, so take this time to move to the other side of the hall where no one can connect you with us. You must dance with other gentlemen, if you can. When is your next free set?"

Elizabeth thought for a minute. "I believe the supper set is still free."

"May I claim that dance?"

Elizabeth nodded, smiling uncertainly. Darcy hoped she was not in too much distress. "Thank you. Now go."

Darcy opened the door and shut it after she disappeared on the other side. With a deep sigh, he moved to where Mr. Herman was sitting. "Your family is old and well-respected, but do not think that will save you. If one word of this spreads, I will use my considerable reputation to ensure your family is never welcome in London again. Do you understand?"

"Yes," Mr. Herman said weakly.

"Very good. I hope never to see you again, although your father is a worthy gentleman. He clearly missed something somewhere in your education."

"I was not going to compromise her."

"And yet, that is exactly what you did. Did no one tell you that you cannot kiss a lady until she is your wife?"

"They might have."

"You are despicable."

"No more than most men here. I knew we were alone."

"Did she wish for you to kiss her?"

"She had enjoyed our time dancing. She had seemed receptive, until she started pushing me away. I thought she would learn to like my kisses."

"I doubt anyone can learn to like something that is forced upon them. In future, you must secure a lady's permission. A guardian would have the right to call you out for such an act."

"I am not a terrible person," Mr. Herman responded, terrified at the thought of being in a duel.

"That is only a matter of opinion. There are some who are worse than you, certainly, but you are far from a good person in my book. I will leave you now. Enter in three minutes and find a married partner or your family to keep you company for the evening. Until you can control your actions, you ought never to dance with a maiden again."

"You have no control over that, but I will attempt to follow your advice. I value my life."

Darcy walked away. He looked inside the ballroom and immediately saw Elizabeth speaking with his aunt. Her smile was still forced, but he doubted anyone else would notice. He opened the door and stepped inside, picking a lady to dance with at random. They were at the end of the set, so Darcy had ample time to think. He had kissed Elizabeth. He had been as impulsive as Mr. Herman, but she had not pushed him away. Was he as ungentlemanly as Mr. Herman?

"Mr. Darcy?"

Darcy looked up to find his partner had been talking. He switched gears. "I apologize for my inattention. What were we speaking about?"

Half an hour later, he was free of his partner and looking for Elizabeth under the pretext of searching for his next dance partner. This time, however, he could not find her so easily. When he was about to ask the footman if she had left, he spotted her dancing with Colonel Fitzwilliam. He smiled. If anyone could coax her into a good mood, his cousin was the best person for the job. He watched her from the sidelines for a few minutes, and, sure enough, Elizabeth's smile turned into a short laugh. A laugh that was not forced. It signaled improvement.

He would get to talk to her later. For now, he needed to find his dance partner.

23: ACCEPTANCE

"This is our dance, Miss Bennet." Darcy held out his arm to escort Elizabeth to the dance floor. He had been waiting for this chance for what had seemed like forever. After much thought, he decided he must press his suit once more. He had compromised her, and he could not go back to simply being her friend after that.

Her hand felt so wonderful in his, even through both her gloves and his. The gentle pressure was nearly his undoing. Walking over to the dance floor, he took his place and looked at her. Her smile had faltered, but she was watching him with that inquisitive look she used when she was working out a puzzle. Instantly, his mind started wondering what she could be attempting to understand. She was clearly not angry with him, and that mere thought buoyed his resolve. When they first came close enough to speak, he gave her a chance to begin their topic. She smiled but did not speak.

They moved away again, and Darcy took matters into his own hands. When they came back together, he said, "You seem to have recovered remarkably well."

After the next return, Elizabeth responded, "I had a wonderful teacher."

"I doubt that."

"I suppose..." Elizabeth laughed as they separated again. "I suppose then you gave me reason to hope for a future that had been quashed not minutes before."

She had spoken so fast that Darcy had to process her words twice before he could respond. "I am glad to be of service in any way I can."

"I do have one question." Elizabeth moved away. "I hope I am not overstepping my place as your friend."

"That is impossible." Darcy's breathing was becoming erratic as he walked away.

"Very well. From our encounter, I found out that what I know about love is... wrong. What is love like?"

"I do not think this is really a conversation for a ballroom," Darcy said uncomfortably.

"I have no wish to make you uncomfortable. Jane and Charles are so well-suited for each other. Their love for each other has been visible ever since their second or third encounter. The books describe love in terms that relate entirely to them."

Darcy contemplated her words as he waited to return to her side. "Some people are not so able as you to see their love so soon."

"Was that because you did not see it, or because you did not want to see it? I remember you back then."

"And I remember you were the reason that I did not want to see it. Very well, you have asked me a question. I will see if I can find an appropriate response." Darcy was grateful for the break in the dance this time. When they reconvened, he was still unable to speak. It was another two turns before he could muster a word, and even then he could not finish his thoughts in time. "When we first met, I thought you were plain. Your face lacked symmetry. Your hair was dark. But then I saw your eyes, and I was lost... Your eyes captured my soul when you walked three miles to Netherfield to see Jane, although I did not know it at the time... I now know every freckle on your face, including the three which appeared at Pemberley. There is not one part of you that does not make my heart rush."

Darcy paused long enough that Elizabeth was about to speak again, but now that he had started, he could not let her take over. "But it is not just your looks that I love. You have challenged my mind. Conversing with you is never dull, even when we are talking with my aunt Catherine. Whether we agree or disagree, you force me to think harder. You have changed my mind countless times. I cannot imagine running Pemberley for the rest of my life without you by my side."

Darcy sighed as he looked to her again. What more could he say?

"But what does love feel like?"

"My heart races when we touch, even through these despicable gloves. I lie in bed thinking of you. In all of my thoughts, you are there. The best part of every day is the part when I can spend time with you. I long for a day when I can wake up beside you. A day when I do not wonder when I will see you again. A day when I know you will be on the other side of the door whenever I want to stop and say hello."

Darcy noted a small tear forming in Elizabeth's eye, and he realized he had one more thing to say. "But not if it costs you your happiness. If you are happy, I will support you and be your friend as much as I can. It tears my heart in two when you smile at another man or laugh during a dance. I dread the day you truly give your heart to someone, for I fear mine may never recover. However, if you chose to remain unmarried, you will always be welcome at any home of mine. If you chose to marry someone else whom you love, I will be the first to wish you joy, however much pain it might bring me."

They made another two turns before Darcy spoke again. "Is there anything else I can do to explain?"

The first song ended. They stood there for a few moments, and Darcy watched as Elizabeth's face changed from apprehension to determination. He felt he was about to step up to the gallows. His future was about to be determined. Suddenly, he was afraid. Could he stand to hear her refusal once again?

"I do not like either of the choices you have given me.

After our... discussion in the garden, I have no desire to be alone, but neither do I want to marry someone else. I want to marry my friend. My friend whom I never thought would have me after I refused him so many times." Darcy's breath caught, and he was certain his heart could not wait until the next turn brought them together again. "I prefer spending time with you to spending time with Jane. When something amuses me, you are the person with whom I am eager to share my memories. I have been worried about returning home and losing our connection. I love you." Darcy's heart was about to leap out of his throat. He stepped faster than he knew he ought, eager for her next words. "I know it is unconventional to expect another proposal, so I will not wait for you to gather your courage to either propose or walk away. Will you be my husband?"

Darcy stopped in his tracks. The music had died for him. He looked at Elizabeth, her eyes glowing in anticipation. "I have no words. You have made me the happiest man alive."

Elizabeth took his hand and pushed him in the direction he was supposed to go. Darcy followed willingly. She smiled as she said, "You have not answered me."

"Of course, yes."

The music ended, and everyone applauded, preventing Elizabeth from responding immediately. Thankfully, it was time for supper. They would be able to converse together while they ate. Darcy escorted his betrothed through the hall. He found them a table in the corner where they were unlikely to be disturbed. "I do want to ask one thing, if I may." Darcy waited for her nod. "How long have you loved me?"

Elizabeth paused to consider. "I have no idea when I started loving you. The feeling is so fresh, but at the same time, so familiar. I suppose the first time I cherished time with you was when we watched the sunrise on the beach. I wish I had realized I was falling in love." Elizabeth laughed lightly. "I was so worried I would break your heart at Pemberley, I did not bother to see how much I cared about you. I have missed out on so much time with you; if I had only known my own heart before."

"Well, then we shall have to make up for lost time once we are married."

"I look forward to that time. I suppose you will not ask for a long engagement." Elizabeth arched her eyebrows at the suggestion.

"I will request a special license tomorrow if you will allow."

"No. You must speak to my father first."

"I will ride to Hertfordshire tomorrow and obtain the license on my return. Would you prefer to marry in Hertfordshire or London?"

"I think we should discuss the particulars another day. Your sister is coming."

"Are you hoping to keep this secret?"

"No, we should have no secrets from our sisters."

Darcy smiled and kissed her gloved hand. At the sound of a few sniggers at the table beside them, he dropped it. "We should not tell too many people tonight. Without your father's permission, we are not truly engaged."

"You sound as though you fear he will not approve."

Darcy paused as he remembered his conversation with Mr. Bennet.

"You are smiling. What are you not telling me?" Elizabeth laughed at his playful nature.

"Your father has already promised his consent. He saw how I watched you at Pemberley."

Elizabeth released a sharp breath of air. "Was I the only one who did not know we would be together? Am I so stubborn as to not see what was right in front of me? I expected stars would dance when I fell in love. Jane was so clearly in love from the beginning that I was certain I would feel the same."

"You did not see what you did not want to see."

"How many times did I hurt you?"

"Not as often as the times you gave me hope."

Elizabeth nodded as she accepted his answer. Georgiana sat beside her brother and leaned forward to speak with Elizabeth. Darcy chuckled as he leaned back to give them space.

Georgiana was eager to speak about a friend of hers who had become engaged on the balcony during the previous dance. Elizabeth and Darcy shared a short look before Elizabeth engrossed herself in Georgiana's narrative.

"I wish I had been there to see Lady Emily nearly faint. It is so romantic. I hope that when I fall in love, my man is just as romantic."

Elizabeth sighed. "I hope you will have more wits about you than to faint or to nearly do so. It is more fun to enjoy the time with your betrothed."

"I suppose. Why do books not write about that?"

"Maybe the people who write them have not experienced real love," Darcy suggested.

"Oh, how tragic! To dream and write of so much love and not experience it for yourself."

"There is time for everyone," Darcy said as he turned to smile at Elizabeth. "Even for us."

Georgiana's smile dropped. "You mean... you and Elizabeth... she said yes!" Her smile resumed ten-fold.

"She did not have to. She asked me to marry her," Darcy stated with pride.

"That is romantic too! Oh, Brother! You have found me a sister! I must congratulate you." She threw her arms around his neck before realizing that they were in a crowded room. "Lizzy, thank you for wanting my brother! I love you so much, and I could not be happy if I did not see my brother so happy as he is when you are near him." Georgiana continued in the same happy manner for the next minute or two.

Darcy took this chance to slip his hand under the table and was thrilled when Elizabeth grasped it. They each tried to calm Georgiana down, but she did not stop until their aunt came to see what had occurred. Her response was more subdued, but she congratulated them both.

When the dancing resumed, Darcy sighed in frustration. He escorted Elizabeth to her partner and left to find his own. He was a few feet away from Elizabeth's partner, and he watched her for the majority of the dance. His own partner never stopped talking or batting her eyes at him, but he did not care.

24: PREPARATIONS

Darcy awoke the next morning, instantly ready to jump out of bed. He was so excited to spend time with Elizabeth in the library. His valet congratulated him while helping him dress quickly. After sending his valet to request his horse be readied, Darcy hurried downstairs only to find the library empty. He turned to look out the window, wondering if he would be able to see Elizabeth before he needed to leave.

He was so wrapped up in his thoughts that he was unable to hear her enter. She was able to sneak up to him and wrap her arms around his waist before he realized her presence.

"Good morning, Fitzwilliam. I trust you slept well."

"Good morning, my dearest Elizabeth. Yes, I slept very well. My dreams were filled with our future." Darcy placed his arms over hers and stroked her fingers. "I will need to leave soon if I am to return in time for the theater tonight."

"Then you should go. The road is waiting for you."

"I have very little desire to leave my current situation."

"Neither would I, except perhaps to have you turn around," Elizabeth sighed against his back. When he started to turn around, she stepped back to give him room.

Darcy placed his arms around her and looked at her carefully. The majority of her hair was pushed back, but a few curls had been left down to frame her face. He noticed for the first time that one of her eyes was slightly smaller than the other as she observed him. He remembered saying her face lacked symmetry. How he loved her unique look now. Her eyes danced with affection and shined with happiness. Her cheeks were blushing, and that same blush was now spreading down to her neck.

"That is a better view," Darcy said. He moved his hand to her cheek and leaned forward for a delicate kiss. Elizabeth met him halfway and returned his kiss as he deepened his.

Darcy did not even know how long they had been kissing when he heard sounds coming from the doorway. He stopped quickly, but when he pulled back, he noticed Elizabeth had not noticed the intruders. Her eyes were half-closed, and she looked completely at ease and happy. Darcy could not help thinking how lucky he was.

"I suppose you enjoyed the ball," Jane said, bringing Elizabeth out of her haze.

Elizabeth's blush deepened as she leaned in to hide her face in Darcy's chest.

Darcy smiled as he held Elizabeth close. "Yes, we enjoyed the ball. Miss Bennet and I have agreed to be married in the spring."

Jane and Charles finished coming into the room and congratulated the happy couple. "I am sorry we chose not to go. If only I had been feeling better, I would have loved to have been there." Jane rubbed her growing midsection lovingly as she spoke.

"Yes, I am certain Elizabeth would have loved to have you with her, but she has you now, and I must ride to Longbourn this morning. I hope to return in time to escort all of us to the theater. Will you take Elizabeth in to the dining room for me?" He paused and pulled Elizabeth out of his arms. Her color had returned to normal, and she happily hugged Jane and Charles before returning to Darcy. "Have a good day, dearest Lizzy." He placed a kiss to her forehead before he turned away in time for the butler to enter and announce that his horse was ready.

"Ride safely, Fitzwilliam, and good luck speaking with my father."

Darcy sighed. He did not want to leave, but he had no choice. He said his farewells once more and left for the stables where his horse was waiting. He thanked the stable boy for holding his horse, before mounting and departing.

The ride to Hertfordshire was short and uneventful. The land had been covered in a soft blanket of snow the day before. He paused at the gate, looking at Longbourn stretching out before him. The house was much smaller than Pemberley, and the stone faces were deteriorating, but it was still attractive. Darcy could tell the gardens were well-tended to, even though they were coated with snow. He was about to move forward when the front door opened and Mary and Kitty walked out together, covered in thick clothing to keep out the chill. They turned and headed behind the house, carrying a basket and trimming shears, laughing lightly as they went. Darcy instantly had a vision of Georgiana and Elizabeth acting in the same manner at Pemberley.

Darcy lightly kicked his horse to spur him the remaining distance to the stables. Once he had dismounted, he headed for the house, only to find Mr. Bennet on his way out to meet him.

"Good afternoon, Mr. Darcy. I trust I know why you are here," Mr. Bennet said as he shook Darcy's hand.

Darcy nodded, suddenly lost for words.

"You had best gather your wits about you, for you are about to embark on a journey that will never end with a woman who will remember everything you will ever say and use it against you every chance she gets."

"I will keep that in mind. Have you any questions for me?"

"Will you treat her with respect, even when you are arguing?"

"Yes." Darcy did not hesitate.

"Then you have my blessings. I know that for her to give

her heart away, you must truly deserve her. I am sorry to lose her, but I am relieved that such a deserving man has won her hand. Come, I will show you one of her favorite paths in the park, and then we will give my wife the good news. The house has been so calm with just the two girls that it is about time my wife had some news to delight her. Tell me Elizabeth's thoughts on the London season."

Darcy recapped the places they had been and described Elizabeth's opinions on the places and the people. Mr. Bennet was not cruel with his laughs, but he enjoyed how silly the Ton could be.

The path led them from an open area to a small, frozen stream, bordered on both sides by a few oak trees. Each of the trees was woven with dormant vines climbing up their trunks, making for a sheltered walk. Mr. Bennet described how the place had been a haven for Elizabeth to sit during fine weather and read away from her mother's nerves. Darcy could see the love Mr. Bennet held for her and wondered how difficult this moment had to be for him. After a few minutes, he felt he could no longer delay his purpose, so he asked for refreshments.

"Very well, you must be eager to return to your betrothed tonight. Join me in the parlor with Mrs. Bennet and the girls for half an hour, and then you may return to London. I do not envy your having another few hours on your horse, but your bones must be better adapted to it than mine. Have the two of you decided on a date for the wedding?"

"No, however, we are thinking of marrying in the spring here."

"It would be best to have the wedding sooner rather than later. Jane is planning on returning north to have her baby. My understanding is that they will travel no later than March. My Lizzy would want her sister to be present. That gives the two of you just over a month to enjoy your engagement. Just don't enjoy it too much. I remember how it feels to be young and in love. My Lizzy…"

"…Will only be treated with respect, before and after our

wedding. Allow me." Darcy skipped the last few steps and opened the door for Mr. Bennet. He did not need to be spoken to in such a way, but he knew that Mr. Bennet loved his daughter and only had this one chance to ensure her safety and happiness. "You will be welcome to come to Pemberley or visit my London home at any time. I recall you enjoyed the library on your last visit."

"Thank you. I hope you never come to reconsider your invitation, for I did enjoy your library quite a bit. I miss some of the books, but I do not have room to buy more here. My tenants have agreed to change their crops this year to replenish the earth, as I had read about in your library. They are a little skeptical, but since I promised to help them in the transition if necessary, they are willing to risk it. While they might not see the benefits for a year or two, once the increased output comes, they will hopefully then come to benefit from the profits."

Darcy attempted to continue this subject, but Mrs. Bennet had noticed his entry and welcomed him profusely. Tea had been prepared for the family, so it was only a matter of requesting an additional cup, which was brought quickly to the table. "Mr. Darcy, it is so good of you to come visit with us. I trust all is well in London. Are Lizzy and Jane enjoying the season?"

Darcy answered in the affirmative.

"Have there been many balls?"

Darcy confirmed that there had.

"Has my Lizzy behaved herself? She can be very wild and outspoken when she wishes."

Darcy stuttered a bit, but he was careful to say that Elizabeth had been a model lady.

"Oh good! I worry about her. I did my best to teach her the ways of society, but her father spoiled her. With all that reading, she thinks she is as clever as a man. I tried to tell her that men do not want wives as intelligent as they are, but she won't curb her tongue. I sometimes despair that she may never win a husband. I suppose you would not know of any suitors for her?"

Darcy smiled as Mr. Bennet laughed. "Actually, I do know of one." Technically, he knew of a few men who had shown an interest, but he had no need to explain that to her now. "Mr. Bennet has just given his blessing for my betrothal to Miss Bennet."

Mrs. Bennet's eyes widened at this pronouncement. In all her machinations for her daughters, she was surprised that Elizabeth would have such a catch. The silence was broken by the entrance of Mary and Kitty, who had just returned from the garden with their baskets of flowers from the hothouse. They had heard the announcement from the hallway and offered their congratulations freely. Darcy was pleased with their comportment.

This interaction allowed Mrs. Bennet the time to recover from her shock. "Oh Mr. Darcy! I should have seen your interest in my Lizzy! She is a good girl. She will be a good mother for your children. Is your estate entailed?"

"No, ma'am."

"That is good. I know I was such a burden to Mr. Bennet, only giving him daughters, which is why I have sought to find good men like you to marry them. With you and Bingley, I know my daughters will have a good home should we be thrown into the hedgerows when Mr. Bennet dies." Darcy only had time to nod his assurance. "Oh, I will enjoy having such a son as you, Mr. Darcy! But, surely you must wish to return to London and my daughter tonight."

"I do wish to escort Miss Bennet and my sister to the theater."

"Then you had better hurry. I will send a message to the stable to ready your horse." She left the room in haste. The girls shared a glance as they listened to their mother shouting down the hallway that they were saved.

Darcy focused on his teacup, wondering what he ought to say to the two ladies before him. Mr. Bennet had hidden in his library once he had his cup of tea, so he had no help from him. Remembering that Mary played the pianoforte, he decided to commence a conversation about music. Apparently, Mary had been teaching Kitty to play duets with her. Darcy could see that the two had grown close, and both appeared influenced by the other for the better.

When Mrs. Bennet returned, she appeared calm and gracious. Her excitement must have been spent in telling the staff the news. She sat quietly beside Darcy as Kitty picked up the conversation. She chose to describe the music she had been practicing. It was a piece Darcy knew, as he had purchased it for his sister a few years earlier. He had heard it countless times. He remembered a few things about the composer, and he was able to continue the conversation until Mrs. Hill entered to announce that Darcy's horse was ready.

"Thank you for your hospitality today. I hope to see you again soon." Darcy bowed to the room before following Mrs. Hill to the front, hoping that he still had time to make it to London. Unfortunately, the snow had begun falling quickly, making it hard for him to see. Believing the snow could not yet have made the roads unsafe, he struck out, thankful for his warm outerwear. Ten minutes in, he was buoyed by the fact that the snow was very dry and blew off his coat without soaking in.

As he proceeded though, the journey became more treacherous. Indeed, he was quite certain when the third tree on the road slowed him further, that he would never reach London on time. He slowed his pace as he looked around to ensure there were no highwaymen. The weather was the likely cause of the trees falling. He moved around the last one and was able to return back to the road on the other side. He did not dare move beyond a trot for the final three miles, knowing that London was nearly upon him. When the cobblestone streets came into view, he hoped his troubles were behind him.

The roads were icy, but the ice was thin enough for him to keep going without injuring his horse. He said a prayer of thanks when he made it to the stables. He was even more grateful to see that the carriage was still present, ready with the horses harnessed for the evening. He entered the house and rushed to his room. Davies was able to tell him that the ladies had chosen to delay their departure in the hope that he would arrive. After a warm bath, he was able to dress and head downstairs in good time.

He barely made it to the bottom step before Georgiana wrapped her arms around him. He laughed as he picked her up and spun her around. "Yes, I am safe! I would have never returned if I had not thought myself perfectly safe."

He put her down and turned to Elizabeth, who was standing off to the side. He wished he could embrace her in the same manner, but that would have to wait. "My trip was a success. Your family are well. Miss Mary and Miss Catherine are getting along well together. They are enjoying each other's company more than I thought possible."

"They were not the best of friends, but Kitty is very impressionable. With Lydia away indefinitely, she needed someone to follow. She had better hope that Mary never marries; she would then have to fend for herself."

"She could always come and live with us," Darcy said as he walked up to her. He smiled as he took her hand for a gentle kiss. He did not release it until he had aided her entry into the carriage, and even then it was only to help cover her, Jane, and Georgiana with blankets as he sat opposite them with Charles. He hoped this was what the future would look like.

"How did you manage to capture him?"

Elizabeth looked over at the lady who was talking to her. She was barely listening, but she thought her to be someone important that she may have met once before. The lady had been talking for most of the intermission about how upset she had been to learn that Mr. Darcy was now unavailable. "I did not capture him, for he is not a fish. I fell in love with him because he is the very best of men, and the most deserving man I know."

"Awe!" Was the only reply that the lady could offer, then she huffed and walked away saying that she should have compromised him the season before.

Darcy, who had been listening to the conversation, laughed as he came over. "You charmed her very well. Her older sister tried to compromise me a few years ago. I knew to always keep to open areas full of people, and to keep a friend near me to corroborate my innocence. I think she tried to lock me in her uncle's study, but since her uncle and mine were in the room at the time discussing business, the plan failed."

"Have we really disappointed so many people?" Elizabeth asked, her eyes still sparkling from merriment.

"I doubt it. I am an old catch, not to mention too reserved to really be considered."

"You look neither old nor reserved. You have been quite the conversant with me tonight, and with the twenty or so people who have come to speak with you during the intermission."

"I have the right inducement. What do you think of the play?"

"There is no contest; it is one of my favorite plays and has been for some time. The actors are splendid, and your box is in an excellent position. When I would come with my aunt and uncle, we would sit almost directly in the middle of the room, where you can hear so many conversations that are not on the stage that you cannot hear the actors. This is so much better. I am starting to see the benefits of accepting a proposal from a rich, handsome gentleman."

"So all this time, I could have won your hand, had we only been in London for the theater."

Elizabeth scrunched her nose at the thought and turned back to the stage, upon which the performers were resuming. "If that were true, I would have accepted Mr. Williams."

Darcy growled as he claimed her hand possessively. "I am very glad you did no such thing. It was hard enough listening to him and worrying I had lost you this summer. Then you rejected him, and he continued to speak as though you had no alternatives."

"Much like another gentleman I know."

Darcy rolled his eyes before returning his attention to the stage. "I was surprised at how blunt you sounded when I heard you speak to Mr. Williams, and I could not help wondering how I could have been so daft as to not recognize your dismissal before I had made a fool out of myself."

"I would not worry too much about that. You are a very handsome fool." She squeezed his hand to let him know she was teasing.

"Charles, why are you insisting on traveling north? You have no need to visit your relatives so soon again, and your family are healthy. Jane is surely too close to confinement to travel. Elizabeth wants to be here with Jane after we marry. Jane has also stated she would prefer to be here." Darcy sighed. He had agreed to speak to Charles because he knew Elizabeth was worried for her sister. There were only a few weeks left of the season, and the banns had been read. They were planning on a trip to Hertfordshire for the wedding, and now it seemed that the Bingleys would not remain after that.

"We are trying to fix a problem."

"What problem requires you taking your very pregnant wife on a very long journey in potentially inclement weather?"

"Lydia."

Darcy stopped in his tracks. He had nearly forgotten about her. She had been left in the north. "How is she? I know I should have asked sooner, but I was… distracted."

"Lydia is healthy. My aunt is sending me letters about her; she is claiming that she has been imprisoned. She has conveniently forgotten that her behavior is precisely what put her there in the first place. Mr. Bennet has refused to allow her to return home until all of her sisters have married. He does not even allow Mrs. Bennet to speak of her."

Darcy could not entirely convince himself that this was a bad move on Mr. Bennet's part. "I see. How can you help the situation?"

"We cannot abandon her or my aunt. We must return. If we can return before the birth, we are hoping to claim Lydia's child as our own.

"How would that work? Jane is about to have a child."

"She will have twins. Twins do not always look alike. A midwife we spoke to at my aunt's home believes that Jane and Lydia will come into confinement at about the same time."

Darcy nodded, relieved that this was not his burden. "What if Lydia has a boy? Will he inherit your fortune?"

"Jane and I have agreed to raise him as our own. It is the only way Lydia would agree to give up her child. We are hoping that, in a few years, we can present Lydia as a sister who has been away at a distant finishing school. She is so young, so it should not be too hard. We have found a governess who will accompany us to my aunt's home and has agreed to be discreet. Lydia will learn some accomplishments and proper behavior, or she will be... I do not know what will happen if she refuses. I suppose I am relying on Jane to be able to convince her sister that this is for the best. She will grow into a fine woman if she applies herself. But, for this to work, we need you to marry Elizabeth soon so that we can head north. Jane and Elizabeth will have a few days together before we need to leave. The weather is fine now. We cannot wait much longer, or we will struggle to make the journey safely. The babies will come in about two months."

"Very well, I will speak with Elizabeth. I doubt she will complain about hurrying our engagement. She will understand that this is the best for Lydia." Darcy could not help thinking that he would not mind hurrying the engagement for other reasons as well.

25: BETROTHAL

Darcy watched Elizabeth's carriage depart with apprehension. He had grown used to Elizabeth's presence in his home. His daily routine had barely shifted with his engagement. In the early morning, he and Elizabeth could still be found in the library, only instead of sitting in separate chairs as they had done, they would sit on the sofa with his arm around her shoulders. During the day, they took walks together, either as an entire group or just Elizabeth and him. Rarely was he unable to arrange his day so he could spend the majority of it with her. Their evenings had not changed much either, as there were still plenty of balls and dinners to attend.

Darcy enjoyed introducing Elizabeth as his betrothed. He also enjoyed Elizabeth's laughs when they were alone or watching the titters and tuts of desperate ladies and their even more desperate mothers upon finding out he was no longer eligible. He still had to watch others occasionally dance with Elizabeth, but he could enjoy more dances with her also.

It was only two days until he would travel to Netherfield to be with her. The day after, the church would bind their lives together forever. He ought to have been happy that it had come to this. The carriage turned around a corner and out of sight.

A voice bellowed from the other side of the street. "You must not mope about her absence! You are worse than Bingley!"

"Richard, I see you have been granted leave again. Will you travel to Hertfordshire with me?" Darcy attempted a welcoming smile.

"To see you move around like a love-sick mooncalf? I would never miss such a scene."

Darcy was about to complain, but then he remembered that he was still standing outside in the rain watching an empty street. Three days seemed much longer as his thoughts grew in anticipation.

"Come inside. Tea should be ready soon. Georgiana will be pleased to see you now that her sisters have departed. They were almost inseparable. I believe I have only had three private moments with my intended in the past month."

"You mean in the past day. I doubt they were as inseparable as you and Elizabeth are. Every time I have visited you in the past fortnight, you were discovered embracing her. It is good that her father was not here, or he might have called you out for the liberties you took with his favorite daughter."

"You visited once, for the record." Darcy smiled as he remembered her soft form in his arms. Richard had a point, though. He should not have allowed himself that much liberty until after the wedding. He opened the door for his cousin and followed him to the parlor, where Georgiana was slowly sipping her tea.

"Two days seems like a very long time," she said, putting her tea aside to serve her brother and cousin.

"Oh, not you too, Georgiana," Richard sighed.

Darcy laughed at Richards melodrama before changing the subject. "Georgiana, have you thought of your plans for after the wedding? Will you join us at Pemberley or remain at Longbourn with Miss Mary and Miss Catherine?"

"You are not planning a wedding tour? They are all the fashion right now," Georgiana informed him.

"We will tour the Lakes in the summer, which is a much

better time for traveling. It is too cold now for long days in the carriage. I am glad Elizabeth was not able to tour the Lakes over the summer, for I had been longing to show her them myself for some time."

Georgiana thought about her options. "I believe I will return to Pemberley with you."

Richard applauded her choice. "As will I, even though you have not invited me."

"Do you have leave for such an extended trip?" Darcy asked.

When Richard did not respond right away, the Darcys prepared for a very grave answer. They were shocked when Richard responded, "I have resigned my commission. My purpose in traveling to Pemberley is to visit Lady Julie. She and I have formed an attachment."

"I remember you telling me that you abhorred the idea of running an estate. The boredom would be the death of you," Darcy stated.

"Yes, just as you were a confirmed bachelor for so long. All it takes is meeting the right woman at the right time, and all your carefully made plans completely go out of the window. We are considering a June wedding, if we can trespass on your hospitality for that long."

Darcy agreed with all his heart, and Georgiana squealed with delight. She had become acquainted with Lady Julie over the season and was now very excited to get to know her better. "Shall we invite her to dinner tomorrow evening? We have no current engagements, do we Brother?"

Darcy thought about this. Having company would help pass the time. He had not thought much about Lady Julie this season or at Pemberley, other than his aunt's requests for him to dance with her. She was the heir to the Harlow's estate, although she could not inherit the title. He would be happy to see Richard so well settled, especially having him close to Pemberley where they could remain in contact frequently. "No, we have no fixed engagements tomorrow, although we must leave early in the morning the following day."

Richard laughed. "We will not trespass on your hospitality too late in the evening. Lady Julie is a true romantic. She would not delay your return to your beloved Elizabeth at any cost."

"I would not have offered the invitation if I had thought it inconvenient to my plans. Your mother must be over the moon to have finally brought both of us to the altar, although in your case I am certain she is more relieved that you resigned your commission."

"There is plenty of truth in that. I am looking forward to the cessation of her pleas for marriage. That was one of the inducements that led me to my proposal."

Georgiana laughed gaily before looking out the window longingly. Darcy picked up on the behavior, but he knew better than to ask her for information in front of Richard. If she had been willing to share, then she would have spoken openly. He waited until after supper when they were alone in the music room to ask her about it.

"What has you so melancholy, my dear Georgiana?" He said, after she had finished one of her slower performances.

Georgiana fiddled with the keys as she thought out what she ought to say. "I have nothing to cause me to feel melancholy."

"And yet you do. We have been close for too long for you to be able to hide from me. Does Richard's news upset you?"

"No... and yes. I am thrilled for him and for you, and I know it is too soon to be thinking of marriage for myself, but I feel left out."

"You must remember that we are much older than you. It is well past time for Richard and me to have found wives, our aunts would say. Your time will come. You must be patient, for my sake at least, if not for your own. I do not know if I could ever find someone worthy to be your husband."

Georgiana nodded. "I know I am just being silly. I truly have no desire to marry."

"But you have a desire for romance, is that not it?"

"If I agree, you will tell me that romance is dangerous."

"No. It can be dangerous, but you already know that from

your and Lydia's interactions with Wickham. You must take the time to think through potential encounters before you can really begin to play on your romantic notions. Take myself and Elizabeth. I thought I was in love with her over a year ago, and I impulsively proposed to a woman who intrigued me, where in truth I barely knew her. I am grateful that she refused me. She forced me to reevaluate what I wanted in a future partner. Being her friend over the past year, while it had seemed a hardship at the time, was the best way for me to court her and get to know her. My love for her is so much stronger and truer now because of it. I wish for everyone to experience the romance Elizabeth and I share, at the right time."

Georgiana began a new tune as she collected her thoughts. Darcy recognized the piece and moved behind her to play his violin. Half an hour later, Georgiana was ready to say, "Thank you, Brother, for explaining everything so fully. I look forward to a time when I may feel the same as you do for Elizabeth."

"Hmph. So long as that time is somewhere in the distant future, I shall agree with you."

The siblings shared a warm embrace before he led her to her chambers for the night. "Sweet dreams, Georgiana." He kissed her cheek affectionately before turning to his own chambers.

The Bingleys had opened up their home for the Darcys, but Mr. Darcy was only in residence for a quarter of an hour before he asked for his horse to be saddled. They had left early in the morning to arrive just after breakfast, and Darcy had no intentions of breaking his fast with anyone but Elizabeth that day. She had hinted that she would be waiting for him at Oakham Mount this morning, and he could not wait to see her again.

Mr. Bingley laughed as he bid his friend goodbye, remembering his own feelings the day before he had married Jane Bennet.

Darcy rode quickly through the fields along the trail where

he expected to find Elizabeth. He only paused when he found her running ahead of him towards a grove of trees. Delighting in her form, he picked up his pace again until he found where she had disappeared from the trail. Here, the branches hung low, making it hard for him to follow her. He tied his horse to a tree out of sight of the road and began walking around the grove, calling out to Elizabeth as he went.

She did not respond to him at first, but he heard the cracking of twigs ahead of him. After a minute passed without hearing any trace of her, he began to worry that something must have gone wrong. He stepped around a tree, only to be captured in a strong embrace as Elizabeth leaped from around the other side and enveloped him with her arms. His face was instantly covered in her soft curls as he noticed her bonnet had been removed.

"Oh, my darling Lizzy. How I have missed you," he whispered in her ear, before he pulled her away just far enough for a proper kiss that did not allow her to speak of her feelings for some time.

"Come over here; our feast awaits," Elizabeth said as soon as she was able. "I have all of your favorites, excepting coffee, for that would not stay warm, and I know how you detest cold coffee."

Darcy kissed her once again before he allowed her to lead him to a small clearing where a blanket had been laid out. "Is it not too cold for a picnic?"

"That may be the case, but I am certain we would not have had the peace I crave at either Longbourn or Netherfield."

Darcy looked around as he settled himself beside her on the blanket. The trees were bare, although he could see miniscule buds had begun to grow. The snow had melted the week before, according to Elizabeth's letters, and the ground was covered with soggy, dead grass and bushes. They were completely secluded in the heart of a winter wasteland. Thankfully, the blanket was thick enough that they remained dry.

"Have you contemplated your surroundings enough, or

shall I watch you for another quarter of an hour?"

With a small chuckle, Darcy turned to Elizabeth, who was handing him a lemon tart. "I am at your command, my dear, although I am worried you will be cold out here."

"I am not afraid of the cold. Indeed, I hardly feel cold at all when you watch me like that." Elizabeth blushed but did not look away. "I feel as though you might devour me whole."

"There is no fear of that, for I intend to remain a gentleman for the next twenty-four hours." Darcy thought about how unfamiliar he felt. "I am not used to these feelings. In time, my ardor for you will become commonplace. This face which you seem to think I make will become familiar to you, especially when we are alone together, as we are now."

"You may wish to remain a gentleman, but I prefer the more passionate side of you that was kissing me earlier." To prove her point, she moved towards him to offer another kiss.

Before he acquiesced, he warned her. "You know not what you are about, Elizabeth. I have no wish to remain a gentleman. I am only doing so for your sake." He moved to pull her onto his lap as he kissed her with less restraint than he had ever shown before. He continued to move his hands down her sides as he felt her curves until she stiffened. "Do you see what I mean?" He gently kissed her forehead as he lifted her back to her own seat beside him.

Elizabeth took a few breaths to calm her racing heart. "I am still not afraid of you, partly because you have shown me how well you are under control, and partly because I wish you had not stopped. However, I see the importance in waiting until tomorrow for such attentions, for my own sake." In an attempt to hide her discomfort, she picked up another tart. Instead of handing it to him again, she asked him to close his eyes.

Darcy closed his eyes as he opened his mouth to accept the food. He was thrilled when he noticed her gasp as he closed his mouth around her fingers, but then she startled him by kissing his cheek in response.

"Tomorrow seems too far away just now," she whispered in his ear.

"Much too far," was all he could think to say as he tried to regain his senses. He coughed as he realized how close he was to the edge of his self-restraint. "What are your plans for today?" His stomach growled despite having just eaten two tarts.

Elizabeth laughed and handed him a biscuit. "I am not used to someone who is as hungry as you are so often in the morning. At least half of our discussions at your home were interrupted by that grumbling. Perhaps I should store some biscuits beside the bed in the future."

"There is no purpose in that. When I am..." He paused, knowing he should not be saying such things. "When I am in your bed, I will have other, far more pleasurable things to distract me. My stomach must simply learn to grumble and be done with it." He was about to admit to being hungry for another kiss, but he heard the distinct whinny of a horse in the distance, signaling that it would not be proper to remain out any longer. "As much as I am enjoying my time with you, I believe it is time I returned you to Longbourn. Your father surely knows that you came out to meet me. I should not betray his trust any further."

Elizabeth agreed and began to pack up the basket. Once all the napkins were returned to their place, she found Darcy waiting to lift her to her feet. Taking each of his offered hands, she leapt up and into his arms once again. "One more kiss to prepare me for the day," she said, as she wrapped her arms around his shoulders and accepted his very thorough kiss.

Darcy pulled her away once again and quickly moved to pull the blanket as he regained his senses. He was starting to believe he could indeed turn into a love-sick mooncalf. "I look forward to many such picnics at Pemberley, and only some of them will be among the daisies. The rest must be in secluded glens such as this one." Once the blanket was draped over his horse's back and the basket was fastened to the saddle, Darcy took Elizabeth's arm and escorted her home.

A saddle-hand came out to tend to the horse when they reached the house. Darcy gave strict instructions for how to care for the spirited mare. Elizabeth laughed, "You are not the only landowner with such a mare. I am certain that he already knew your instructions."

"You may be correct, but such is my habit, as is yours to point out my faults."

"It is enough that you accept your faults. Miss Bingley could never be counted on for such a purpose. You were so perfect in her eyes."

"I would not want to be perfect for…" Darcy was stopped as the front door burst open to allow Mrs. Bennet to come through.

"Mr. Darcy! This is such an honor. We are so thrilled to have you join us. I had almost doubted your returning."

"Good morning, Mrs. Bennet. I am sorry to have caused you to worry. My business in town could not be concluded before today. Please, have faith that nothing will prevent my marrying your beloved daughter." He bowed low to mark his deference for the mother of his future bride.

Flustered by such behavior, Mrs. Bennet giggled before inviting her guest into the house. Once they were all settled in the drawing room, Mrs. Bennet began lamenting the coming loss of Elizabeth.

"Mamma, I have not wed yet." Elizabeth attempted to calm her down. "Save your lamentations for tomorrow, or better yet, save your lamentations for after you have spread the word of the wedding finery to all of your neighbors the moment we leave the house tomorrow.

"Oh, very well," Mrs. Bennet sighed. "It is too easy for me to think of your leaving us with all of your trunks laying packed from the moment you arrived."

Mr. Darcy smiled. "You never unpacked your trunks."

"I only wished to be prepared. It is a good thing too, for Kitty wandered through my closet yesterday to claim my prettiest dresses. She was mortified to learn I had already packed them away." Elizabeth laughed lightly at the memory. "My compromise was to give her all my copies of La Belle Assemblée. She and Mary have been pouring over the plates these three days. Mary is better with a needle, so she will be making the majority of the alterations they wish to with their dresses."

"Mr. Darcy surely does not wish to hear about such silly matters," Mrs. Bennet scolded.

"On the contrary, I am glad to hear that Miss Darcy's magazines have had such an effect. It sounds as though your remaining daughters are getting along very well. Would you be opposed to having them join us for the winter season in a year or two, Mrs. Bennet? Elizabeth has expressed her hopes to extend invitations to her sisters."

Mrs. Bennet began to bounce in her seat. Before she could speak, Mary and Kitty joined the group, ignorant of the fact that their futures had been discussed.

Elizabeth used the distraction to address them. "Would you enjoy spending a season in London, Mary and Kitty?" She remembered how much she hated when people would make plans for her without discussing them first. She would not make the same mistake for her sisters. "Miss Darcy has a music master who could help both of you improve your performances. The balls and dinners are extraordinary."

"And they could both find the best of men, for you will be part of the first circles. Your uncle is Lord Matlock, is he not?" Mrs. Bennet could contain her glee no longer.

"Yes, he is. My cousin is also engaged to Lord Harlow's daughter in Derbyshire. Elizabeth, do remember Lady Julie at Pemberley?"

Elizabeth nodded as she remembered him complaining of his aunt's machinations for his marriage to the same lady. Darcy smiled as he realized their thoughts were both running in a similar manner.

Kitty sighed as she replied to the invitation. "That would be lovely, thank you."

Darcy was taken aback by her modesty for a moment. A year ago, she would have leapt for joy at such news, and he would have hated her for it. Now, he regretted that she was not so lively as she had been then. Losing a favorite sister must have been hard on such a young, impressionable girl.

"I do not know what I shall do with myself once all my daughters are out of the house. Six years between my eldest and youngest children and yet in the course of one or two years, all of them will have moved away."

Mary was the first to make sense of her statement. "Have no fear, Mama. I shall return. I doubt London's frivolities will entice me to stay longer than a month or two. I look forward to a more accomplished music master, but I will certainly miss my home."

"Mary Bennet, you must not return home until you have found a husband!"

Mary began to protest, but Elizabeth put a hand on hers to silence her. There was no point responding to such statements. "We can make these plans in the autumn. Mama, the post should have come while I was away. Have you received your letter from Lydia? She is three days beyond her normal writing day. You have been anxious to receive it."

Mrs. Bennet looked at the door as if to gauge how far her husband was from the conversation. She had been instructed not to mention Lydia in the presence of any guests. Surely Mr. Darcy was nearly family, though. "Yes. She is bored but learning to cope with her daily routine. She is continuing to practice the pianoforte. Miss Darcy has sent her music sheets that have confused her, but she is determined to become proficient, if only to escape Mr. Bingley's aunt. I think they are treating her very poorly, but I am not allowed to complain."

"They are attending to her comfort, from what I hear. Mr. Bingley purchased that instrument for her when he learned of her desire to continue practicing," Darcy interjected. He would not allow the Bingleys to be considered lacking in their treatment of Lydia. Indeed, they had done much more than other families would have.

"Oh, I suppose they are." Mrs. Bennet was still not comfortable disagreeing with such a wealthy man. Thankfully, she was interrupted from explaining her discomfiture by the Bingleys' entrance with Georgiana.

Elizabeth rushed to embrace first her sister and then Georgiana. Knowing she would be nervous to meet Elizabeth's family, Elizabeth took her hand and made the introductions. Mrs. Bennet returned to her best manners, while Kitty and Mary began soft conversations about the fashion plates and music. With the three girls engaged in conversation, and the Bingleys speaking with her mother, Elizabeth could share a private moment with Darcy.

"It would appear that you look forward to the morrow," Darcy stated.

"You know I do. I have been preparing to be your wife ever since I returned."

"You did not tell me this in your letters."

"I did not feel it relevant."

"Thank you."

"Whatever should you thank me for?"

Darcy smiled. "For giving me the chance to prove myself worthy of you."

"Pish posh! I could say the same to you. I abused you and your friendship so much this past year that it is a wonder you remained in love with me at all. I must have wounded your heart so many times that I would not have blamed you for leaving."

"You never wounded me intentionally, except for upon my first proposal, which I most likely deserved. I cannot say it has been a terrible year. Being your friend helped me to understand you more than I would have before. I am even more in love with you now as a result."

Elizabeth was feeling playful. "How did you fall in love with me? I was certainly not attempting to garner your attentions."

"You were the only one not to do so, which caused me to notice you. I very much liked what I saw. You will not flatter me in the way almost every other lady does. I feel more like a person with you, and not an untitled, rich landowner with a house in London. You see me, and you accept who I am. I can be myself with you." For effect, he kissed her hand.

"You can be certain I will never flatter you unduly. You are very handsome and even more intelligent, and you are almost without fault. I did not want to see that before we met in Kent."

"Then I am doubly thrilled to have gained your affection. To have you declare me almost faultless is praise indeed."

"You should not think too much about it, or I will have to remind you of your terrible proposals."

"Technically, I only proposed once.

"But I knew you were about to propose at least twice. I stopped you because I knew you would say more than I would have liked to hear... but let us speak of other things. Shall you be happy to remain at Netherfield for the next week?"

"So long as you are at Netherfield, I will be happy to remain. You wish for this time with your sister, and I am eager to grant this. We will return to London in a week, where my aunt will host a ball in our honor, and then we will travel on to Pemberley, where the rhododendrons should be about to bloom. I look forward to many rambles through the countryside."

"Would you have me neglect my duties as mistress of Pemberley to ramble every day with you?"

"No, but your duties shall not overwhelm you. I am certain you will create a routine that will allow for your daily walks, and when the weather does not permit being outdoors, we shall tour the various wings of the house together. You shall never feel cooped up again."

Elizabeth laughed. "You know me so well."

26: WEDDING

When Darcy opened his eyes on the morning of his wedding, he smiled and looked over at the large space in the bed beside him. This was the last night he would spend alone. It was customary for a husband and wife to have separate bed chambers, but he would not follow this custom unless Elizabeth insisted. He did not believe that she would. Their picnic the day before had taught him that she wanted to be with him almost as much as he desired her. Ready to face the day, Darcy rose and rang for his valet, surprised Davies was not present already.

Finding a clean bowl of water and a trough, he began to wash his face. The light was dim, so he fumbled a bit as he dried his face on a nearby towel. He felt bad for leaving a mess of water on the floor, but there was nothing to be done now.

Davies entered with an apology for his tardiness. It was only at this time that Darcy realized how early it was. He did not need to dress for another three hours. "You have no reason to apologize, Davies. I had not realized the time. I believe I will walk to Longbourn when I am ready. By the time I arrive, the family should be ready to head to the church."

"Very good, sir." Davies worked in silence as Darcy donned his best pantaloons, waistcoat, and cravat.

After half an hour, Darcy was ready to begin walking to Longbourn for his wedding. He walked faster than he had expected, and was standing at the gate, unsure if he should enter or not. The Bennets would barely have risen. It would be rude of him to arrive so early. Knowing he could not remain at the gate, he opened it and strolled through the path by the creek until he found a clean stone bench under a thick oak tree. Claiming the cold seat, he watched the water meander over and around the rocks. Looking at the banks, he could see the new spring life beginning.

The scenery was fitting for the day upon which he would begin the rest of his life. He was not aware of how long he had been sitting, watching the water, until Elizabeth took the seat by his side. With the fallen leaves, he had not heard her approach. "What dark thoughts plague you, Sir?"

"No dark thoughts." He looked up to see that she was dressed in a green gown that had been fashioned from the gown that she had worn at the ball at which she had proposed. It had been altered to have long sleeves and ribbons decorating the front. "You are wearing the gown you wore when we began our betrothal."

"It seemed fitting."

"You look lovelier every day."

"Then I am more than tolerable, now. Perhaps one day I will aspire to beautiful."

"I will not qualify that remark. You know you are beautiful to me."

"Then we had best hurry, or my parents will beat us to the church and will have to wait for us. We need not lose that time."

Darcy could only agree. They met the rest of the Bennets at the gate and walked with them to the church. The villagers threw herbs and rushes before them as they walked and wished them well.

At the church, Colonel Fitzwilliam, the Bingleys, and Georgiana were waiting inside. Once everyone was seated except the vicar, bride, and groom, the vicar began the ceremony. Darcy could not help but steal glances as he listened to the words of prayer. He was glad to see Elizabeth seemed almost as often to be looking at him as at the vicar. He thought he felt elated when Elizabeth promised to obey, serve, love, honor, and keep him, but it was nothing to when he triumphantly placed his ring on her finger.

He was so happy, he almost forgot to remain passive and calm. Thankfully, only Elizabeth recognized the upturn at the corner of his lips. The majority of the observers wondered how happy Elizabeth could be marrying such a stern man. Darcy occasionally glanced at them to see their expressions of curiosity. He did not mind being the subject of their stares. Not today.

As they rose after the prayer, Darcy felt a rush of finality. Just a few more prayers and blessings and they would be forever joined together. He was so lost in his thoughts that he almost missed the final blessing and announcement of the marriage; almost, but not quite.

Darcy took her arm in his and smiled, his love nearly overflowing. They followed the vicar to a small room off to the side to sign the registry with the vicar, Colonel Fitzwilliam, and Mr. Bennet. Upon leaving the small room, Mr. Darcy claimed her arm again. "Hello, Mrs. Darcy."

Elizabeth smiled her brightest smile. "Hello, husband."

Leaving the church, they were stopped by all of Elizabeth's neighbors, who had come to wish them well. Darcy moved as quickly as he could through the gathered group, not allowing Elizabeth's arm to leave his. He greeted a few neighbors with warmth and politely nodded to those he had not met. At last, they made it to the carriage waiting for them. The rest of the group moved to another waiting carriage. Darcy sat beside Elizabeth and took her hand warmly in both of his. "I thought I was happy at the ball when you asked me to marry you, but this is infinitely better. You look absolutely radiant, Elizabeth Darcy."

He began to move forward to kiss her, but the carriage jostled in a rut, forcing him to switch tactics to remain in the seat. Elizabeth, more familiar with the Hertfordshire roads, held onto her seat and remained unperturbed. "It is a short distance to Lucas Lodge. Lady Lucas insisted on hosting our wedding breakfast. Hopefully, we will only need to remain there for an hour or two, before we can go to Netherfield to settle into our rooms."

"An hour or two, Elizabeth, will not pass soon enough. However, for you, I will endure it. You must be allowed to enjoy your time with your friends." Feeling more secure in his seat, he moved to kiss her again. This time, there was no impediment.

The following morning, Darcy opened his eyes to behold Elizabeth with her brunette hair scattered over the pillow lying beside him. Her eyes were closed and her breathing relaxed. She was still asleep. Unable to resist the temptation, he stroked her cheek lightly with his hand. He was rewarded as her head shifted closer to him. "I am too comfortable to wake now, dear husband. I hope you do not think I will really obey all of your orders. I intend to sleep a while longer."

Darcy laughed. "Of course, my beautiful wife. Sleep as long as you wish." He kissed her forehead as she snuggled into his chest. He wrapped his arms around her belly and said a silent prayer of thanks for all that he had gained.

EPILOGUE

Fitzwilliam and Elizabeth stood on the front porch to welcome the Bingleys to Pemberley. This was the first time they would meet their two nieces. Fitzwilliam kissed his wife's hand as he thought of his own child growing inside Elizabeth. Elizabeth had arranged for this visit so that her sister would be with her through her confinement. She might have also done so to ensure a prolonged visit from her sister, who had refused all invitations so far, claiming difficulties with traveling with two babies.

Three carriages stopped in front of the building, and Elizabeth rushed down the steps with her husband following behind. He had long ago ceased telling her to slow down to protect the baby. She insisted she knew her body better than he did and that she could handle the speed well enough. The midwife's agreeing with her had frustrated him, but he relented. They had proof of her safety when they saw how graceful her movements were, even though her belly was quite large now.

"Jane! Charles! How wonderful it is to see you again!" Elizabeth exclaimed as she threw her arms around both of them simultaneously. Once she stepped back enough to wipe the tears of joy from her eyes, Fitzwilliam welcomed his guests to Pemberley.

The group then turned to the second carriage, from which two sleeping infants were being carried by their nursemaids. Elizabeth quietly kissed their foreheads before allowing them to be taken to the nursery.

"Come inside. Refreshments will be waiting for you as soon as you are ready." Darcy reclaimed his wife's hand as he led the way up the stairs. "Mrs. Reynolds will escort you to your room."

When their guests left the hall, Elizabeth turned to her husband. "I suppose you will tell me to rest while we wait for them."

"Only if that is your inclination. Certainly, rest would not delay your first chance to speak with your sister. You are more tired than you let on. I can tell by the way I supported you on the stairs."

"Hmm. Your words have merit, but I believe I shall sit with Georgiana instead. She is beginning a lovely piece from the new set you gave her. She will be delighted to perform for us tonight. That will give me all the rest I shall need."

They walked to the music room where Georgiana was hard at work on the pianoforte. After two runs through the song, Jane entered and claimed Elizabeth's attention for the rest of the day. Darcy had to wait until after evening to speak with his wife again, and even then he was speaking in hushed tones as she held her sleeping niece.

"You seem enamored of little Letitia. I hope you know that she is only your niece and will be leaving in two months."

"Of course, I do. That is no reason to stay away from her now. Besides, in less than two months, I shall have my own little one to love." She turned her attention back to her niece as she opened her eyes sleepily and smiled at her aunt. Elizabeth then began to make cooing noises and was rewarded with an adorable laugh.

Fitzwilliam tried again to get her attention. "Do you think she looks more like Lydia or Jane?"

Elizabeth looked thoughtfully at her niece again. "I cannot

tell. Both have very similar features. Jane looked very much like Lydia when she was her age. Besides, I think it is pointless to try to tell which one was born to which mother. It was providence that they were born at the same time, and very smart that they chose to have the confinements in the same room. The Bingleys will never know which child is theirs by blood, so they will love both equally, not that I ever doubted such generous people as Jane and Charles could be anything but perfect parents to both girls. I have no wish to find out the truth, for it serves no purpose."

Fitzwilliam scowled as he contemplated her words. Could he forget that Wickham was the father of either Letitia or Joanne? Would it serve any purpose to remember the father? Most definitely not. They are not responsible for his sins. "May I hold her?" he asked as he reached out to his niece.

Elizabeth laughed as she handed the now alert baby to him. "You will fall in love with her yet."

After a minute of holding her and watching her expressions change as she contemplated him, he said, "I already have." He smiled brightly at Letitia, and she rewarded him with a laugh before she squirmed to be let down.

He set her on the floor, and she claimed his fingers as she began to walk around the room. It took her twenty minutes to arrive across the room where her mother was sitting with open arms. Fitzwilliam laughed as he finally was able to stand up straight and shake his arms out. He then spent a few minutes congratulating Letitia's parents on their success.

"If you had met her a few months ago, you would not have seen such a darling child. She could not sleep unless she was being held. I had to double the nursemaids' salary to keep them during that month. Then she became ill and could not keep her food down. This is the first time we have been able to travel or sleep peacefully."

"I am relieved you were able to travel, or Elizabeth would likely have had us traveling to you. She does not appreciate that I do not want her in a carriage at this time for her own health. What news of Lydia?"

"She remains with my aunt. She has learned some manners, although she still spends her time thinking about the local gentlemen. Three have taken a fancy to her, and she is allowing each to court her. Thankfully, my aunt has an excellent set of servants who keep her out of any real danger."

"Perhaps she will fall for one of them, and they will accept her current state."

"If only she had a dowry to encourage the men."

"She will. I have already set aside five thousand pounds for her. If there is interest, you could let her know. She would then be free to choose them. I know it is not much, but it will make the marriage more tenable."

Charles nodded. "I believe they are serious about her. Her liveliness is refreshing to them. The days are shorter and colder in the north, and yet she keeps bouncing with full vivacity through every drawing room she is invited to."

"I did not know that there were so many parties to attend with Mrs. Campbell."

"There are not. She is attending dinners and a few small gatherings. In the past year, only once did she attend an assembly, but my aunt longs for company, and she is well respected in the village. She is frequently attending dinners with her close neighbors."

"Then I am glad for her. She deserves a bright future despite her past."

"What have you heard of Mary and Kitty? The last I heard was that Mary might have a suitor." Charles changed the subject.

"She is engaged to the vicar's son in Hertfordshire. They are planning on marrying after the new year when he will have a post that can support a family. Kitty will be joining us here in a month and will remain with us for the season. She has requested a drawing master as she has found a new favorite pastime. I cannot help being pleased with how well they have turned out. Lydia could have ruined them."

Charles nodded. "Our family has had a lucky escape. At least one of Mrs. Bennet's daughters will be living near her."

"What about Jane? You live at Netherfield."

"Jane and I have decided to find a more suitable estate to purchase. Netherfield is only a lease. We cannot own it, for the owners have no intention of selling. We are hoping to find a home in Derbyshire. Jane is hoping to live closer to Elizabeth."

"Elizabeth will be pleased to hear this. I will write to my solicitor tomorrow, and we shall see if any estates are for sale."

"This will not make Mrs. Bennet happy."

"Perhaps it will. It is easier to embellish our status when we are not present to prove her false. Our letters are read throughout Meryton with alacrity, according to Kitty."

"One can only hope."

As Charles said this, Fitzwilliam noticed his wife coming towards him. He broke away from Charles and took her arm. "Has Jane indicated their intent to move?"

"No, she has not. Why should Netherfield not be their home?"

"Because they cannot own it, and they would prefer to live closer to Jane's favorite sister."

Elizabeth's eyes lit up with delight. "I should love to have her close to me. Will you find them a house? Julia was telling me the other day that one of her older neighbors is looking to move to the seaside. Perhaps they will be willing to sell. It would be so wonderful for us all to be so close."

"I shall do my best, my darling, but for now, you must think of your health. It is far too late for you. I can see how tired you are. Do not argue with me on this. You need your rest. Say goodnight to your sister so that she may put her little ones to bed."

"That is an excellent idea, Fitzwilliam." Jane agreed. "I am very tired, and I long for a comfortable bed. Elizabeth, we shall speak more in the morning."

Elizabeth relented and allowed her husband to lead her to their chambers. She tried to fall asleep, but a pain in her abdomen began. She tried to ignore it, but the pain grew steadily worse. After three hours, she woke her sleeping husband and asked for Jane and the midwife. "She has rested enough, I hope, because I believe it is time for our little one to make his or her appearance."

Fitzwilliam leapt from the bed before he realized what he was about. Elizabeth had to call after him to remind him to put a robe on before calling the servant and shocking the staff. He returned for his robe as Elizabeth cringed once again as the pain returned. "My darling, how much I wish I could ease your pain."

"You can ease my pain by bringing Jane to me. She will know what to do until the midwife arrives. Now go, for you have your orders. The pain is easing again, so I must rest until the next wave."

Fitzwilliam kissed her forehead and left the room. He crossed the house to the guest wing in record time, and Jane woke instantly when she realized Elizabeth's time had come early. "There will be time for sleep later. You two must try to rest." She looked back at her husband and Fitzwilliam and laughed. "If you cannot rest, then go to the library, so that we know where to send updates to you. Some wine should help you rest. If you come anywhere near your rooms before you are summoned, you will be sent away. Men are not strong enough for this." She then darted out of the room to find Mrs. Reynolds waiting to escort her to Elizabeth's chambers.

Fitzwilliam stared at the door. He knew he could not follow her, but he wished dearly to do so. Charles took the reigns after donning a robe and clapped his friend on the back. "Let us raise a toast to fatherhood. Have no fear. In an hour or two, you shall be back in your room holding your heir."

Fitzwilliam nodded and followed his friend down the hall. Charles drank one swallow of brandy before he settled down and slept. Fitzwilliam, on the other hand, downed two drinks, and still he was alert. He paced through the hallway, but no news came save for the appearance of the midwife an hour after he had settled into the library.

Charles prediction of a speedy labor did not come to pass.

In the afternoon of the following day, Fitzwilliam received a message from above stairs that all was progressing as normal, but that it would be some time yet before the baby came. The servants who were not assisting the delivery offered Charles and Fitzwilliam refreshments on schedule, but only Charles partook of the delectable offerings of food and tea. Charles repeatedly stated that all would be well, but it was of no consolation to his friend. Fitzwilliam paced back and forth, wondering how much longer it would take for the babe to come, worried that the delay meant something had gone wrong. He did not expect frequent updates, but the lack of news worried him greatly.

As the clock chimed midnight, his resolve broke. He dashed out the door and up the stairs before the footmen assembled outside could stop him. At the top of the stairs, he found that the door to their shared sitting room had been locked. He was about to knock on the door when he realized everyone inside must be busy. He would not bring even one person away from her task. He leaned against the door and tried to hear inside. Knowing there were two doors between him and the commotion in the bedroom did not help him. He could only hear faint moans and occasionally doors opening and closing. They must have been using the servants' doors, for they never opened the door he desperately wanted open.

He paced in the hallway when he tired of listening at the door. Around three in the morning, a maid came up the stairs with a candle, forcing him to squint away from the seemingly bright light. "Sir, I could not find you in the library. Mrs. Darcy is ready for you now. Follow me, if you wish to see her."

Fitzwilliam released a quick breath of relief before stepping away from the door, so the maid could open the door which had already been unlocked. He silently cursed himself for not noticing someone unlocking the door from the inside.

Once inside the chamber, he found Elizabeth laying on a clean bed, propped up with fresh pillows. The windows were open, allowing a breeze to drift through the room, cooling the air. In Elizabeth's arms was a tightly wrapped bundle. She was so lovely and radiant, he forgot to breathe. Elizabeth smiled at him. "Come here, my darling, and meet your heir."

Fitzwilliam needed no other encouragement, and he quickly stepped over and settled beside his wife. He pulled back the coverings to look at the small face on the perfect baby boy nestled in his wife's arms. Even in the dim light, no one could doubt the love that shone from his face as he watched his son sleep.

He could barely spare a thought to his wife until he felt her kiss his cheek. "Have I done well, Husband?"

Fitzwilliam laughed. He would have responded, but a cry caught his attention. He looked down at his son and noticed the boy had not made the noise. For the first time, he looked around the room and found Jane standing beside the bed holding another tightly bound bundle. Jane smiled at him. "You must be quiet, Fitzwilliam, or you will wake your daughter. Would you like to hold her?"

"My daughter?" Tears slipped down his cheek as Jane gently handed the small bundle to him. His arms shook as he held his daughter. She weighed almost nothing, and he feared he might accidentally hurt her. Jane patted his shoulder momentarily before announcing that she would retire. Fitzwilliam barely heard her as he looked back at his wife. "We have a son *and* a daughter. My dear, you have done very well, indeed. I could not be prouder of you than I am at this moment."

They held their babies for some time, until Elizabeth yawned. "Have you had any rest, Elizabeth?"

"Only a few minutes here and there." She whispered, too tired to speak clearly.

Fitzwilliam gently rose from the bed, but then he was not sure what to do. He could call for a maid to come care for the children, but he found that he did not wish to leave them just yet. Instead, he pulled the pillows down and set the babies between Elizabeth and himself on the bed. Elizabeth shifted onto her side as she kissed her son before drifting off to sleep.

When Fitzwilliam woke, he found Elizabeth was already

awake, although she had not risen from the bed. He looked down at the space between them and found it empty. "Where have they gone?"

Elizabeth laughed. "Mrs. Reynolds has taken them to the nursery to see the wet nurse. She will return them when we ask for them. Are you happy?"

"Undoubtedly so. I would have to say this even tops our wedding day, which I was not certain was possible."

"This is only the beginning, my dear."

"Indeed it is, my friend, my love, my life." Fitzwilliam leaned forward and gently kissed his wife as he continued to gently show her how much she meant to him. He was very careful to avoid the places where she was undoubtedly sore.

"Thank you, Elizabeth."

She pulled away at hearing his thanks. "Why are you thankful, Fitzwilliam?"

"Because you rejected me when I needed it most. If you had been mercenary and accepted me in that field all those years ago, I do not believe we would be where we are today. I did not know what love was or how great and powerful it could be. Becoming your friend first was the best thing that could have happened to me."

"Then you are very welcome, dearest Fitzwilliam. Now, I believe I shall rest again. Will you hold me?"

Fitzwilliam shifted his weight so he was directly behind her and curled around her small form. "Forever and always, Elizabeth Darcy. Now, sleep."

THE END

ABOUT THE AUTHOR

I am a part-time writer, mostly with fanfiction variations of Jane Austen's Pride and Prejudice. I work full-time teaching high school students science at a local school. My specialty is marine biology, studied at Oregon State University.

Writing fanfiction is my way of unwinding at the end of a very busy week. Writing takes me out of the real world, and I can enter a fantasy where I can make things either flow smoothly or add all the angst that I feel my characters deserve.

New books are being tested on fanfiction.net and beyondausten.com before they are published. My ID is LoriH, if you want to preview future books.

Made in the USA
Lexington, KY
25 October 2018